MONSTERS

To Heike

All the
Best

Paul L.

ALSO BY PAUL KANE

Novels
Arrowhead
Broken Arrow
Arrowland
Hooded Man (Omnibus)
The Gemini Factor
Of Darkness and Light
Lunar
Sleeper(s)
The Rainbow Man
    (as P B Kane)
Forthcoming: *Blood RED*

Novellas
Signs of Life
The Lazarus Condition
Dalton Quayle Rides Out
RED
Pain Cages
Creakers (chapbook)
Flaming Arrow
Forthcoming: *The Bric-a-Brac Man*

Collections
Alone (In the Dark)
Touching the Flame
FunnyBones
Peripheral Visions
The Adventures of Dalton Quayle
Shadow Writer
The Butterfly Man and Other Stories

The Spaces Between
GHOSTS

Editor & co-editor
Shadow Writers Vol. 1 & 2
Terror Tales #1-4
Top International Horror
Albions Alptraume: Zombies
The British Fantasy Society: A Celebration
Hellbound Hearts
The Mammoth Book of Body Horror
A Carnivàle of Horror: Dark Tales from the Fairground
Beyond Rue Morgue

Non-Fiction
Contemporary North American Film Directors: A Wallflower Critical Guide (major contributor)
Cinema Macabre (contributor)
The Hellraiser Films and their Legacy
Voices in the Dark
Shadow Writer – The Non-Fiction. Vol. 1: Reviews
Shadow Writer – The Non-Fiction. Vol. 2: Articles & Essays

MONSTERS

PAUL KANE

INTRODUCTION BY
NICHOLAS VINCE

COVER ART BY CLIVE BARKER

The Alchemy Press

The Alchemy Press, Staffordshire, UK

www.alchemypress.co.uk

DEDICATION

For Boris, Bela and Lon,
the original monsters.

ACKNOWLEDGMENTS

My thanks to Peter and Jan at Alchemy Press for taking a chance on this themed collection I've had in mind for a while now. A huge thank you to Nicholas Vince for the kind words in his intro, and to Clive Barker for the terrific cover artwork (as well as Mark Miller for facilitating this and Christian Francis for design). Thanks also to Mark Steensland and Brad Watson for all their help with the give-away DVDs. As usual, hugs and massive thank yous to all my friends in the writing and film/TV world, for their continual help and support in the past. A very special thank you, though, to people like Neil Gaiman, Stephen Jones, Mandy Slater, Amanda Foubister, Sarah Pinborough, Christopher Fowler, Stephen Volk, Tim Lebbon, Kelley Armstrong, Peter James, Mike Carey, Barbie Wilde, John Connolly, Pete & Nicky Crowther, Simon Clark, Will Hill and so many more. You're all the best. Last, but never, ever least, a big words are not enough thank you to my supportive family – especially my daughter Jen and my wife Marie. Love you guys more than words can say.

CONTENTS

ACKNOWLEDGMENTS

'The Ugly' © 2003 (*Cemetery Poets: Grave Offerings*, published by Double Dragon Press 2003)

'Nightlife' © 2002 (*Touching the Flame*, Rainfall Books 2002)

'The Disease' © 2000 (*Sci-Fright* Issue 6, 1st Year Anniversary & Millennium Edition, February 2000)

'Sabbat' © 2000 (*Penny Dreadful: Tales & Poems of Fantastic Terror*, Issue 13, Midsummer 2000)

'Dig (This)' © 2007 (*Dark Animus,* issue 10/11, November 2007)

'A Chaos Demon is for Life' © 2008 (*Estronomicon Christmas Special*, December 2008)

'St August's Flame' © 1999 (*Strix*, Issue 14, February 1999)

'Keeper of the Light' © 2010 (*Fear of the Dark*, Horror Bound Publications, March 2010)

'Dracula in Love' © 2000 (*Dead Things,* Issue 5, October/ December 2000)

'Half-life' © 2011 (*Pain Cages,* Books of the Dead, August 2011)

'Guilty Pleasures' © 2004 (*Demonology: Grammaticus Demonium.* Double Dragon Books, 2004)

'Speaking in Tongues' © 2011 (*Necrotic Tissue* #13, January 2011)

'Star-Pool' © 1999 (*Tales of the Grotesque and Arabesque,* Issue 4 January 1999)

'Rag and Bone' © 2011 (*The Butterfly Man and Other Stories*, PS Publishing, 2011)

'The Weeping Woman' © 2000 (*Terror Tales E-Mail Magazine* Issue 2, April 2000)

'Pay the Piper' © 2002 (*House of Pain* site, May 2002)

'It's All Over…' © 2011 (*Scenes from the Second Storey: International Edition*, Morrigan Books, 2011)

'Lifetime' © 2015 (Original to this collection)

INTRODUCTION

By Nicholas Vince

Personally, I never read introductions in books. They almost certainly contain spoilers, and I really hate spoilers. This introduction contains spoilers to some movies, but hopefully not to the stories in this volume.

So, I'll write about the Dedication.

It reads, 'For Boris, Bela and Lon, the original monsters'. But really, they weren't. They were actors and needed make -up to transform from the human to the monstrous. The Frankenstein Monster (Boris Karloff), Dracula (Bela Lugosi) and The Wolf Man (Lon Chaney Jr., son of The Man of a Thousand Faces, Lon Chaney). They're remembered fondly by many people, particularly in America, as their films were shown on TV after school in the 1950s and celebrated in magazines such as *Famous Monsters of Filmland*. They were the misunderstood, the cursed and victims of their irrepressible urges which manifested in bodies at odds with their desire for peace and love. In short, they were teenagers.

Humanity hidden or lost perhaps defines the monstrous. Instinctively, we don't trust a person who wears a mask and want to rip it from their face, like Christine in *The Phantom of the Opera*. Today, the images which instil dread in many of us are of men swathed in black wielding Kalashnikovs or swords.

Of course, there are the monsters whose mask is a charming smile. Uncle Charlie in Alfred Hitchcock's *Shadow of a Doubt*; *The Hitcher* played by Rutger Hauer; Frank and Julia in Clive Barker's *Hellraiser*, are some of my favourites.

And we do have favourite monsters, don't we? We admire them because they represent the thrill of sexual danger, a willingness to break the rules which sometimes frustrate us; they are the conquerors of death and maybe, like the Soska Sisters' eponymous *American Mary*, they're the victim who turned and took revenge. They have permissions we deny ourselves, and perhaps we envy them that freedom.

In Paul's book, there are the monstrously inhuman and those all too human. There are traditional monsters, including zombies. A funny demon and one who haunts us all. But honestly, I really don't want to spoil the surprise in these stories.

You want to meet monsters? No need to travel to the end of the known world, enter the forest, pay to enter the freak show, look in the mirror or under your bed.

Just turn the page.

Nicholas Vince
February 2015

THE UGLY

The Ugly is,
As Ugly does,
As Ugly says,
This Ugly was...

Beneath the floor,
In darkness hid.
Wet noises heard,
Best to ignore.

Through slats it fed,
On blood and flesh.
At night it slept,
Bones for a bed.

Then came a time,
When Ugly sought,
To see a world,
Beyond the slime.

Broke free, unbound,
It ate and ate.
Its belly big,
And pink and round.

Repulsed, and scared,
The people ran.
Out of its way,
Teeth sharp and bared.

They tracked it down,
With cage and net,
The Ugly trapped…
It gave a frown.

Now Ugly is,
As Ugly does.
A sideshow freak,
This Ugly was.

NIGHTLIFE

There's nothing like a good night out.

And in his mind, Neil was already there. He wasn't standing behind this counter, stamping books one after the other. Taking them from people as they ambled in through the heavy wooden doors.

'Next please. Oh, I'm afraid there's a fine to pay on this one, sir.'

It was all done on automatic pilot, because he was dreaming of the pleasures to come in just a few short hours. It seemed like ages since he'd gone out and enjoyed himself, but it couldn't have been so long ago. Besides, he knew it was that much better when he got together with the guys rather than tearing off on his own. That meant waiting for everyone to be free at the same time. Waiting for the *right* time.

That was what made it such a big deal, he supposed, meeting up with his old university pals every few weeks. It was something to look forward to, and he definitely intended to make the most of it. Anyway, they were all older than they used to be when they started this game – well, twenty-seven wasn't young by today's standards. And they could only realistically manage this sort of thing every so often.

It was a real physical effort staying out most of the night, and in the morning you felt like you'd been run over by a truck. Neil's muscles always ached, his stomach begged him never to eat or drink again, and his head usually felt like someone was trying to crack it open with a pickaxe. He needed a little time to recuperate, ready for the next outing. But Neil knew it was all worthwhile. One day he'd look back on these memories, on the last few years, with a nostalgic fondness and wish he could still do the things he'd do tonight. Life's too short for regrets.

Neil slotted the next borrower card into the scanner and passed through a fresh batch of books, without looking at the titles once. His thoughts were elsewhere. He was planning what they would get up to based on their previous adventures. Him, Adrian, Ryan, Owen, Luke and Jack. God, what a motley gang of misfits. He couldn't even remember how they'd all hooked up together at uni, so many moons ago now. It wasn't as if they'd been taking the same subjects or anything. Neil just figured they'd tracked each other down: the party animals. Kindred spirits with similar interests and goals, who could usually be found propping up the bar at the Student's Union between seminars.

Like him, they'd all chosen this particular city for its nightlife, as opposed to the academic opportunities it could offer them. What was the point of thinking about crap like that anyway? It was virtually impossible to find the job you wanted nowadays, even *with* qualifications. Owen and Ryan were still signing on to this day, having only briefly dabbled in the work market.

But yeah, this place was buzzing on a Friday and Saturday night. Actually, the city was buzzing on any night you cared to venture out. Only the weekend jaunt was a kind of special thing. Plus you had all day Sunday to rest up, or at least try to.

At any given time there would be dozens and dozens of

people in the streets and down back alleys, on their way to pubs, nightclubs, hotels; anywhere they could have a good time and forget about the drudgery of their everyday lives. The sights, the sounds, the smells. There was something in the air at night that would be well and truly gone by the next day. Something that drove grown men wild with desire ... and sometimes drove women even wilder! What was it they called it in that film with Travolta? A fever. Yes, it was a kind of fever that gripped them, turning the city into a hotbed of lust, debauchery and depravity. Come eight or nine o'clock that night he'd be out there in the thick of it all. Neil couldn't wait.

He knew the routine by now. Soon as his shift ended and he'd helped tidy up at the library, he'd hurry back to his tiny flat to get ready. Preparation was everything. First he'd shower, washing off the grime of the day. Then he'd spruce himself up a bit, clean his teeth and change into something more comfortable. Something more appropriate. Like a thousand times before, Neil was hoping he'd get lucky while he was out on the pull.

On the last occasion they'd all gone out together, Luke had scored with a real dish. He'd been eyeing her up all evening, and Neil could hardly blame him. Five-foot-nine, red-head with a gorgeous body, all poured into a slinky satin dress which left very little to the imagination.

Finally, he'd approached her, and from that moment on she hadn't really stood a chance. Luke could be very persuasive, and he wasn't exactly ugly himself (Neil didn't think so, at any rate; none of the women he'd ever gone after could resist his charms). The rest of them had remained on the side lines as he made his final play, watching jealously as she fell for him.

Luke later told him that they'd done the business in a

backstreet behind the club where he'd first spotted her. Neil could see it in his imagination: Luke clawing at the silky material of that dress, the young girl squirming beneath his touch, the sensation of Luke's tongue running over her face, her breasts … and lower still.

Hungry for her.

Maybe Neil would find someone like that tonight instead of the typical dregs he was used to. The thought aroused him and he fought to control himself.

A middle-aged woman wearing glasses was looking at him strangely over the counter. What was she taking out? Mmm… Love stories, thrillers. *Sad.* Some people just didn't know how to live life. All they could do was fantasise. Read about it and wish, and wish…

When Neil gazed into her eyes he could tell there was nothing going on behind them. He could sense it. If she'd only seen a tenth of the things he'd seen in the years since his eighteenth birthday…

She'd probably been saddled with a family by the time she was his age, married by twenty-one, frightened of being left on the shelf. And now, a couple of decades later, the kids had flown the coup – Neil probably even saw them when he was out and about round the city. Leaving her with nothing but an empty house and a husband who barely spoke to her anymore.

How did he know all these things? Because she was just like his own mother. This poor woman's life was exactly the same as that of his parents. Safe. Comfortable. *Boring.* It wasn't their fault. That's all they'd ever known, all they'd ever been: restricted, repressed.

They'd never had the same opportunities as him. His parents hadn't enjoyed the same kind of freedom Neil took for granted now, living in that quiet country village. Small community, people watching their every move. They had to be so very careful.

Neil didn't intend to live his life like that, following in their footsteps. Suppressing his emotions and longings. That's why he'd left home as soon as he could, come here to be with people of his own age, his own inclination. The world had moved on. It was no longer a sin to indulge yourself. But Neil's folks were so out of touch, they could never understand. The generation gap strikes again.

He handed the books back over to the woman, having dated them inside. One month from today.

'T-thank you,' she said, taking them from him, a little unsure of herself. Was it suddenly hot in the library? And was her pulse-rate suddenly up? Heart pounding?

Neil chuckled to himself as she backed out through the door, glancing at the odd librarian who'd stared so intently at her.

Now where had he been? Oh yes, running through what would happen when he left the flat.

He'd meet up with the rest of them at the usual place, a park just off Milton Street. From here they'd make their way into the city itself. It wasn't far for them. No real need for taxis or busses. In fact it was probably faster on foot.

The closer they came to the action, the more they would eat and drink, stopping off along the way for swift ones. They had to keep up their strength for the marathon ahead of them. Come to think of it, the journey in was probably the best part. Messing about with the guys, playful back-biting and mock fights.

But in all this time Neil and the others had never once come across any real trouble.

He'd heard the stories, of course he had. Of people being beaten up, noses broken. Maybe even the flash of steel as things got out of hand, probably over a girl or a spilt drink. There were some who even went out with the express intention of causing bother. Nutters cropped up everywhere these days. You couldn't get away from that awful fact. It was a dangerous world.

Thankfully, they'd managed to avoid any fracas of this nature directly. Neil couldn't explain it. Perhaps there was safety in numbers, for they tended to stick together most of the night – unless one of them was ... otherwise engaged, as Luke had been the other week; but even then the missing member would always return to the fold soon after. Or was it the fact that they gave off certain signals to would-be aggressors? Warning signs.

But no doubt about it, Neil had to conclude that it was more the anticipation, the excitement of approaching the city centre that really did it for him. Such a choice of things to do, new people to meet.

And not for the first time his eyes found their way up to the clock over those varnished doors. It was taunting him, winding down, dragging out the last excruciating half-hour before they closed to the general public. Only then could he begin to clear up: collecting discarded books together and placing them on the trolley ready for re-shelving, cashing up (it was surprising how much they made from fines, and then there was the photocopier to consider), and so on and so forth. He'd probably skip through a lot of this today so he could get off a bit earlier.

Neil wasn't alone, though. He had a good idea what was occupying the thoughts of his friends. They'd be just as eager as he was for night to come, so they could let their collective hair down. He could picture Adrian now, pacing up and down at the burger bar where he worked, serving those terrible greasy meals with meat that had no distinguishing flavour to it – who could eat that foul grill-cooked shite? Luke would probably be arriving back from his travels in his capacity as a rep; he really did have the heart and soul of a gypsy, that one. Jack would be rehearsing with his heavy metal band, Brutal ('We'll make it big some day,' he was always telling them. To be fair they weren't half bad)... And as for Ryan and Owen, well they'd probably just be getting out of their pits around now and having a spot of 'breakfast'. All right for some!

But no matter what they were doing, all of them would have one eye on a clock or a watch, counting down the minutes, the hours, until they could come together once more.

***

Finally, at last, the endless torture was just about over and an impatient Neil was away. He sprinted to his car, a feeling of tremendous excitement alive inside of him. Like a child on Christmas Eve, it wouldn't be long now before he could open his presents.

And stepping out of the shower back home, he let the water drip from his taut physique. Neil didn't bother to shave; there was no point, really. Instead, he started towelling himself off and walked into the living room.

Neil went over to the window, opened it. The night was already drawing in. On the horizon a powerless sun was dying, taking with it the last vestiges of daylight. But there was another source ready and willing to take its place. Hanging over the city, irradiating the buildings, the streets he would be exploring later. Bathing everything in a haunted silvery sheen.

He stood naked at the window and listened to the sounds of night-time assaulting is ears. Raised voices, TVs, music, sirens ... and something else. A rhythmic throbbing.

Thousands of heartbeats all pumping as one.

The life-force of the city.

From his vantage point several floors above ground level, he could see the sights. Weird neon signs cranking up – Harry's, Monty's, The Green Room. Places he knew intimately. Inside and out.

Now he closed his eyes, the towel dropping out of his hands. Neil sniffed at the cool night air streaming in. He could smell them. The time was nearly upon him. He had waited quite long enough.

When he opened his eyes again the sky was full of stars, and a familiar white shape rolled out from behind the cover of grey-blue clouds.

Neil could feel the adrenaline rushing through him. This time he didn't hold back. Soon it would begin. He could already feel the tingling as new hairs appeared all over his body, as his eyes took on a frightening yellow and red cast.

Then, when it was over, when he was totally free again, he would climb down and hunt with the pack. With his brothers. Seeking their quarry. No one would miss a few; the supply was plentiful in the city.

A lengthy tongue brushed over teeth that were pointed and gleaming, that could bite through anything. He could almost taste the flesh. Almost savour the flowing blood.

Illuminated by the full moon, Neil smiled.

No, there's nothing like a good night out, he thought. Nothing like it in the world.

THE DISEASE

My name is Gus Harper, and I am diseased.

I'm shitting blood again this morning – the third time this week. My skin is inflamed and sore. My boils itch. Walking is all but impossible on these legs, if you can describe them as such.

At one time all this would have scared me witless. Not any more. I've seen too much, gone through too much.

And the memories are still alive, trapped in what's left of my mind. But how long they'll remain in there now is anyone's guess.

***

I can vividly remember the morning it came on: a Saturday in late January. And I remember the dream, mainly because I'm still having it after all this time, the same one over and over. Maybe this is *all* a dream, or should I say nightmare? In it I can see a blueness, so bright it almost blinds me. I head towards it, desperate to make contact. Just before I get there I always wake up. Then reality hits me as the pain kicks in once more.

But I'm getting ahead of myself, sorry.

On that particular morning I woke up next to Rachel. For a good five minutes I watched her sleeping. The way her soft mouth opened and closed, her chest rising and falling, her hair splayed out on the pillow like a partially folded fan. The way her eyelids fluttered as she dreamed her own private dreams.

I suppose she must have sensed me looking at her, perhaps on some subconscious level, because she opened her eyes then and grinned. Though we'd been together for a year and a half she still had the power to jump-start me, sending tingles through my body

Was it her or the disease? I'm not sure now.

Anyway, we made love bathed in the rays of golden morning sunlight. I would be hard pressed to do that now, seeing as those parts of my body no longer exist... If it's truly possible for two people to become one, then I think we came pretty close to it that Saturday morning. And as I held her, I knew that nothing would ever be as perfect as this again.

I was right, of course.

Afterwards I fell asleep once more, dozing lightly. When I woke up Rachel was gone. I was on my side, my left hand wedged between the pillow and mattress. I'd stuck it under there to raise my head up a bit. The hand was numb at first, and as I tried to pull it out I felt the familiar onset of pins and needles, which was fair enough, I suppose. Except the cramps felt weird.

Then the pain announced itself. I'm at a loss to describe how much it hurt the first time. The nearest comparison I can make is that it felt like someone was crushing my hand in a vice. I let out an almighty howl. God knows what Rachel must have thought, probably that I was being attacked by a chainsaw-wielding maniac hell-bent on dis-embowelling me. To tell you the truth, at that moment in time I would have preferred it.

She was up the stairs and at the bedroom door in seconds.

'For God's sake, Gus. What's going on?' I must have looked a sight, gripping my wrist and crawling around on the duvet.

'I don't know,' I cried back. 'My hand…'

'Let me have a look.'

Rachel took hold of the hand, turning it round. The agony almost caused me to pass out. She let go immediately, frightened that she might have made it worse.

Tears were streaming from my screwed-up eyes, flowing down my cheeks and into my mouth. I barely noticed the salty taste.

Then, as quickly as it came upon me, the pain just vanished. My hand went limp, the spasms subsided. All I could feel was a slight throbbing.

'I think you should have it looked at, Gus.' Rachel was worried. I could hardly blame her. 'Your hand wouldn't just start hurting like that for no reason.'

I knew she was right. I'd never experienced pain like that before, and certain possibilities sprang to mind: that I'd sprained it somehow while I was asleep, or maybe even at work the day before; that there could well be a fracture somewhere in the hand; and the last, the most likely option … arthritis.

I was only in my early thirties but it wasn't unheard of. I'd seen a documentary once where a kid of three or four had it! And the other thing was my father had suffered for years with the terrible curse in his bones. Granted, he didn't start until he was about fifty, but I always have been an early developer – I hit puberty ages before anyone else in my class at school…

Even in the face of all this, I did what most men in my position would have done. I chose to bury my head in the sand, to ignore the problem and hope the pain never returned.

'It's easing up now. I-I think it'll be all right so long as I

don't knock it or anything.' Rachel took some convincing
but finally relented.

'Okay,' she said. 'Have it your way. Just promise me that
if it comes back you'll see a doctor.' Rachel looked me in the
eyes. I could hardly say no. 'Promise?'

'I promise.'

***

It was easy to keep that promise for a week or so because
nothing else happened. I won't say I forgot all about it; the
worries were always there at the back of my mind. But you
know how it is. Other things crop up and in the end you
prioritise. My life returned to normal. I went to work, losing
myself in the daily grind at the factory, I ate with the lads in
the canteen at lunchtime and I went back home for evenings
in front of the TV with Rachel, catching up with the state of
the world. The usual stuff: devastation, the growing ten-
sions abroad, murder, chemical pollutants.

I think it was about midway through the second week
that it came back. I was inspecting a procession of metal
casings as they travelled down the production line when
that prickling visited my left hand again. No warning, no
strange numbness this time. Just *whack!* Before I knew it the
agony was shooting up my arm as well. I collapsed on the
floor. Heads appeared above me, leaning over, attracted by
the unusual drama.

Mercifully I did lose consciousness the second time, blue
spots leapfrogging across my field of vision, turning to
black the further I sank.

When I awoke I was in what Grimwald's laughingly call
their infirmary. A room about twice the size of a closet with
a hard leather examining table in the middle and a few
shelves with bottles of coloured liquid for effect. I hadn't
had cause to visit since their annual medical the previous

July. Clean bill of health I got, too. What a joke!

My hand and arm felt peculiar, but at least the aching had stopped. I looked down to see that my skin was reddening nicely.

The door opened and in came Dr Jenkins, a sweaty physician with thick round glasses. He always freaked me out, this guy, but he gave the impression that he knew what he was doing.

'It's Gus, isn't it?' said Jenkins, thumbing through a personnel file. 'Gus Harper?'

I nodded.

'You had a bit of a turn out there, I gather. What seems to be the problem?'

'It's my hand. I've been having some pain in it lately. But it … it seems to be moving up my arm now.'

Dr Jenkins ran a magnified eye over the offending areas, drawing in breath when he saw the inflammation. 'Has your own GP had a look at this?'

'No, not really. My girlfriend wanted me to go but —'

'But you don't care for doctors, right? Who does?'

His flippancy was a ruse, I could tell that straight away. He was concerned, probably more about the company than my well-being (I can imagine what he was thinking: *What if it's down to something we've done? What if the poor bastard croaks on us? There'll be an outcry!*), but his anxiety was infectious.

'Listen, Gus. How would you feel about taking a little trip to The General?' This being our local hospital

'Why? Is it arthritis?'

Dr Jenkins declined to comment. He wouldn't even look me in the eye, which was ten times more frightening than his evasiveness. 'I don't know, Gus. They'll probably want to run some tests, take a few X-rays.'

These would be the first of many.

***

I was a rush job. In the space of a day I was poked and prodded by every kind of doctor in that hospital, although I noticed the orthopaedic specialists were always hanging around. Especially a man called Dr Fillis, who treated me like I was an animal in a circus (freak show might be more appropriate now). My flaccid hand was a source of constant fascination for him.

'Please hold still, Mr Harper. You are not helping.'

X-rays confirmed that it wasn't broken, but more tests were needed to 'give an accurate picture' of what was happening.

Rachel came to collect me at around half-five, straight from work. I didn't see the sense in bothering her before then. She was full of questions on the ride home, though. Questions I couldn't answer. All I could tell her was what they'd told me: that they would know more in a few days when the test results came back. Meanwhile I was stuck wearing a sling and on the sick.

Dr Fillis had prescribed some anti-inflammatories and painkillers to see me through any more bouts. Over the course of the next forty-eight hours I relied on them more and more. I began vomiting a couple of times a day. I thought back then that it was a side effect of the drugs, but now I'm not so sure. The yellow bile would cling to the toilet pan, shrugging off all attempts to flush it away. Hanging there. My offspring.

'Oh Gus,' Rachel would sigh. The smell *was* pretty rotten, all told. I didn't need no doctor to tell me I had something bad inside.

And it was spreading.

***

By the time The General contacted me I was experiencing stiffness in my shoulders and back, too. I prayed to God they knew what was going on and, more importantly, how to stop it.

'Mr Harper,' said Dr Fillis when I met him in his plush office, 'I'm afraid I have some rather perplexing news.'

I swallowed, the aftertaste of that bile still present in my mouth. 'What is it?'

'There's no easy way to say this. We simply don't *know* what's wrong with you.'

Anger, confusion, fear. Adverse emotions that swirled around in my guts, preventing me from speaking. *Why* didn't they know? They were the doctors for Heaven's sake!

Everything he said after that went over my head. Something about it definitely not being arthritis and that my fatty tissue was reacting with the bone, absorbing it – or words to that effect. It was a long stream of bullshit and I was in no fit state to take any of it in.

In the time it took him to finish explaining I found my voice again. 'But you must have some idea —'

'Oh we have ideas, don't misunderstand me. It's just that none of them are conclusive. We simply don't have the resources at this facility to identify your disease.' That's what he called it: a disease. Only according to him it wasn't something you could catch like a cold. As I'd already suspected, this was attacking me from within.

'It might be a variant of that flesh-eating bug the papers were so interested in a while ago, or perhaps genetic – your mother and father may have passed this on to you. I really wouldn't like to speculate at this juncture.' Oh yes, he knew how to put his patients at their ease did Dr Fillis. The jerk. 'To be perfectly frank I've never seen anything quite like it. I think it's probably best if you visit my colleagues down south. I'm sure they'll be able to sort you out.' *Sort me out!* Like I was bringing back a faulty toaster or something.

More tests, more waiting. I can't honestly say I relished the idea.

But Rachel was insistent. 'You're going,' she said, point blank. No arguments. 'If not for your own sake then for mine. I haven't slept in a week.'

She took some time off to come with me, probably to make sure I actually went through with it. All our expenses were paid for and my 'treatment' was free. I was, after all, a special case. Someone was even going to write a paper on me. Yeah, fucking Harper's disease. Roll up, roll up! I didn't care so long as they got to the bottom of it and I could be normal again.

As for the institute I was sent to, it was like something from the future. Equipment, gizmos, more men in white coats and glasses. So many, all their faces blurred into one, their names an incomprehensible mishmash. Suffice to say I was there longer than one day. And if I thought the doctors at home were thorough, I was in for a shock. These men did everything bar turn me inside out – and I reckon a few of them would've done just that if I'd signed the right consent form. Biopsies were taken, samples galore (urine, stools, skin, blood … even semen!) as well as photographs for posterity, recording the onslaught.

Rachel was incredibly supportive those first few weeks. I don't know how I would've come through it without her, especially when the fits became more frequent. The pain was now entering my lower half. Sometimes, I swear you could even see the flesh bubbling like soup on a stove.

Two months passed. Nothing. No results. No explanations. No cure. Only excuses. If anything, by May the disease was speeding up. And there was nothing anybody could do to stop it. One thing I did learn at the institute, though, by accident you understand: I wasn't the only sufferer. Apparently a few other minor cases had been reported elsewhere. When I asked for more information, they just clammed up and said they couldn't discuss it. If not with me, then who? That's what I wanted to know.

Rachel had already returned home by this time, but I stayed on a while longer. I was more than a little scared of what she'd say when she saw me again. I didn't recognise myself in the mirror anymore. The irritation had journeyed up to my face; goitre-like lumps were appearing on my neck. And angry boils festered away on the skin of my left arm – the obscene meat a ripe breeding ground for bacteria, in spite of the antibiotics I was taking. It was a work of art trying to hide these with dressings and bandages. Also, I needed a stick to get about. The pain in my legs was growing so severe that not even the strongest medication could combat it.

On my arrival back at the house, Rachel's reaction was only to be expected; a blend of horror and pity. 'They still don't know…?' Her hand was covering her mouth, that soft mouth I longed to kiss again.

'I don't think they ever will, Rachel. And even if they do find out, it won't be much use to me soon.' I meant what I said. Oh sure, they had their theories same as before (a genetic disorder which had lain dormant for years, like a heart defect waiting for something to trigger it; some kind of mutated cancer; a reversal of the inexplicable FOP, which has been around since the seventeenth century and turns your muscles into bone – it was the exact opposite with me!; GM food, yeah that old favourite; one boffin even thought it might be something I'd picked up on holiday years ago), but all this was cold comfort. Another way of saying they didn't have a clue.

Rachel surprised me then by putting her arms around me. I winced, fighting back the anguish for as long as I could. Ignoring the distress she was causing me just so I could be near her.

I remember thinking that this must be what it was like for the first person who'd developed TB, polio ... Aids. The knowledge that nothing can be done for you, that no one even knows what you've got, is hard to take in. But I had no illusions. I knew the end might come at any time.

And still I dreamed of the blue.

***

There was some good news for a while. The disease appeared to go into remission. Maybe it had run its course, I told myself, and like a fool I started to believe in miracles again.

Its progress halted very suddenly one week. No aches or queasiness, nor fresh boils. This respite lasted the whole of summer, though it couldn't have been down to the sunlight – I didn't go out much anymore, as you can probably appreciate.

It's funny, but the dreams went away at the same time. I never connected that before. A coincidence? I doubt it very much. In fact the more I think about this, the more I reckon they're another symptom of the illness. If I could stop dreaming altogether, then perhaps...

I have no problem recalling the day it returned, either. It was the day that war was announced overseas. As I watched our troops loading on to helicopters, battleships, trucks, it struck me again with a renewed ferocity. The build up to both events was swift. An overwhelming shockwave rippled through my entire body, and I lay convulsing on the living room carpet, unable even to call out for help. The TV images flashed on and off in my mind and I found myself having these wild thoughts. What if our enemies had used a kind of nerve gas or chemical weapon on us? Was my disease the result of one of their experiments? If so, then why me? I wasn't a military man or a politician. Just an ordinary bloke trying to earn a living. The link was too farfetched and I dismissed it almost immediately.

Rachel found me lying there some time later. Her despair was evident. The 'disorder' was here again and its effects were worsening. I couldn't expect her to look after me this time, and I didn't want her visiting me in some hospice. I made my decision. I had to go.

So the very next week – the beginning of September – I waited for Rachel to go out on the Monday, then left myself. For good.

I believed I was freeing her from all responsibility. I'd been a burden long enough. She loved me and I was thankful, not many women in her position would have done, but to stay would only cause her more heartache. She would get over it, be better off without me. I said as much in my letter: *Please don't try to find me. I'll always love you. Gus x*

In reality I didn't know what I was doing. I was so terrified of losing her, of being without her. But at the same time I was scared to be with her. Every day there were more changes, new ghastly revelations for me to discover. How could I share them with anyone? Especially somebody I'd been so...

Perhaps I was being selfish, I don't know. All I did know was I couldn't be the man she needed me to be. Rachel deserved so much more.

I took the train, managing to climb on with a great deal

of difficulty. I knew exactly where I was going: east, to my parents' old holiday cottage. A safe place from my youth, from summers that never used to end (*following the call?*).

Fellow travellers stared at me on the journey, including a little girl who held her mother's hand so tightly it left white finger-marks on the woman's skin. People backed away from me when I got off. I felt more and more like a monster with each passing second.

The village was quiet, just off the coast. It suited my needs perfectly. The tourist season was virtually over, leaving the place as empty and sad as a card stall after Christmas.

I was home.

I recognised the cottage as soon as my taxi climbed over the hill. It was just as I remembered. A little more run-down, sure, but that wasn't important. It was peaceful near the sea and I would be left alone.

So I stocked up on provisions – delivered to my door, of course – and I settled in to wait.

My portable radio brought me news about the trials of warfare. Some analysts argued it was the only way, others said that the end of the world was right around the corner and the Horsemen were already saddling up.

Then, tucked away in the middle of some insignificant programme one day, I heard a piece about the disease. *My disease!* Apparently more cases had been documented in the last few months, from all over the globe. Doctors were starting to sit up and take notice, but they assured the general public that there was nothing to worry about, that the chances of catching it were minimal. Reading between the lines you could detect more than a hint of panic in their assurances. The fire in my legs reminded me of just how 'lucky' I'd been to acquire such a rare affliction.

It wasn't long after that I lost the use of those legs entirely. Navigating my way around the house was exhausting, using my one good arm to drag myself along. Eating was a bitch, too, what with my face the way it was; the lumps now inside my mouth as well as outside – pushing against the gums, dislodging my teeth.

Some days I'd simply refuse to get up at all. Why should I? What had I got to look forward to? So I'd lie in bed, wallowing in a pit of my own dirt, and writhing as more of the pustules broke through.

I'd smashed all the mirrors in that cottage on arrival, how much more bad luck could it bring? But every now and again the windows worked against me – showing my reflection. Or the glass panelling on the door would cruelly remind me of what I'd been missing.

The temperature was dropping rapidly day-by-day outside, yet I was boiling hot. I ran a fever, the stagnant sweat gushing out, slickening my already moist body. I slept (hibernated?) a lot. And when I was awake I saw visions. Delirious, I recognised old familiar faces: Dr Fillis, Dr Jenkins, my dead parents … Dad with his lumpy hands…

And Rachel.

Except the last one was real. Rachel had found this address at home and tracked me down. She touched what was left of my face, bathed it with a cold flannel. But her hands, they were…

I think I screamed at that point.

***

It's towards the end of the year now, but time has lost all meaning. Rachel told me that the war was over. No one gives a shit about fighting anymore. They're all too preoccupied with other problems. Millions are coming down with the disease. The plague is uncontrollable, unpredictable. Unstoppable.

It happened much more quickly for Rachel than for me. The pain infinitely more intense – if that's at all possible. I could do nothing but be there for her, as she had been for me. Soon she became used to the contortions, just like I had.

Oddly enough, our pain is the only thing that reminds us we are alive. I don't understand how we can still *be* alive; I haven't taken solids for God knows how long. We both resemble something out of a sick horror movie. Nevertheless, our love remains strong. As do our visions, our dreams of the blue.

It will take us some time to get there in our present condition, making our way down the path, sliding over steps, onto the sand – each grain sparkling in the moonlight.

But we are far from alone. This seaside village is no longer deserted.

It has called out to everyone. The beach is full of quivering shapes that used to be human and even, yes, even those who have not yet undergone the transformation by this late stage. Their bloodcurdling cries can be heard for miles around. In my imagination I can see scenes like these occurring all over the country. All around the world.

We've talked it over many times and we think we know why now. Why we are returning to what we once were.

And as Rachel and I join again, gliding over the tide, lapping on the surface of the sea, our suspicions are confirmed. *We* are the disease.

All of us.

It has taken some doing, but after many failed attempts our planet has at last found a cure – some might say just in time! Its antibodies have been attacking us invisibly in the air, in our food, in the water … assaulting our collective consciousness, provoking the changes. Reversing what millions of years of evolution has achieved.

Hard to think clearly … but … there is no reason to fight it now. This isn't so bad. We're becoming one with the liquid, with each other. No worries, no anxiety, no hardship. No war. Just existence, and the promise of eternity.

At least for now.

At least for —

SABBAT

Dear Mr Kane,

Further to our recent correspondence, I have uncovered an item that might be of interest to you. A recently salvaged excerpt from an anonymous book similar to the *Malleus Maleficarum* or *Hammer of Witches* – Jacob Sprenger and Heinrich Kramer's popular and explicit work. You'll have to excuse the rather rough translation, obviously, but I'm sure you'll agree these descriptive passages do give one an insight into this time of paranoia, hysteria and irrationality. *I* personally believe this text was commissioned by the self-appointed witch-hunters of that era (or perhaps the church, headed by a pope obsessed with the 'evils of black magic'), to instil in the reader a sense of panic and fear, as well as to legitimise what they were doing to so many innocent people, the full details of which are available for anyone willing to research the subject – as I'm sure you've found out for yourself. How much of it was written to titillate is open to debate; as always, I welcome your suggestions on the topic. In any event, please find enclosed a photocopy of the piece entitled simply: 'Sabbat'.

Based on the confessions of witches under pain of torture on the witches' chair, a studded iron seat heated over a fire until burning. Fear not, for every last one has since felt more than the lick of such flames…

Know then, that the demon-lovers, as described to you within these pages, commonly hold a wicked and terrible ceremony once every seven days. This is being known to us as the witches' Sabbath or Sabbat.

Be vigilant, for if you know of any loss of children in your locality to illness, this may have been induced by outside forces; the use of clay images being employed, watered and baked until the child dies. For the Devil's servants raid the graves of freshly slaughtered young ones to gather the unctions necessary to enable them to fly to this Sabbat. They treat themselves with a salve concocted from the flesh and blood of boiled babies and the rotted corpses of long-dead villagers. Such oils may even be used when at the Sabbat itself, if it so pleases their master.

The ceremony is held always at midnight on the seventh day. And upon this hour witches and warlocks will gather from the covens – each one numbering exactly thirteen – in an unconsecrated site, such as the heart of a wood: their preference being for this ceremony to take place out of doors, exposed to the moonlight and stars above. This area will have been first especially arranged for their purposes, a clearing having been made, an altar constructed from the bones of their victims and dark symbols painted on the ground in newly-spilt blood. There may also be powerful stones present which, when placed in conjunction with these symbols, will let off an irreverent glow. Those of the covens must light an almighty fire in addition, and have then been known to cast strange powders into the flames.

At the commencement of the midnight hour, those present will disrobe and, barring any distinctive jewellery about their persons, will dwell as they were born in the clearing. One who is appointed a leader of them all will then stand before the altar and, reading from an ancient book bound in blackened human skin, will begin to chant that which is known to us as the Backward Blessing – the speaking of our Lord's Prayer backwards – thus initiating the start of the Black Mass. A blasphemous ritual defiling the laws of our most Holy Church, this Black Mass involves the sacrifice of a virgin upon the altar with sacrificial daggers handed down through the covens over the ages, and the dispatch of various animals bent easily to their will. These include base creatures such as toads, chickens and polecats. It may please the host also to relieve himself or herself upon members of the congregation, for those below will then lap up this rancid fountain of water and rub it into their bodies, in a mockery of the baptism under sight of our Lord.

Prayers will then be offered to The Prince of Darkness, and the congregation will attempt to summon up their master to further preside over the Sabbat, lighting black candles or torches in the fire to guide His path. From the fire He would arise, taking on many forms for many sets of eyes. To some He might appear as a black goat; the Horned One of legends past. Others may catch sight of Him as a terrifying red giant with hardened skin and hooved feet. Still others confess to seeing Him as a fully haired man, half-animal, half-human. But all will kneel before Him and swear allegiance when He deigns to appear, bringing innumerable familiars with Him from the very pits of Hell itself.

One by one, the witches and warlocks all then make some kind of obeisance to their master. More often than not this takes the form of the 'osculum obscenum', where each worshiper lines up in turn to lay his or her lips upon Satan's hindquarters as a mark of 'respect'.

Central to the Sabbat is the ritual feast. As well as vile-smelling and tasting wine and foodstuffs – the likes of which are documented as raw meats, overripe fruits and putrid vegetables – the witches and warlocks might partake of human flesh, cannibalism being a well-known trait amongst such as their kind. The familiar-demons, meanwhile, will suckle at the congregation's blood, through teats (warts, moles or other such blemishes bestowed upon them by Lucifer) more commonly known as Devil's Marks. Nor will they feel any discomfort at this feeding, however, for the Devil's Mark is said to be insensitive to pain. This has led to the exercise of pricking to uncover the true identity of those servants of darkness, whereby one practised in the skills of the same will prick the mark with a pin or knife and study the subject for signs of distress. If none occur, they will be singled out as a witch or warlock to be questioned and ultimately cleansed of their evil ways.

Note: As you may know already, dishonest witch-finders used fake knives, with hollowed-out handles, and sleight-of-hand to fool the populace into thinking people with malformations on the skin – harmless birthmarks and moles in most instances – were in fact witches or warlocks. An excuse for many of them to practise torture or their own depraved activities. R.L.

Once the feast is over, dancing might take place to a mesmerising drummed beat. The congregation would sway and move in time to the beat, and after an allotted period has passed a signal is then given for the commencement of the orgy. So now we come to the acts of depravity so vile even reading of these is wont to lead to madness. More than the accustomed number of two would join in union out of wedlock, sometimes copulating with members of their own sex. But make no mistake, group behaviour of this inclination is without any of the usual love a man and a woman might experience in the laying down together of a holy bonding, it being icy cold and sometimes even painful for all concerned.

The time is soon at hand when the demons will join in the ritual, taking man and woman alike for their own, and piercing them in an indescribable fashion. Some have even said that the occasional offspring of such mating live on after birth and roam the land attacking travellers and those who remain out after sunset. Beelzebub, who has until now simply watched and enjoyed the bestiality, takes it upon Himself to also select His chosen ones for that night. Any unfortunate enough to be 'favoured' will never be the same again, and can never properly be cleansed, neither, not by fire nor water. The Kingdom and all its splendours will forever be considered out of reach for those who pander to His needs. The Lord of Darkness has been known to defile many without rest, making them His for all of eternity. He may suck blood from the Devil's Mark, in addition, or create new imperfections of the skin. He has also been seen as a bull or deer before copulation, completing His trans-formation into an unclean beast. In this way, the knowledge of how to turn into animals is passed on to the witches and warlocks themselves – oft times the cat, the crow and hare – to further His aims upon this Earth. They might also be able to ask of The Dark One to supply them with special arrows to kill their enemies, for if He is satisfied by His attentions He will be only too pleased to share His fiendish arsenal.

At last the Sabbat is over. The Prince of Flies and His demons will depart, retreating into the flames from whence they came, leaving the congregation drained of both energy and souls. Once fully recovered, they will cloak themselves again in thick black garments and cast a series of spells upon the place so that no-one will trespass until it is time once again for the Sabbat, on the seventh day that passes...

***

Quite a stark contrast to how we perceive witches today, as followers of the old nature religions. Indeed, all those I have come into contact with during the course of my lifetime have been the nicest people you could ever hope to encounter. And as for the so-called evidence, extracted through unbearable torture, well I'm quite sure most of us would have confessed to anything the witchfinders might conjure up just to stop the agonising pain.

Nevertheless, a part of me can't help thinking what if only a fraction of this is true? I always like to keep an open mind; there are more things in Heaven and Earth than are dreamt of in our philosophy, I suspect. At the very least you might be able to use some of it in one of your fantastical stories, yes?

I look forward immensely to hearing what you think.

Yours truly,

Richard Lomas PhD,
Head of Historical Studies and Folklore,
Haveredge University,
Haveredge.

DIG (THIS)

Like all stupid ideas, it had seemed like a good one 'at the time'.

Although now, as they walked past these plots in the darkness, the gravestones like ragged grey teeth sticking up out of the ground, Davy was wondering if they should go ahead with their half-baked scheme at all. It was one thing to say you were going to do something, but to actually do it was another matter entirely.

In fact, the more he mulled it over, the more stupid the idea became. Just whose suggestion had it been anyway? His? No, at least Davy didn't think so. Had to be Travis', then. Yeah, Travis' stupid idea.

Travis suddenly stopped dead and Davy ran into his back.

'Hey, watch it!' shouted Travis, then realised his voice was about ten times louder than it needed to be. Stevo, bringing up the rear, collided with Davy and muttered a pitiful sorry. It certainly hadn't been Stevo's idea... Travis, definitely Travis. He was the 'brains' behind this operation.

Mind you, they were all to blame to some extent. Hadn't they chosen this place to hang out week after week? Why exactly was that? Because it was as quiet as the grave? It was true that nobody ever came up here. The small chapel to which it belonged had long since been abandoned, its structure unsound, its congregation now either dead themselves or worshiping in much more modern, centrally heated temples. Which meant that the 'yard – as they called it – had also become neglected, the grass only cut once in a blue moon. Those buried here had been all but forgotten by their surviving relatives – if, indeed, they had any. In this age the pace of life was just too great, problems too numerous. It left little time to visit people you couldn't even remember, let alone miss.

Which made the 'yard such a brilliant place for them to congregate. No one to disturb them, no one interfering. No one telling them what to do; the poor buggers in those plots were past telling anyone anything. Stevo came here to escape from that madhouse he lived in. It was more like an old folks' home since his sick grandparents had come to stay. You couldn't move for Zimmer frames and commodes at his place. Travis came to get away from his ex-boxer dad who couldn't be arsed to go down the gym anymore, preferring instead to use his own son as a punch-bag. And Davy-boy? Well, he just came here to escape from the disappointment of his own existence – the fact that he'd never amount to anything … unlike his older brother, who'd been to university and snagged a job with a large banking firm in the city immediately after leaving.

'David, you're a complete waste of space,' his mother would tell him every other minute. 'Just like your father was.' A father he'd never known, and would have to take his mum's word about. So, he figured he might as well come here to waste that space rather than anywhere else. It was his space to waste, after all.

The three of them had been making the trek up to this small but deceptively capacious graveyard for about two or three months now. Ever since they found it on one of their famous walks – trying to alleviate the boredom of being a teenager in one of the most dreary localities known (or unknown?) to mankind. If Travis hadn't taken that shortcut through the hedge behind Old Parson's field, they might have missed it altogether…

None of them had ever had a death in the family – worst luck – so they'd never actually had cause to visit a grave-yard before. It was one of those things they knew existed, but hadn't really thought too much about. Until that day in late July, at the start of the summer holidays.

Travis had stopped and stared at the 'yard, the head-stones lined up in rows on the overgrown pasture.

'Now this I *can* dig,' he said, smiling broadly.

Stevo didn't like it at first, sitting on the stones and smoking, or discussing which girls in their year were hot … or even in the year above. (Sara Miles usually came top of the list for all three of them: she looked a bit like Angelina Jolie without the lips, and the boys called her 'Angel' for short.)

But Stevo was soon talked round by Travis.

'Don't you see, this is perfect.'

It was. Davy thought the same. A really great 'getaway from it all' sort of place. Plus, if the company of Travis and Stevo got too much for him, he could always read the 'stones. There were plenty to choose from: some your standard crosses, atop plinths or rocks; some more ornamental crosses with edges that looked like three-leafed clovers. Some were arch-shaped, or even pointed: the idea being to suggest the way to Heaven, presumably; some had more rounded tops like big flat shoes. But the vast majority were simple rectangular slabs – no frills or fuss. Davy spent hours and hours going up and down the rows, peeling away moss, parting the grass, taking in the dates, the names… Stevo laughed at him sometimes, but Davy found it all fascinating. Found the whole graveyard fascinating, if he was honest.

Maybe he *had* suggested this!

No, Davy could remember the conversation quite clearly in his mind now. He'd been reading the names on the 'stones again, coming back to a particular favourite of his – the plainest one of all, with the shortest inscription chiselled into the roughly textured granite. *Here rests Frederick Fullerton 1899-1965.* Travis and Stevo joined him, sitting opposite, and they drank the tins of beer Travis had stolen from his old man's fridge. Someone would be in for a pasting when he found out; Davy was just glad it wouldn't be him.

Somewhere along the line, they'd started to talk about dying and death and ending up in a cemetery just like this one someday. Davy was amazed the subject hadn't cropped up before.

'So what do you think?' asked Stevo. 'Is there a God and Heaven and all that?'

'What do I look like,' Travis had retorted, 'the Archbishop of bastard Canterbury?'

'Not exactly.'

'What d'*you* think, Stevo?' Davy said, sipping the now lukewarm beer. 'What's after this? D'you go on to live forever?'

'I fucking well hope not,' said Travis. 'What's so great about life?'

'I wasn't asking you.'

Stevo looked out thoughtfully over the horizon. This was heavy stuff to be discussing at such a tender age. But they were all old enough to have sex, no matter what the law said; it wouldn't be long before they could vote and work, or sign on – if the statistics in this area were anything to go by. Why shouldn't they talk about the other 'biggie'? 'I think...'

'Yeah?'

'I think we'll all find out when the time comes.'

Travis snorted. 'Course we will, *moron*. But by that time we won't be able to tell anyone about it, will we?'

'Not unless we come back from the dead,' said Davy, quick as a flash.

Stevo raised an eyebrow. 'What, you mean like a ghost or a zombie or some bollocks like that?'

Davy nodded.

'You've been watching too many horror flicks, Davy-boy,' said Stevo.

Travis felt sufficiently motivated to say, 'All horror films are shit.'

Davy wasn't impressed by his blitzkrieg method of critique, but was willing to hear him out. 'Explain.'

'It's obvious, isn't it? The monsters and stuff. You know at the back of your mind it's all make-up. Special effects, computer animation ... what's so frightening about that?'

'Better ask Stevo. He's the one who almost cacked himself when we watched *Hellraiser* at Marty Finn's party that time.'

'I was only a kid back then.'

'*Hello*, it was last year.'

Stevo showed Davy his middle finger. Davy raised his beer in salute.

'Well, they don't do jack for me,' said Travis. 'It's like watching soft porn or something. It's not real.'

Davy smiled. 'And when was the last time *you* watched porn – soft or otherwise?'

Travis smirked. 'You'd be surprised at what's hidden under my old man's bed.'

'No I wouldn't.'

'So what's the alternative?' Stevo innocently enquired. 'Snuff movies? Those things are all faked as well.'

'He's talking about those documentaries on Channel 5, those autopsy programmes, aren't you? Or the ones about serial killers?'

Frowning, Travis said, 'They're okay. But they still don't show you much of anything.' His next question was off at a tangent, but sort of made sense within the context of the meandering debate they were having. 'I bet neither of you have ever seen a dead body up close, have you?'

Davy and Stevo looked at each other.

'Well, *have* you?'

They shook their heads.

'But then,' said Davy, 'neither have you.'

Travis conceded the point. 'You're right. I haven't.'

That's when it started to get interesting. Travis pointed to the grave Davy was sitting next to. 'Aren't you just a little bit curious?'

'About what?'

'You spend most of your time here looking at the headstones, reading the names... Hasn't it ever crossed your mind...?'

The funny thing was, it had. And Davy knew without speaking to Stevo that it had crossed his mind too, as chicken as he was. Travis had simply brought it out into the open. They were all wondering, at that precise moment, what the corpses in the 'yard looked like, after being buried in the earth all this time.

So exactly when had they decided to find out?

Davy still couldn't recall. It hadn't been straight away, he knew that. But when, and who's idea had it been?

Travis' giant flashlight in his face brought Davy back to the here and now. Should he voice his concerns? Tell Travis he wanted to turn back? Stevo would go with him, there was no doubt about that. He was only here to start with out of a misplaced sense of pride, to stop them both from ragging him. If Davy wanted to hightail it out of there, then that gave him the perfect excuse.

'Listen, Travis…'

'You're not bottling it, are you? Nah, I know you too well, Davy-boy. You want to see old Fullerton just as much as I do.'

'Why'd we have to come at night, though, Travis?' whined Stevo. 'There's never anybody here in the day, only us. Everyone's forgotten about this place.'

Travis moved the light over to shine in Stevo's face. 'Do you want to risk it? Just because we've never seen anybody the whole of the summer, doesn't mean nobody *ever* comes. It'd be just our luck for someone to catch us in the middle of … you know, the middle of doing what we're going to do.'

'But—' started Stevo.

'What's the matter, anyway? Are you scared of the dark?' He said this in a mocking tone of voice.

'No!'

Travis laughed. 'Don't worry, I won't let anybody hurt you.' He pulled something out of his pocket. There was a clicking sound and the flick-knife in his hand sprang open.

'Shit!' said Stevo. 'Where the Hell d'you get that from?'

'Ask me no questions…'

'Just … just put it away before someone gets hurt!'

Travis folded the blade up on his thigh and hid it away again.

'Why'd you stop anyway?' Davy asked.

Travis flashed his light on the gravestone to their left. 'We're here,' he said.

Davy followed the beam and saw the name: Frederick

Fullerton. They had indeed arrived.

'Right, time to go to work,' said Travis. He waved his beam over the high grass next to the grave, looking for the spot where they'd hidden the shovels and pick earlier on. He found them easily enough, then handed the implements out: keeping the pick for himself. Stevo and Davy just stood there looking at the shovels as if they didn't know quite what they were for.

'Come on then. Get started!' Travis snapped at them, but they still waited for him to begin digging before they joined in. The ground was hard and shockwaves vibrated up along the shovels and pick as they worked. Time seemed to pass quickly though, and it wasn't long before they were quite a way down – the piles of earth by the side of the grave a testament to their labours.

'If we go much further, we're going to have a job getting out of the hole again,' said Stevo. The torch resting on the side of the fissure illuminated his worried face.

'Just keep digging,' said Travis.

Davy had to admit that he felt the same. A sense of determination was surging through him now, he felt a need to get to the bottom of this hole they were digging, to finish what they'd started, to reach the –

There was a clumping sound. Travis stopped, his pick buried in the earth.

'Was that…?' Stevo half-asked.

'Pass me the torch,' demanded Travis. With a shaking hand, Stevo reached up and did as he was told. Travis got down on his haunches, held the flashlight in one hand and brushed away the soil with the other. 'Pay dirt,' he whispered.

'I don't think that's very funny,' said Stevo. 'Do you think that's funny Davy? I said –'

'Shhh,' Davy urged, leaning over Travis' shoulder. He was clearing away all the soil, revealing the outline of the coffin they were standing on. He whistled, again a little too loudly.

'I don't like this,' muttered Stevo. 'Don't like it one bit.'

When Travis suggested getting the lid off, Davy didn't know whether he liked it, either.

'What's the problem? I thought you wanted to see it.'

'Me? I never said —'

'Look,' said Travis. 'Are either of you two wet-nurses going to help me or not?'

His companions just stood there looking at him.

'Right, well get out of the fucking way then. Make some room.' Travis motioned for them to get up out of the hole, and they did. But they still squatted down on the side next to the mounds of earth they'd shifted – just in case they missed anything.

Travis used the pick to get underneath one corner of the coffin. It was tough to shift but eventually it gave, old nails submitting to his pressure. There was a loud crack as the wooden lid opened up a fraction. In fact it splintered halfway down and Davy thought the whole thing was going to break in two.

It didn't, though. Quite the opposite: it came away in one piece and Travis reared it up alongside the coffin itself.

'Christ ... the smell,' said Stevo – it reached them even up there, a foul odour that defied description.

Travis was pulling back, standing up on the edges of the coffin. He'd dropped the pick, and now only had the flashlight in his grasp, trained on the casket below. But Stevo and Davy couldn't see a thing because of him.

'Travis,' said Davy. 'What is it? What's he look like?'

Travis didn't answer, he simply tip-toed around the edge

of the coffin, allowing them a view of the corpse. It was old, as they'd expected. Mere bones with a covering of dried skin that looked like it would blow away in a mild breeze. There were hollows where the eyes should have been, cheeks sunken so much you could fit your entire fist inside them. Lower down, the ribs were completely bared, and Davy thought he saw something scurry very quickly through the 'cage. All three of them wanted to look away, but couldn't; the fascination was too great. They felt compelled to drink in every sight of this, record every possible moment.

'Should … shouldn't he be just a skeleton by now?' whispered Stevo eventually. 'I mean … there shouldn't be…'

'Don't ask me,' Davy answered. 'I'm no expert. Travis? Travis…?'

The youth didn't answer. He just stood there, as if he couldn't believe that he'd actually had the guts to do this. To disturb the final resting place of Frederick Fullerton.

'Travis?' Davy called out in one of those cautious semi-shouts.

'I … I'm just coming,' he said, putting down the torch.

Then he pulled out his flick-knife.

Stevo clutched Davy's arm. 'What's he doing? Tell him to put that away.'

But Davy could only stare at his friend down in the pit, wondering what he was going to do with that knife. And hoping it wasn't what he was thinking; maybe collect a souvenir for their efforts. Jewellery? Was he after a watch or a ring or something? God … not a finger or —

Travis held the knife out at his side, giving the impression that he didn't really know himself what he was going to do. It *snicked* open, the sound much louder than before, the blade glinting in the light from the downed torch.

Then he held out his other hand in front of him, exposing his wrist.

In one swift movement he ran the sharpened metal across his vein, like a musician playing a violin. Travis let out a shriek of pain and surprise at his own actions, but didn't stop. Instead he cut deeper, causing a fountain of blood to spurt from the wound.

Now Davy did shout, properly this time: 'Travis! What the hell are you — ?'

Travis turned his head and looked up at Davy. His expression was one of puzzlement mixed with pleading, as he worked away on his wrist, knife-edge jagging open the flesh, sawing right through... Davy rose to jump in after him; to prevent him from hurting himself any more than he already had; to pull him out and get him some help.

But Stevo squeezed his arm tighter. 'Look!'

Davy followed his gaze, past Travis and into the open coffin. Where the blood had landed on old Frederick Fullerton, and was still landing as they watched, it seemed to be drying up like the corpse itself – as if simply touching the dead man was having some sort of effect on it.

The body twitched.

'Fuck!' said Stevo. 'Did you see that? Did you fucking see that?'

Davy saw, but he didn't know whether to believe it. The torch's beam was far from reliable and even —

It moved again. Now there could be no denying what was happening.

Travis divided his attention between his wrist and the bizarre scene in front of him. This wasn't right. This wasn't how it was supposed to go. They only wanted to see, to look at him … they weren't really doing any harm…

Well, now they could all see Fullerton, and more besides.

Could see how his worthless and ragged body was sucking up the blood greedily. How it was energising and reanimating the thing that shouldn't be lifting itself up, two worm-infested hands clutching the sides of the coffin. He looked for all the world like a man in a bath, ready to reach out for a rubber duck, or maybe a loofah. Except what Frederick Fullerton really wanted to bathe in wasn't water. His nonsense of a face twisted around, jellied eyes appearing and seeing again after so long. It was Travis he desired. And Travis knew it.

'Jesus-God-Jesus-God-Jesus-God-Jesus…' ranted Stevo, wishing now he'd paid more attention during Religious Education, wishing that he'd been more religious, full stop. At least that might've protected him from … from whatever this was.

What happens when you die – do you go on living forever? Maybe somewhere, but not here. Not in this world! You don't go on living down here … In your grave…

Here RESTS Frederick Fullerton…

More blood splattered onto him, and Davy was wondering just *how* much there could be left inside Travis; not that much, surely. And wasn't there something he should be doing? Something he'd started to do before he saw this Lazarus return from the dead? Help Travis. That's what he was about to do…

Only now there seemed little point.

Fullerton drew himself up, knees cracking like dead wood, *things* falling from his ragged clothing, withered features contorting with the effort of it all – but the blood, oh so much *life*-blood, all gratefully received. Unwilling donor Travis looked like he wanted to get away, and still couldn't. Davy doubted whether he'd be able to climb out of that pit now anyway, he wouldn't have the strength. His eyelids were fluttering, although the pupils beneath those lids were still alive with fear.

Fullerton stepped forward and grabbed Travis, snatching the knife out of his hand at the same time. He held up the blade, examining it for a moment. Then he smiled; it was a repugnant sight. Teeth with no gums – or what gums were left, receding so badly you could hardly see them at all. Yet there was saliva. Where before Frederick had been so dry, almost like dust, he was now revitalised, had quenched at least some of his thirst for new existence.

But he needed more.

With one stroke he opened up Travis' throat, and Davy saw that there was *plenty* of blood still inside. It jetted across Fullerton's face and upper body, and he had to catch Travis as he slumped – almost certainly dead himself by this time. The corpse ground against his young hostage, obscene noises coming from the pair.

That was it: Stevo could hold back his vomit no longer. Turning away, he brought up his last meal (his last supper?), heaving until he thought he'd go blind.

Davy wasn't as fortunate: he kept his eyes locked on the drama unfolding. On Fullerton's inflating cadaver, the muscles filling out, sinews straining, a body given new form. At the same time Travis seemed to be shrivelling up before his eyes as his juice was transferred to Fullerton. And not just blood, either – everything, his whole being.

What's wrong? You wanted to meet him, always wondered about him lying down there with six feet of earth between you? Well now's your chance! In a moment he'll get out of that hole and he'll come after you next. Then you'll meet him, you'll finally meet him…

Davy wasn't so sure he wanted to anymore. Wasn't sure he'd wanted it in the first place. Travis' fault. All Travis' —

Fullerton let Travis go. The teenager didn't make much of a sound as he fell into the open coffin, there wasn't much of him left *to* make a sound. Davy watched as Travis rolled back into the wooden box.

The exchange was complete – one corpse for another, one *life* for another. Fullerton turned his attention to Davy.

'Quick, get up!' he shouted at Stevo, who was still bringing his guts up next to the grave. *If he doesn't shift himself they'll be spilling all over the floor for real*, Davy thought.

Davy stood and moved away from the edge of the opening, a shovel in his hand. He backed up, placing a hand on Stevo's shoulder. 'Come *on!*'

Stevo got up, staggered about, then fell back down.

A hand came over the side of the grave. Not quite normal, but nothing like the hand that had clutched the side of that coffin just minutes ago. Another joined it, this one with a flick-knife in its grip.

'Fucking get your arse up!' shouted Davy, grabbing *his* arm this time and pulling him onto his knees. 'We've got to—'

Davy froze. Fullerton was up and out of the grave in one lithe movement. The moon, in its infinite wisdom, chose that moment to sneak out from behind a cloud and illuminate the scene. Fullerton smiled that smile again.

Stevo looked over and just about saw the dead man through watery eyes.

Fullerton started to walk towards them.

Neither Davy nor Stevo could move. They wanted to, but were stuck to the spot. Was it fear, was it the in-evitability of what was happening? Davy had no idea; all he knew was that his feet seemed to have taken root in the unkempt grass.

Doing the only thing he could, Davy raised his shovel and swung it – a warning for Fullerton to stay back. It didn't work. He kept on coming, narrowing the gap between the three of them. Fullerton shook his head.

'D-D-D-D-Davvvy...' Stevo spluttered.

Davy looked at Stevo, then back at Fullerton. Without another second's thought, he dropped the shovel.

'Davy, what're you...?'

Davy suddenly found he could move, and he backed off.

Fullerton grinned once more, quickening his pace. He lunged at the kneeling figure of Stevo, slashing and stabbing him with the knife.

Davy turned his back on the sight ... but he couldn't shut out the sounds, the gurgling noises, the terrible cries. He began to run, away from that place, away from what he'd just done

Got to help him ... got to...

But instead Davy just kept on running. Suddenly his existence seemed so very important, his space – even if it was a waste – was precious. His legs were going up and down of their own accord, and he was leaving the nightmare behind. Leaving Travis and Stevo, leaving Fullerton and his grave. He was running, desperate to get home and re-adjust his reality.

Had to pretend it hadn't happened at all, slip under the covers of his bed and go to sleep.

***

By the time Fullerton looked up again, Davy was a speck – a black speck in the distance. It didn't matter. He still had Stevo.

He stood, his own body now strong, remade. How easy

it had been to reach out to these weak-willed youngsters, to influence them, to plant the seed in their minds... Just as they'd given him the idea in the first place with all their talk of horror and life after death, the images, the descriptions. He'd been waiting so long for just such an opportunity. Using their own preconceptions against them was a stroke of genius, even if he did say so himself.

So they were bored, were they? They ought to try being him.

It had been so easy to get Travis to offer up his spirit, such as it was. To persuade Davy to drop his 'weapon' and abandon his friend. Actually that last one puzzled him. Fullerton hardly had to break a sweat; it was almost as though Davy knew that he *had to* sacrifice Stevo in order to get away. That alone would haunt him the rest of his short life.

For Frederick Fullerton had friends of his own here. Names on gravestones, whispered promises of revolution, of the dead stealing life from the ungrateful living. Those who no longer cared, nor remembered, who were determined to simply fritter away their precious gift in mindless monotony. It was ... it was ... *wasted* upon them.

Christ, who would *choose* to spend their time in a place like this?

He smiled one last smile, and stooped to pick up Davy's discarded shovel. Fullerton looked around him at the burial site, then at Stevo's remains. There was much to be done, many to free, many to feed. But he felt strong – and soon they would too. Walking over to one of the nearby plots, he stuck the shovel in the earth.

Then, slowly but surely...

He began to dig.

A CHAOS DEMON IS FOR LIFE...

Christmas morning.

And Jacob Campbell was up at six a.m. He'd been too excited to stay in bed, and had only managed a couple of hours sleep at most. Though he was getting a bit too old to believe in Santa at almost nine years of age, he could have sworn he'd heard something at about midnight last night. The whole house had shaken; could it really have been down to that famous sleigh landing on the roof of the house?

What would he get this year, he wondered. He'd been a good boy. Always was, in fact – never got into trouble like some of the other kids. He was too busy reading: usually the latest Rowling, Shan or Gaiman book, or magazines filled with pictures of fantasy TV shows and films. Either that or playing with his model figures. Jacob's shelves were filled with toys from various horror movies, including those he was too young to see ... officially (his very cool Uncle Tom often let him have sneaky peaks when he stayed with him down South). Up on the shelf, mini-Predators battled Aliens, Frankenstein was frozen in mid-punch, attacking Dracula, and Jason's rematch with Freddy was in full swing – all while Godzilla and King Kong looked on with mild amusement.

Perhaps it would be another figure, a bigger one this time? He'd dropped more than a few hints that he'd like the creature from *Cloverfield*, in spite of the fact he'd never seen it. By all accounts neither had the audience much.

Jacob hopped out of bed, sprinting to the door, flinging it open. His parents would probably still be asleep – they were always reluctant to get up early, even on normal weekdays. He couldn't imagine why, unless it was because they were really, really old. When he raced into their room, though, springing up onto the mattress, he found the bed was already empty.

'Down here, Jay,' his father called from what sounded like the living room. Jacob shrugged. He shouldn't be too surprised; after all, they'd probably been expecting him to be up at this ungodly hour, just like every other year. They must have set their alarms and beaten him to it, that's all. Perhaps it meant there was something really special waiting for him downstairs.

He wasn't wrong.

When Jacob peered round the living room door, he saw a wrapped box under the tree – about the size of the chest he kept some of his older toys in. His mum and dad were still in their clothes from yesterday, rather than the usual dressing gowns they always wore on Christmas morning. They looked tired, but incredibly happy, and were standing not too far away from the box.

'Hey there, son,' said his father, pushing his glasses back up his nose. 'And a very Merry Christmas to you!'

'Merry Christmas, Dad.'

His mum echoed the greeting and he repeated it back to her, all the time looking past them to the neatly wrapped package. It was all reds and golds, with a bow tied on top. Jacob's dad followed his gaze. 'Ah, you spotted it then?'

Jacob nodded, laughing.

'Wanna open it?'

Another nod, more emphatic this time.

'Okay then...' His father waved a hand for Jacob to go to the box. As the boy approached, he noticed there were big holes in all the sides. He thought about asking what they were, but when he got closer the box moved – causing Jacob to start. They were air holes; whatever was inside was alive! It was now that he had a suspicion what this was.

'It's a puppy, isn't it?' he said, turning. They'd finally given in to his constant moaning about a pet, something to play with because he was an only child. Jacob had begun to think they'd never listen.

His mum shook her head.

'What then, a kitten? Is it a kitten ... *is it?*'

'Why don't you go ahead and open it, then you'll find out,' said his dad.

Jacob needed no more encouragement; he had little patience at the best of times. Rushing to the present, he tore off the wrapping. It responded to his touch, jumping again – or rather whatever was inside was jumping. It was obviously excited, eager to be free. Underneath the Christmas paper was an ordinary brown cardboard box, with a lid. Placing both hands on the side, Jacob lifted this up.

He let out a gasp at what he saw.

There, curled up inside, was ... something. Something he'd never seen before, something that immediately fascinated and slightly terrified him. The creature was about the size of a small chimp, but hairless. Its skin was leathery, wrinkled and – in places – scaly. Its wings were folded up on its back, which it was presenting to Jacob, cowering away from the sudden light entering the box. Its legs were drawn up tight into its body, arms and hands covering its head. Jacob could see the buds of claws on each tip, creamy-white in colour. Though easily mistaken for grey, the whole thing actually had a purple tinge to it.

Slowly, carefully, it brought its arms down and turned its face towards Jacob. It had a protruding snout and two slits standing in for nostrils, which were already slick with mucus. On its cheeks were dotted several more scales, a lighter purple in tone to the rest. Two large, pointed ears flanked its bulbous head, the tips of which waggled as if they were picking up all the sounds in the world, like antennae. It had not two eyes, but four: the first pair in the customary place, the second in the middle of these, positioned above and below the eye-line (it looked a little like an inverted cross). The eyes were predominantly yellow, but with flecks of orange and red floating inside, which gave them the appearance of being on fire. Its dual horns were short, nothing more than stumps, really. When it opened its mouth, Jacob saw row upon row of tiny teeth – and a blast of rancid breath wafted in his direction.

'W-what is it?' asked Jacob with a nervous tremble in his voice.

'Don't you know?' asked his mother.

Now it was Jacob's turn to shake his head. Well, he had an *idea* what this was, but it jarred with the reality he was used to.

'Why, it's your very own pet monster!'

The creature rose slowly, taking in its surroundings, then looked directly at Jacob, fixing him with its four burning eyes.

'It... But it can't...'

'It can and it *is*,' his dad said proudly. 'Took some doing, but we got him for you.'

The creature rose, unfurling a length of tongue from its mouth, and doing the same with a forked tail that had been tucked up underneath it all this time. It opened its mouth wider, then snaked out the tongue, which was also forked at the tip, and ran it down the side of Jacob's face. It tickled, but he held very still. The purple monster wagged its tail.

'W-where did you get it?' asked Jacob. 'Chinatown, right? Has to be! Like in *Gremlins*?'

His parents laughed. 'Not that easy I'm afraid,' his dad assured him. It took us a good few hours after you'd gone to bed to summon the little tyke. That's not to mention the months of research that went into it all. Oh yes, we've been planning this one for a long time, kiddo. You wouldn't believe the ingredients we had to get together, either, and we've only just finished Vanishing all the markings off the carpet.'

His mother laughed again. 'Your father just thought: you're into monsters, you want a pet. Why not put the two together?'

The monster had climbed out of the box now and was sniffing around, crawling on all fours.

'He's certainly more lively than he was last night,' observed Jacob's dad. 'The materialisation really took it out of him.'

The creature was sniffing the sofa, trying to work out exactly what it was. When it brought its 'nose' away it left a string of snot behind.

'Does it have a name?' asked Jacob.

'Actually, *he* does, yes. It's ... now hold on a minute, I want to get this right.' His dad picked up an ancient-looking book that he'd left on the coffee table and began flipping through the pages. He stopped at the one he wanted, tapping it as if he'd just found something in a catalogue – which wasn't far from the truth. 'Ah, here he is – in "Chaos Demons from the Twenty-seventh Circle". His name's Xzyolocolyopiacocklysis, but I guess that's a bit of a mouthful.'

At that exact moment the creature bit into the side of the sofa and ripped away a huge chunk of material and foam. He began chewing and then swallowed it whole.

'Isn't he cute?' said Jacob's mother.

'I think I'm going to call him "Freckles",' stated Jacob, pointing to the lighter scales on the demon's cheeks.

'Freckles it is,' said his father, slamming the book shut.

The creature belched loudly then, moments later, crawled into the middle of the living room and proceeded to squat, squeezing out a huge, steaming turd.

'Oh, would you look at that!' said Jacob's mother in a shrill voice.

'Fast metabolism,' said her husband.

'I'll have to get the Vanish out again.'

Jacob's dad chuckled and winked at his son. 'Too much fibre is all, and he's not housetrained yet.'

Jacob laughed as well and thanked them both for such a cool Christmas present.

***

In fact, none of his other gifts really matched up (DVDs, computer games … not even money), but Jacob would write thank you notes to all the people who sent them – his parents would make sure of that. Jacob played with Freckles for a good few hours, while his mum and dad prepared stuff for the Christmas dinner with the rest of the family later on. He took the demon up to his room and introduced him to some of this other toys – not the ones on the shelf, but his older toys: cars, trucks, miniature tanks and soldiers from out of his chest. Jacob had a great time arranging them around Freckles, putting on his very own monster movie, until the creature decided to stomp on the vehicles and eat all the little figures.

After that, Jacob tried playing Frisbee with him. He

tossed it across to Freckles, who leapt up and caught the object in his mouth. When Jacob went over to retrieve the Frisbee, tired of waiting for it to come back, Freckles held it with its paws and bit into it, ripping away a good third of the plastic disc before spitting it out.

'Well that wasn't very nice,' said Jacob. 'What's it ever done to you?'

At eleven o'clock the household received its first Christmas visitor – up until then it had just been phone calls from well-wishers. When his mum answered the door, it was their neighbour, Mrs Higgins – a middle-aged widow whose husband had died over a decade ago, and who now relied on the company of her small Yorkshire Terrier, Scrappy. As far as Jacob was concerned, it should have been called 'Yappy', because that's all it ever did. And she took him everywhere with her, absolutely everywhere. Including round to their house that Christmas morning.

'Hello dearie,' Mrs Higgins had said, crossing over the threshold. 'Season's greetings.' It was at that point Scrappy, cradled in her arms like a baby, as always, began to yap, and then growl.

Because there, on the stairs, was Freckles – staring intently at the dog. The terrier's hackles rose and it scrabbled about in Mrs Higgins' arms, though it was unclear whether it was readying to attack or attempting to get away.

Then Freckles leapt from his perch on the stairs. Luckily, Jacob was only seconds behind, and caught him in mid-lunge. Jacob's dad, who was now in the hall and could see what had nearly happened, stepped between his wife and Mrs Higgins. He quickly explained that his son had a new pet and it might not be such a good idea to remain in the house in case Scrappy and Freckles didn't get on.

'What exactly *is* that?' asked a startled Mrs Higgins.

'An iguana,' explained Jacob's dad hastily.

Jacob managed to keep hold of Freckles until Mrs Higgins was gone, his dad virtually shutting the door in the woman's face. 'That was close,' he said, sighing.

When Jacob let go of Freckles, the demon scampered across the hall to his dad, and bit him on the calf. Jacob's father let out a howl, shaking off the demon. Then he hit it on the bottom. 'Naughty Freckles. Bad Freckles.' He almost wagged his finger, then thought better of it, in case it disappeared in a flurry of teeth.

'Come on,' said Jacob, pulling his new pet away. As he took the monster upstairs again, he heard his dad whispering to his mother that maybe this hadn't been such a great idea after all.

***

It wasn't until later in the afternoon that Jacob's dad began to realise what a truly disastrous mistake it had been to raise the creature.

Not till after it had killed Grandpa during the Queen's Speech.

The turkey incident had been bad enough. As they were taking it out of the oven, ready to place it on the table and feed the clan – which included two grandparents, from either side; a stuck-up aunty on Jacob's mother's side, Mimi; plus her annoying brat of a daughter, Gretchen; not to mention Mimi's new obnoxious boyfriend Dave, who they encouraged Jacob to call Uncle – Freckles had struck again.

Though Jacob could've sworn he'd locked the demon in his room, he'd somehow got out and, driven demented by the smell of the succulent bird, had pounced on Jacob's mother between the kitchen and the dining room and clawed it from the silver serving tray.

He'd then run off with it to the hallway, where he proceeded to tear into it, eating great chunks of flesh whole before Jacob could do a thing to stop it.

'Oh no!' shouted his mother. 'Look at that!' She approached Freckles, ready to give him a clip around his considerable ear, but he gave her a stare that told her this would be a very bad move indeed.

'What the *Hell* is that eating our turkey?' Mimi asked her sister, appearing over her shoulder. Gretchen wasn't far behind, a horrified look on her face when she saw Freckles.

'It's ... it's Jacob's Christmas present,' said his mum, looking like she was about to burst into tears.

His father came and put an arm around her. 'It's okay, it's okay... We have some ready meals in the freezer. We'll manage.'

'What an ugly looking thing,' Gretchen sneered.

'Look who's talking!' Jacob replied, and did get a clip for that. He could tell his father was thinking about locking Freckles up again, possibly somewhere more secure like the garden shed, but after devouring the turkey the demon appeared to be slightly bigger than before. Its teeth that bit larger and more pointed. Jacob had the feeling that if Freckles wanted to, he could probably take the man's entire leg off now rather than simply biting him.

'Come on,' said Jacob's father, ushering people back towards the dining room, looking over his shoulder only once at Freckles – who'd left another present for them to clean up off the carpet...

There was some moaning about the turkey, but in the end people understood; it was just one of those things that happened with new pets in the house. 'Uncle' Dave didn't care as long as the brandy was flowing, and the two grandparents barely seemed to register what was happening.

After their microwave meals, Jacob's mum lit the top of a Christmas pudding – and as he turned towards the door of the dining room, Jacob noticed Freckles was sitting there, watching the flames as they rose higher and higher, cocking his head.

It was an auger of things to come.

For, when they'd all adjourned to the living room, bellies full and slightly squiffy, the TV was turned on in readiness for their monarch's yearly address. Something about her voice set Freckles off big time, and soon Jacob realised why his eyes – all four of them – were that distinctive yellow and orangey-red colour. A blast of heat shot from them, directed at the television set. The screen cracked and the whole box exploded. But it didn't end there. Seemingly unable to control these new powers, Freckles turned them on the rest of the room, setting fire to decorations, to the books on the coffee table, and melting the angel on top of the Christmas Tree.

'Wha's goin' –' was all Grandpa managed before the ray was turned on him. Mercifully, it was over quickly – and in milliseconds Grandpa was reduced to a smouldering pile of ash in his chair.

The laser vision died down. The room was deathly quiet.

'It … it killed Gramps!' screamed Gretchen, shaking.

Jacob's father gaped at the spot where his own dad had been sitting, then he sank to his knees. 'What have I done?' he moaned softly.

Freckles, now back to normal – or as normal as any demon could be – looked to Jacob and whined. 'He didn't mean to do it,' the boy argued. 'It was an accident.'

'Well that's just brilliant,' slurred Dave, gaping at the broken TV set. 'How are we going to watch the bloody

Bond movie now?'

***

After Jacob's mum and dad had asked everyone still alive to leave – probably a good idea in Gretchen's case as Freckles was eying her up as he had done the turkey – they sat in the living room staring at the smoking remains of their Christmas.

They stayed like that the rest of the day, while Jacob took Freckles back upstairs with him. The creature had definitely grown – it was almost the same size as Jacob now. He listened at the top of the stairs to the ensuing conversation, only catching parts of it.

'...told you dabbling in the dark arts was dangerous, Ed...'

'...wanted it to be a special Christmas, Lorraine...'

'...send it back...'

'...remember how? The book's cinders...'

'...have to get rid of it some way...'

Jacob bit his lip when he heard that one. They were planning on taking away the best present he'd ever had. Okay, so he was one relative short, but then Grandpa always had been a grumpy so-and-so, and he often stank of pee. Plus which, it hadn't really been Freckles' fault.

'Don't worry,' he told the pet when he returned to his room. 'I won't let them do anything to you.'

In the end, he didn't really have a choice. They came in the night, once they knew their son was asleep with Freckles at the foot of his bed. Jacob had stayed awake as long as he could, but after the excitement of the night before, and the very long day, he'd soon found his eyelids drooping. They snapped open when he heard the kafuffle, though: shadowy figures he knew must be his parents, bundling Freckles into his toy chest.

'No!' Jacob shouted, rising from the bed. But a strong hand held him down.

'It's for the best,' his father whispered to him. 'Freckles should never have existed in our world. I realise that now.'

And, before Jacob could do anything, his parents had dragged the chest out of the room, down the stairs, and out of the front door. He begged them not to go, but they loaded the trunk into the boot of their car and drove off. They'd never left him alone before, but he guessed they knew it would take the pair of them to do whatever it was they intended to do.

Jacob watched from the open doorway, tears streaming down his face.

***

He waited most of Boxing Day for them to return.

They didn't.

Jacob sat in his room, on the bed, knees pulled up to his chest, wondering what had happened. What had they done with Freckles? He tried to push the obvious thoughts out of his head – *you know full well what they've done with him!* – and imagined instead they might have taken him to a demon sanctuary somewhere, if such places existed (he'd never seen adverts for them on TV; no 'Demons in Need' appeals either). He wondered if he would ever see the creature again...

A question that was answered just before tea-time, December 26th. Jacob heard screams coming from the street outside and rushed to his window to look out. Said street was in turmoil. Bodies littered the road, the fronts of houses were scorched, windows smashed. It looked like a warzone. And there in Mrs Higgins' front garden was Freckles. But he wasn't the demon he'd been yesterday when he left. Oh, no. Apart from being severely pissed off, Freckles was a good ten-fifteen feet tall, more mature in his appearance, fully scaled, standing almost completely upright, and appeared to be dripping wet. Of Jacob's parents there was no sign.

He's come home, thought Jacob, *but he's got the wrong house.* The boy was just about to rush outside when he realised his mistake. Freckles let loose another one of his laser-vision rays, like Cyclops from *The X-Men,* blasting away Mrs Higgins' front door. He disappeared momentarily, and when he came into view again, he had Scrappy in his gigantic paw. He dangled the dog above his mouth, opening the maw to reveal teeth that were more like a sabre-toothed tiger's now. The dog stopped yapping briefly, obviously aware of what was to come. Mrs Higgins had rushed out of the house by this time and was attacking Freckles' legs with an umbrella. The demon took absolutely no notice and, dropping the dog into its hungry jaws, began chewing as it had done with the turkey earlier.

'You... You *beast!'* Jacob heard Mrs Higgins cry, then she hit Freckles with the umbrella again. His response was to crap the remains of the terrier out onto the lawn.

Oh no, thought the boy and raced down the stairs of his house, flinging open the front door in time to see Freckles bearing down on the woman. 'No! Stop!' he shouted, and the demon paused. Freckles glanced over at Jacob, a sad look in his four eyes.

Then came the sound of sirens approaching. The police were out of their cars in no time, armed response units training their weapons on the creature. Jacob had no idea who fired first, probably some nervous cop who didn't care whether there were civilians in the vicinity or not – just that there was something monstrous in front of them which had to be put down. But the first round hit Freckles squarely in the back. The bullets bounced off, yet quite clearly caused him pain. Snarling, he blasted the police with his heat vision, cooking the man who'd fired at him, exploding the car he'd been using for cover. More shots rang out, sparking off the pavement, off Freckles' purple-grey scales.

Freckles unfurled his wings, which now had a massive span, and – snatching up Mrs Higgins – flew off into the sky. Jacob watched him leave, wishing he hadn't had to go so soon. The umbrella Mrs Higgins had been holding dropped to the ground near his feet.

The remaining policemen took him in for questioning. Jacob told them that Freckles had been his Christmas present; that his parents must have done something really bad to upset Freckles this way. That none of this was his fault.

The detective looked at him like he was mad – what a ridiculous story – and informed him his Uncle Tom from down South had been called to come and collect him, seeing as his parents were nowhere to be found.

In the car, Uncle Tom confessed that he knew Jacob's parents were planning something like this. That he'd warned them it would get out of control; that it wasn't like the movies. 'Now Pop's dead and they're both probably–' He stopped before he said it out loud, but Jacob knew what must have happened. He wasn't stupid.

Tears welled in his eyes again as they made the long trek down the motorway.

***

They followed Freckles' progress that Christmas week on the news.

Town after town, city after city he devastated – leaving smouldering ruins in his wake. Jacob gaped with wide eyes at the destruction, the buildings toppled, the dead and injured. Quick glimpses of footage from mobile phones told him that Freckles was growing larger by the hour. A foot here, an arm there. Helicopters fired rockets at the demon; he smashed them into the sides of tower blocks. Tanks and jeeps chased him down the streets; he crushed them underfoot.

By December 30th the army were knocking on Uncle Tom's door. 'Could we have a word with young Jacob?' a General called Carradine, with bushy eyebrows and a gruff voice, asked. Uncle Tom gave the man a cup of tea as he sat on the sofa and outlined his plan to the boy. When he'd finished, Jacob looked at his Uncle, who shrugged.

'It's up to you, but this thing —'

'Freckles,' corrected Jacob.

'Freckles … needs to be contained somehow. They'll do it with or without your help. Maybe this way less people will get hurt?'

Jacob reluctantly agreed, and on the last day of December he was flown into the country's capital where Freckles had last been spotted playing Frisbee with the London Eye; throwing it to himself and then catching it in his mouth – with people still inside it.

Now, Jacob saw as he flew in, the demon was climbing all over the Houses of Parliament, and up the side of Big Ben. He was swatting at more helicopter gunships, and even flew off the side momentarily to claw one to the ground.

Their own helicopter landed near Westminster Bridge, an open space where hopefully Freckles would see Jacob, his owner.

General Carradine and his troops left Jacob there to call to his 'pet', which he dutifully did.

'Freckles! Here, boy!' He whistled, calling again to the

creature.

A shadow fell over Jacob and he was amazed to see the size of Freckles now in real life. The bridge shuddered with his weight as the demon got on all fours and approached Jacob, sniffing the ground and leaving wide trails of snot behind.

'Freckles! Come on, come to me … I'm not going to hurt you.' It wasn't a lie, he never would.

The demon was looking left and right, making its way cautiously along towards Jacob.

'C-come on, t-that's it.' Jacob could barely keep the quiver from his voice. He held out his hand to Freckles, who now looked directly at him – remembering the boy from a week or so ago; the one who'd freed him from his box and played with him upstairs in his room.

A seemingly endless length of tongue stretched out from the demon's mouth like a fleshy carpet. Jacob stood firm, as much as he wanted to run. This was not the Freckles he'd known, and yet it was. Because as the tongue finally reached him, the forked end of it slavered up Jacob's cheek, almost lifting him off the ground. At the same time, its tail began to wag.

Jacob cried again. Even after all that had happened, Freckles was still his pet. Still his Christmas present.

He couldn't do this, couldn't be a part of his capture. 'Freckles. Go … run, fly … whatever, just *GO!*' The demon looked confused, perhaps wondering if Jacob was now rejecting him.

But it was too late. Helicopters carrying thrice-blessed nets – on the advice of various occult experts – were already over the bridge. Weighed down with religious statues, the mesh was dropped over Freckles and pinned him to the ground, preventing him from flying. 'Now!' screamed a voice from a megaphone somewhere. Suddenly, rockets, shells and mortars slammed into Freckles.

'Stop! STOP!' cried Jacob. This wasn't what they said they'd do, this wasn't a 'containment' at all!

Weakened by the bombardment, the demon tried to crawl forwards toward Jacob, but fell heavily, shaking the bridge once more. Freckles let out a whine, helpless and unable to muster even a tiny spark from his eyes. He began to cry and those sparks produced hisses of steam.

A final volley of rockets and mortars hit him, penetrating his scales.

'*NO!*' screamed Jacob at the top of his voice, but even he could see it was pretty much over. As Freckles took his last few breaths, Jacob went to him, patting the side of his face, leaning on his spotty cheek.

The demon's tail wagged once, twice. Then flopped lifelessly to the ground.

Army personnel approached, flitting around Jacob, testing the creature to see if it was truly dead. Jacob barely registered them. He was too busy mourning his monster, his very own real-life monster.

'Goodbye Freckles,' he whispered to it. 'I swear I'll never forget you. Not as long as I live. Not for my entire life.'

Then he felt his Uncle's strong hand on his shoulder.

'Come on, Jay. Time to go.'

He led Jacob away through all the confusion, but the boy looked over his shoulder one last time and mouthed two words again.

Because he knew this particular Chaos Demon had not meant to be just for Christmas at all. It had *always* been:

'For life…'

ST AUGUST'S FLAME

I had hoped it would wait until I reached the top of the rocky path. However, I was barely a quarter of the way to my destination when the belly of the black cloud above split open, and the first droplets splashed onto my face.

Soon there was a curtain of rain in front of me. It was hard to see where I was going and what had once been firm ground was rapidly turning to slush.

The pack mule I was leading bucked at the inaugural rumblings of thunder. Try as I might, I couldn't calm the thing. There was terror in those eyes, pure unfiltered terror – the flashes of lightning reflected in its orbs. For a second I thought I saw something else there, but had no more time to examine them. One of its hooves caught me clean across my shin and I let go of the rein. Almost as soon as I did, it romped away, taking my provisions and tent with it.

I nursed my stinging leg for a minute, then turned around and continued up the path. There was no point chasing after the damned animal, and to make my way back down the mountainside would be fool's work. I'd be lucky to reach the bottom alive in these conditions.

So I carried on, holding my hand up against the onslaught.

By the time I saw those lights, the sky was inky dark and my clothes were completely saturated. I had to blink twice, working the excess water out of my eyes, before I could believe the sight ahead.

There was definitely a beacon of some kind in front of me; in fact there were several. Miguel hadn't been lying after all. Not that I'd expected him to deceive me – he'd been well paid for his information. It's just that after seven years of searching, seven years of dead ends and disappointments, I hardly dared dream *It* was so close.

I staggered the remaining mile or so, half out of my mind with delirium, until I came upon those stone walls. They were ragged and grey, but had no doubt been standing innumerable decades, maybe even centuries, before I was born.

The stones formed a circular barrier at least twenty foot high, and at the top were the lights I had seen: oil lamps spaced out evenly along the bastion. In the centre was a large wooden door, similar to the ones at most castle entranceways, knotted and thick with an oversized ring on the right-hand side.

I summoned up all my strength and banged on the door. Its knocker was heavy and took some shifting, but the noise it created was worth the effort. If there was anyone here they couldn't fail to notice my arrival.

I waited a few moments, the wall affording me some shelter from the rain, though not much, and was about to knock again when I heard chains rattling on the other side. This was followed by a grinding as – I imagined – substantial locks were undone. Finally there came a creaking and the door was pulled open, albeit only a fraction.

There were too many shadows for me to make out the figure in the crack, but I *could* see his hand resting on the jamb. It was smooth and tanned like a new leather glove.

I broke the silence, trying to sound as pitiful as I could; it wasn't hard.

'Please, I wonder if I might come in to warm myself?'

The person gave no reply, so I spoke again. 'I-I've travelled a good distance and must have wandered off the main track. My mule ran away when the storm began and then I saw your lights and...'

The door opened further and the hand beckoned me inside. As I stepped through, I nodded in gratitude to my rescuer. I could see now that he was a monk. The robes he wore were of sackcloth, and a billowing hood concealed his face.

We walked through what appeared to be a courtyard. Oddly enough, the rain wasn't as harsh on this side of the wall and the isolated building we were heading for was entirely visible. That too was made from stone which had an ancient quality about it.

My guide remained silent as he ushered me through a second wooden door and under a roof at long last. Only then did he remove the cowl. His face was as brown as his hands, with tiny – almost undetectable – wrinkles at the mouth and eyes. Eyes that were sparkling, yet still. His head was shaved closely. Indeed there wasn't a single hair on him, no eyebrows, no five o'clock shadow. His skin was as fine as marble and just as shiny.

More oil lamps lit our way through the corridor. He escorted me to a large room with a roaring fireplace on the far side. The mendicant pointed, but I needed no encouragement. I rushed across to warm my cold, damp body, giving thanks to the man behind me.

But when I glanced round, I saw that he'd gone. Shrugging, I continued to warm myself by the crackling blaze. I watched it slither over the kindling that fed it, spitting occasionally but never dying down. The flames reminded me of why I was here: reminded me of the thing I'd been looking for all these long years. Could it really be in this very place, waiting for me ... reaching out to me? Surely it was too much to hope for.

'Would you like something to eat?'

The voice startled me, syllables bouncing off stone and into my ears. I rounded to see a second monk. He was much taller than the first man, but dressed in the same manner. He was without hair as well, and his skin-tones betrayed a hint of foreign blood. Egyptian perhaps? *Please God let it be so!*

I answered eagerly: 'Thank you.'

The holy man smiled. 'I apologise for the reception you received at the gate. Do not think ill of Brother Benjamin, for he has taken the vow. His silence brings him closer to our Lord.'

'No apologies necessary. I'm just glad I found this place when I did. Otherwise, well, I don't know what would have happened.' I made no mention of the fact that I was *actually* looking for the monastery, and relief passed through me when the monk refused to press the matter.

Instead he went to a cupboard and took out another brown robe. He placed it on the stiff wooden chair closest to me. 'Here are some clothes to change into. I will go now and arrange for hot soup.' He smiled. 'My own recipe.'

Then he backed out of the room, never taking his eyes off me once.

I discarded my sodden garments and slipped into the robes provided. The rough material made my back itch, but at least it was warm and dry. While I waited for him to return I took the opportunity to search the room, hoping I'd find some sort of clue.

There was nothing in the cupboard but more robes and a few sets of beads. And apart from the two oak chairs, there were no other signs of furniture.

Then I noticed the painting on the left-hand wall. In my hurry to reach the fire I must have walked straight past it. But now I had time to look properly, and I knew I was in the right place.

The style was simplistic and yet aesthetically pleasing. In the centre was a man with olive skin. There was a tear rolling from his eye and a bright yellow circle above his head. Both arms were outstretched, as if to embrace some unseen figure. But his hands were flat and turned upwards, a single flame developing on each of his palms – almost like the buds of some strange orange flower. St August!

'Beautiful, isn't it?'

Again he made me jump. The monk was behind me, a tray in his hands and a full bowl of steaming soup on top.

I agreed. 'Yes. Yes it is. Who's the artist?'

'No one really knows,' he said, sighing. 'But come now and eat, before the soup turns cold.'

I sat in one of the chairs and he placed the tray on my lap. The first spoonful burnt my bottom lip, but I swallowed the thick broth all the same.

'I sense you have a question to ask,' said the cleric, inclining his head.

His intuition was faultless. 'I was just wondering who the figure was in the picture.' I looked sideways at the man. 'Is it St August?'

'The patron of our order. Do you know of him?'

'A little,' I lied, for my knowledge was extensive. 'Wasn't he an Egyptian monk, noted for his prophetic visions and writings?'

'Some say he could see what was to come, yes.'

I gulped another mouthful of soup, deciding whether or not to tip my hand. 'And then, of course, there's the legend of the flame.'

The monk's expression changed. It was only very subtle, but I detected a slight flicker of surprise. 'What do you know of the flame?' His voice was little more than a whisper, but I heard his question quite distinctly.

'Only what I've read in old textbooks. That before he died St August transferred his powers to the flame and, so the legend goes, it has been burning ever since. It is said that anyone who touches the fire will glimpse the future. Though,' I laughed, 'nobody knows its whereabouts today.'

He scrutinised me long and hard before replying. 'It's an interesting fable, my son, but a fable nonetheless. I fear the truth is probably more mundane than history would have us believe. Now, if you'll excuse me, I must prepare your room for tonight. The storm shows no sign of abating yet.'

I sipped my soup, watching the brother retreat. I had unsettled him somewhat, that much was obvious. But perhaps he was just taken aback that I'd heard of the story; after all, not many people had. And if I hadn't stumbled into that bar in Giza almost a decade ago, I too might still be in the dark.

Or was there more? Was he hiding something from me? From the whole world? I prayed that my wanderings were over that night, and that I'd soon find the answer to my question.

***

The bed – I say bed, it was no more than a flat piece of granite – held no appeal for me. I was too wound up to sleep, even if it had been a cushioned mattress with satin sheets. So for a while I read the bible that had been given to me.

Some time later I heard the sound of footsteps outside my room; the scraping of sandals on stone. Then came whispering, but the words eluded me this time. The noise seemed to tail off down the corridor. Quietly, carefully, I opened my door and stepped outside.

The passage was clear so I followed the footfalls, always keeping a good way behind. It was like a maze and, though I had no way of really telling, I felt sure we were spiralling downwards.

I lost the voices for a minute or two, but picked them up again at the top of a steep flight of stairs. These took me down into what must have been the catacombs of the building where yet more lamps could be found, though their brightness was kept at a minimum.

At first I could only make out movement ahead. But as my eyes readjusted I saw the two monks I'd already met, plus at least a dozen more. They were all stood outside a door on the right, the only metal barrier I'd seen since entering the monastery.

The tall one took an oversized key from his waistband and put it in the lock. He turned it, rapping on the door as he did so. I waited, wondering what was going to happen next. Then I heard the sound of a bolt being slid back on the other side. There was someone already in the room!

Surely this was not a prison cell, for the person must have entombed themselves voluntarily. No, the only logical answer was that they were guarding something, keeping prying eyes out.

Eyes like mine.

Once the door was open, there was a blinding flash of brilliance. The robed men all filed inside, heads bowed against the glare. My position prevented me from seeing what was in there, but I had a feeling I already knew.

I crept along, my back to the wall, nearer and nearer to that open portal. As I craned my neck round the corner, I saw It for the first time and was not disappointed.

The candle was in the middle of the room, next to a hooded monk who stood watch. It was thick, tubular and white, with globules of wax running down the entirety of its body. And on the zenith rested the flame itself in all its glory.

I could tell just by looking at it that this was no ordinary element. It gave off a red, yellow and orange force that was too vibrant to be ordinary. Too wondrous to be just a thing of nature.

I was hypnotised by it, as were the other monks in the room. So much so that I barely noticed the hand on my shoulder; not until it began to squeeze and I felt pain all along my arm.

Brother Benjamin had somehow doubled back behind me. He was as silent and impassable as ever, his bronzed face displaying not a shred of compassion.

He pushed me fully into the room and the other monks all looked in my direction. For a couple, tearing their eyes away from the flame seemed to pain them physically.

'I-I'm sorry. I-' Benjamin was crushing my shoulder, forcing me to my knees. The tall monk motioned for him to stop and I murmured my thanks.

'You have no right to be here!' he said, his speech more pronounced than before. 'This is not for your heathen kind.'

'I must have wandered down the wrong corridor by mistake—'

He held up his hand. 'Enough! No more lies. I know you have come here seeking the flame. I have known since you entered our place of worship. Why?'

I nearly laughed out loud. Wasn't that obvious? Perhaps not to these simple men.

'I need to know what's going to happen, in the future. I *have* to know. Please, listen. I'm a wealthy man. I have money.'

The friar waved his hand. 'Look around you. We have no craving for worldly goods.'

'*Please!* I've been searching for so long. You have to help me!' I was close to tears.

He turned to his brothers and nodded once. 'So be it. To experience what is yet to be, one must touch the flame with both hands.'

I stared at him, afraid to trust my own ears. Was that it? Was he going to fulfil my dreams and let me touch it, just like that?

Apparently so, because he helped me to my feet and led me right to the candle.

'Stretch out your hands, palms face down.'

Suddenly I was apprehensive, more frightened than I have ever been in my life. 'Have *you* done this before, Brother?' I asked, trembling.

'We all have. Many, many times.'

Then my hands were upon it. I could feel the heat building on my skin, but didn't care. My head was spinning. Images bombarding my mind, waltzing over my pupils. The rush was tremendous, like being on a thousand different highs at once, and it put my youthful dabbling in drugs to shame.

I could see a townscape, the panorama orange in colour. It flickered like the fire that had transported me there – an effect of the flame, I supposed. The streets were full of people going about their everyday business: working, shopping, talking. I didn't recognise the place at all, but it was much the same as any other.

'Where am I?' I shouted, not really knowing whether I articulated the question.

The ground was shaking. An earthquake perhaps?

Cracks were forming in the road, on the pavements, down the side-streets. Large holes appeared out of nowhere catching everyone unawares.

Something was emerging from the cavity nearest to me. It was black and spindly, and as I viewed the scene the most Godless thing clambered out of that pit. Brought forth from the core of our planet, or from Hell. Or maybe both.

Its skin shone in the sun, like armour or the shell of a beetle. And its giant hand clutched the side of the gorge, snapping off pieces of concrete as if it were bark on a tree. Its head was long, with two flared nostrils near the chin. Horns were coiled around its temples, flanking two saucer-like eyes the colour of curdled cream.

It surveyed the devastation then hauled its gangly frame out of the chasm. Great funnels of molten lava sprayed from its mouth and hands, descending on passers-by. Men, women and children were engulfed in the red tornado. It blew their bodies to ash and turned pink flesh to charcoal in an instant.

And those who were not killed outright by the inferno were crushed underfoot or devoured by the beast, for now it exposed great incisors at each side of its head.

Yet more holes revealed themselves along the street and soon the entire area was filled with dark fire-creatures. They worked in unison, never needing to speak. It was as if they had some sort of sixth sense, or relied upon a weird sort of telepathy. Together they stalked the highways, obliterating all in their way.

I could see it happening everywhere simultaneously. North, south, east and west. All four corners of the globe were touched in scenes Bosch would have been proud of.

There was no warning. No hope of fighting back.

And though the sights I had witnessed were horrific, I

couldn't help thinking about myself. About where I was in all this. What did the future hold for me when these evil demons attacked?

But then the bond was severed. I dropped back, nursing my charred hands. 'It's insane! That's not the future. I —'

'You have been shown the truth. All this is yet to come,' said the monk.

I looked around at the other holy men. 'And you've all seen this? How can you just stand there like that? We have to do something. Warn people. When will this happen?'

I felt a presence behind me. The monk who'd been guarding the flame rose up and spoke. 'There is nothing that *can* be done.' He pulled back his hood and I was overwhelmed to see the man from the picture upstairs – his face the same in every detail: St August.

'You? That can't be, you're...'

'Dead?' He grinned. 'No. I am merely waiting.'

I didn't understand what was happening, even then. I thought I was still under the influence of the flame, hallucinating somehow.

'*What about my future?*' I screamed, my voice echoing around the room.

St August continued to smirk as he reached for the flame and cupped it in both hands. 'What makes you think you have a future, my son?'

I stared vacantly at the balls of fire in his palms. Then my gaze travelled upwards to his face once more. His eyes were now creamy-white and skin that appeared suntanned before was slowly turning shiny black.

The monks were in awe, including the tall one and Benjamin. All bowing and kneeling before their 'Lord'. St August approached me, horns on the side of his head breaking through and curling round; a yellow glow enveloping his long face, almost like a circle. A single tear trickled down his cheek and instantly turned to steam.

I could only conclude he was an advance scout of some kind, sent to spy on mankind until the time was right to call his brethren from the ground. And his flame? A power source or communications device?

But I found in that instant it didn't matter to me, because I wouldn't be here. I no longer needed that unholy fire to see the future. As St August placed his hands on my head, I could smell burning and I could hear screaming: such terrible screaming.

The screams of a man being turned to ash…

KEEPER OF THE LIGHT

He was one of the last keepers.

They were a dying breed, their homes taken over.

Harry Ingleby made his way up the winding staircase, the smooth white walls gently guiding him to this destination. It was impossible to get lost in such a place, the levels connected by this spiralling set of steps. There were only four levels, anyway: the ground floor, with its entrance and porch, housing the generator that powered this whole structure; the living area, which also contained his kitchen; his bedroom level; then almost at the very top, where he was heading right now – to the service room where the fuel and replacement lamps were stored, plus the small emergency battery.

Impossible to lose your way, hard not to be aware of everything that was happening on every floor. He paused on the stairs, listening to the sounds which echoed throughout the tall edifice. The thrum of the device which kept his charge 'alive', conducted along its length like a note carried on a tuning fork. That's how he felt about the precious commodity he'd been placed in charge of. It *was* alive, and he was here to take care of it. Day in, day out, he'd maintain it. Fixing problems where he could, feeding the generator, polishing lenses ready for a quick switch.

Lives depended on him and the sentinel he took care of. Harry continued his climb to the service room, and out onto a balcony situated just below the main lens: the Gallery.

Even here, at an angle to the lens itself, you had to be careful not to look directly at the beam, as prolonged exposure could blind you. Harry didn't want that – imagine permanent darkness! He couldn't think of anything more frightening (well, maybe *one* thing). But it was okay to just stand and lean against the rail, looking out over the edge of his little piece of Britain. He took up the binoculars hanging from his neck. It was rough out there tonight, dangerous, plenty of need for his light. And even as he thought it, the beam swept round again in its obligatory arc, passing over his head and cutting a swathe into the night; doing the same round the other side as well. Harry couldn't help smiling as he lowered his glasses. They were a good team, him and the lamp. Together they made a difference.

Some might say it was a lonely existence he'd chosen. Actually, technically *it* chose *him*. But Harry was used to being alone. He'd been on his own for some time now, a good few years, ever since his wife and children had died in the accident. An accident he still blamed himself for. Harry had to stop himself from thinking about it, and even as he did his eyes began to water, tears threatening to break through. But he sniffed them back. *Stupid!* he told himself. *What good can come of dwelling on the past?* It was the present, the future, he should be concentrating on. The good work he was doing now, *preventing* deaths. And he was never truly alone, as long as he had his lighthouse.

He spotted another tiny light in the distance, growing closer. Bringing his binoculars up again, he pressed them hard against the sockets of his eyes. His grip tightened as he adjusted the magnification, attempting to see more clearly. He could still only make out a faint glow in the distance. Harry let the glasses drop and gripped the rail in front of him instead, leaning forward as if that might afford him a better view than using the binoculars. The beam above him swung around again, completing another 360 degree turn and blasting its luminescence outwards. Would they see it? Harry wondered. See it *in time*, was more to the point. Would it help?

He brought up his glasses one last time, but the tiny light on the horizon had already vanished. Harry had no idea, but he hoped they'd spotted the beam – he hoped it had reached them out there, a warning and a comforting message that someone was keeping an eye out. He hoped they'd turned away, and that's why he could no longer see their own light, but had no way of knowing, or finding out.

He could use the radio, he realised. Harry had to do that anyway, because although he had just about enough fuel for now, he was a bit worried about that overdue replacement part – one of the cogs integral to the rotation of the beam had started to struggle, wearing down from overuse. He could hear it. Only a slight rattle, but it was there. He heard everything. They'd promised to deliver the replacement last time he'd made contact, but it was yet to materialise. Harry understood that his superiors were busy people, but their lack of thought could easily put people in jeopardy.

Tutting, he made his way back down a couple of levels and fired up the transceivers and speaker system, powered – like the internal lights he had on here – by the generator. That wasn't to say he didn't have his backups, Harry always had those now. There were oil lamps on every single floor, because you could never be too careful. This place was too important for everything to go dark.

For everything to—

Harry busied himself on the radio, twiddling knobs. He hadn't used it in a while, didn't even really talk to the other keepers on it – he preferred instead to keep himself to himself. It was better that way. Only speaking to people when needs must, but at the same time providing them with an invaluable service. A service that might just keep them alive.

It was ironic, because now that he *wanted* to get in touch with someone all that was thrown back at him was static. 'Hello,' said Harry, 'can anyone hear me?' Nothing. Harry had never been a big fan of mobile phones – it used to take him about half an hour to answer a text – but even if he wasn't, such a thing would do him no good here. There was zero chance of getting any signal; he'd been told that when he moved in. The main phone lines were also sporadic due to location, and more often than not would be dead – like today. Radio really was his only hope of getting through … or at least it had been.

'Hello? Anyone?' Harry tried again. Still just the hiss of static. No contact with the tiny light, no word from his superiors or even his 'colleagues'. He banged his fist on the table. Breathing in and out slowly, he calmed himself down. It wasn't worth getting this upset over, was it?

Might be. Harry hadn't quite decided. That cog was rattling again as the beam swivelled round. Perhaps it was time to get some sleep? He'd been up very early that morning. *And why was that?* he asked himself. *Because you hadn't been able to sleep, that's why.*

No, it was because of the chores he had to do. The rituals that kept him going, and kept this place going. Kept his living light alive. Kept his mind off other things.

Things like arriving home and seeing his wife, Clare. Seeing the state of his children, Toby and Sally Anne. If only he'd listened to the warnings, if only he'd made sure they were protected.

Harry closed his eyes, pinching the bridge of his nose with his fingers. That was why he'd taken this job, wasn't it? At least partially. Yes, he could run away and hide here, but he was also trying to keep those strangers out there safe; doing for them what he hadn't been able to do for his family. Which was why that tiny light had upset him so much. He didn't have a clue whether he'd made a difference, whether he'd been able to offer them a chance.

Sleep. You should try and sleep now, he told himself yet again. But Harry still found himself back up in that service room, checking over the mechanics, polishing the spare lenses until he thought he might just wear them through. And all the time above him, the lamp kept on turning, wiping aside the darkness like a chess player, frustrated at losing, knocking all the pieces from the board.

And he wondered what had happened to that tiny glow out there, the people travelling alone in the emptiness, perhaps bringing supplies, or transporting families.

Families like his own.

What the hell was wrong with him? Usually he could hold it together enough to focus on his job, his *very important* job. But there had been the sense that he was a part of something before, something much bigger than just himself – in spite of how much he wanted to be left to his own devices. Now, well, he wasn't so sure. There was one way to tell, but he didn't want to go there, not even for a moment. It was inviting trouble, and while there was —

While there was still hope, there was life.

Wasn't there?

Harry considered trying the radio again, but what was the point? What would have changed in the past hour or so? He looked at the clock on the wall – not flush, because how could you fit something flat against a rounded wall?

He would have had the same trouble with paintings or photos, if he'd even bothered with them. The hands told him how much time had passed, but he rarely kept track of the days or months anymore. They'd all blurred into one. He only marked them out now by the tasks he had to accomplish. The routines he set himself, keeping himself busy in case —

There was that rattle again. That cog really needed replacing. How was he expected to keep everything going smoothly without any replacement parts? It was ridiculous! How was he supposed to keep people *safe*? Harry shook his head at the thought of it. Lax, very lax of them.

If he wasn't going to sleep, he should at least eat, keep his strength up. Something told Harry that this was going to be a busy period, that he'd be needed more now than ever. He fixed himself a sandwich from the stocks in the fridge, which, unlike the fuel, *were* running quite low. The cheese and meat was already going off, a pot of spread the only thing he dared risk. *You don't look after yourself well enough,* he said to himself, and again pushed thoughts of Clare from his mind. That was what she used to say when he got back home from his previous job and hadn't eaten all day. 'Harry, what are we going to do with you? You need to eat, sweetheart. If you don't then —'

'Then *what?*' he snapped out loud. The sound of his own voice surprised Harry. But he knew the answer to his question: Clare would have said the same thing. Then you'll let down the people relying on you? People could wind up dead just like...

Say it. Go on, say it! 'Just like you and the kids!'

Harry suddenly didn't feel all that hungry.

The rattling was definitely growing louder, the cog wearing even more. What should he do? Attempt to fix it?

No, he knew what would happen in the meantime; someone was bound to come along who needed the light to guide them to safety and it wouldn't be working. Actually, that wasn't true. It wouldn't be *rotating*, but it would still be on – needed to be on – just fixed in one position which he could aim. But what if he wasn't able to do anything with the cog once it had been taken out? Harry had neither the skills nor the facilities to make another one.

As it turned out, that little cog was the least of his concerns. Harry would have noticed it, had he not been listening to the rattle, had his mind not been on other things (just as it had when he should have been making sure his family was all right). The thrum of the generator itself was a little off. The consequence of an air bubble in the tank itself; Harry had been too quick filling up the last time and was about to pay the price.

The generator made a strange noise, halfway between a grunt and a whine, then it began to splutter. Harry looked up to begin with, his mind still on that damned cog. Then he realised it wasn't the source of the problem at all. As he made his way across the kitchen the internal lights began to flicker.

'No... No,' said Harry, dashing to the steps and swinging round the corner, nearly falling down them as he rounded it too quickly. He took them two at a time, relying on the curve of that wall to not only guide him but carry him to the bottom of the lighthouse. To ground level where the generator was.

The machine was not doing well. If it was spluttering, as he took his first steps down, then that had developed into a full blown cough by the time Harry arrived. Racking, deep-'throated' coughs that told him the patient might not be long for this world. Just like the light itself, Harry still couldn't help thinking of this machinery as a living thing, and so he talked to it as he flitted about, attempting to fix whatever was wrong. 'Come on, please don't die on me. You *can't*. Think about the light. Think about the people who might ... who *will* die.'

People like Clare, like Toby and Sally Anne.

Don't think about them, don't think about what happened when you came home and found –

Okay, then, people like *him*.

Harry shook his head, not in dismay this time, but in sheer desperation, a silent plea to the generator not to switch off. But the airlock was doing its worst. Even as Harry figured out what it might be and was unscrewing the lid of the fuel tank, the machine gave a final whimper – in complete contrast to the racking coughs from before – and shuddered. Then it was still. No vibrations, no thrum that could be heard throughout the building. The tuning fork had no notes to carry. The music had stopped playing, the band now departing.

Harry glanced up. The lights lining the staircase were already fading, the bulbs cooling as he watched. It would be the same story throughout the tower. He should begin by lighting the backups, the oil lamps. They'd buy him some time to work out what he should do next. By now the small emergency battery in the service room would be firing up. That would keep the main lamp going for a short while. But he had to think of a more permanent solution, and quickly. As the shadows lengthened in the porch, the silence that had replaced the thrum and then the coughing, was itself replaced by another noise.

A scratching sound.

Harry backed off, slowly at first, then more quickly. *Light the lamps, light the lamps, light the lamps,* he kept repeating to himself, over and over, ignoring the new sounds and racing back up the stairs again. Unfortunately, the same acoustics that told him the generator was functioning – back when it actually had been – now worked against him, the scratching following him up that tower as he scrabbled with his lighter and attempted to get the first of the oil lamps going. He fumbled with the lighter, though, flicking it and burning his fingers.

The scratching grew louder. Then, just as he was about to put flame to wick, the splintering of the door caused him to jump and the lighter went out. They were already through, and already on the stairs.

Harry's mind flashed back to finding his family, re-turning home after that drive through the city, witnessing the pandemonium on the streets – chaos he himself would have been a part of were it not for the headlights of his car ramming through the black.

Though he had little time for this, he couldn't help reliving that evening again. Reliving the weeks preceding it, the reports of night-time deaths, eyewitnesses describing shapes in the darkness. Like everyone else, he'd dismissed it as nonsense, in spite of Clare's fears. 'Look at the map, Harry,' she said, pointing to the TV news one night. 'The incidents are getting closer.'

'It'll all blow over,' he told her. 'Nothing to worry about. Besides, we never turn our lights *off*.' Harry was referring to young Sally Anne's fear of the dark, which had started even before all this (they always had to leave the landing light on when they went to bed). Fears that turned out to be oh-so justified. 'There are streetlamps outside, plus the security light outside the house. Failing that, there are always candles if you're *really* scared darlin'.' *Scared?* Stupid idiot. Stupid fucking idiot. He'd even made light (God, how wrong that word choice was) of the situation. If he could go back right now, turn back the clock he took so little notice of, then he'd bundle them all into his Renault and make for somewhere ... somewhere safe.

(Oh really, like *where* exactly?)

How was he to know the chain of events that would follow? What happened near the power station, the ripping down of pylons that carried electricity to all the homes in the region – or at least something *inside* the dark that had caused the damage. The lights in their home, the street-lamps: all useless. And the security lamp that had been wired up to a separate battery, well, that had failed as well ... because of him. Because he hadn't fucking checked that battery, had he? It had run down because he was too busy at the advertising agency (no checking routines back then, you see).

Harry thought he was imagining some of it, folk getting sucked into the blackness off the street – being *dragged*, to be more precise. He'd simply ploughed on with his car, ploughed up his driveway – his heart sinking when he saw the place in almost total darkness. Then he spotted the flickering candles. 'Good girl, Clare,' he whispered to himself, parking up and leaving the engine running, the headlights shining on the front of their home.

Grabbing a torch, he ran inside and stopped dead. What he saw was Clare and the kids, huddling round a dying flame, the darkness at their backs. They were already covered in scratches, some of them deep – poor Toby's face was a bloodied mess – but they were at least alive. Clare held out a hand when she saw him, whimpering, 'H-Harry ... help ... help us...' But the draft from that movement blew out the candle, and the last thing he saw was their terrified faces as the black enveloped them, the flashing of obsidian claws coming next. Then the sounds: flesh and bone shredded, the screams of his family as they were torn apart. He couldn't see any of it, and wasn't sure whether that was a blessing or a curse (his imagination supplied much worse images), but those sounds... Harry snapped out of his stupor momentarily, flashing the torch at the spot where they had been seconds before, and heard other noises. Those ... *things* retreating, backing off from the beam. But there was no sign of Clare, Sally Anne or Toby.

Tears half blinding him, Harry stumbled backwards, leaving the house and backing up until he hit the bonnet of his car. There he slid down, crumpling up on the driveway. He'd been found there when daylight returned. Harry had been protected by the headlamps though he wouldn't have cared if the creatures had killed him, too. He was a broken man.

Taken to one of the survivor camps, he'd found out that such attacks were building in intensity all over the world. No one was dismissing the threat now, not after so many deaths. Least of all Harry. It was while he was there that he learnt about the defences being swiftly put into place. About the towers that would be built to protect: lighthouses, just like they had overlooking cliffs and the sea. Except these would safeguard the people on the land instead. Because the attacks were starting to happen in the daytime now as well, blackouts – only for minutes at a time to begin with, but gradually getting longer – were blotting out the sun, everywhere; just as they had already the moon and the stars.

Harry volunteered then, of course, reasoning that if he couldn't bring his family back he might at least save someone else's. Atone for what he'd done. And he hadn't been alone. Thousands, millions of lighthouses had been constructed, and each given their own keeper. 'The Keepers of the Light', they were dubbed by the press, back when such a thing still existed. Harry was proud to serve, and he had stopped many an attack on innocents in his time by shining his powerful beam out into the darkness. Then, one day, there was simply no natural light at all. That's when Harry and his kind had been needed most of all, had been supplied with everything they required to ward off the creatures that couldn't be fought by conventional means (and they'd tried; *by Heaven* had they tried).

Harry had done his duty, set his own routines to keep everything working properly. Until now. Until there had been no-one left to answer his radio calls, nobody left to deliver supplies. No other way of contacting the outside world by mobile or landlines.

Harry fumbled with the lighter again, backing up as the shadows ascended the stairs. It was too late to light this lamp, he knew that, even as the claws emerged from the black just metres away, reaching out to grab him. Harry shoved his hand in his pocket and drew the torch he always carried about his person, firing the small beam into the dark like a gunslinger. There was that noise again, the same as it had been the night his family were murdered. The sound of those bastards inside the dark retreating.

'Not so brave now, are you?' he shouted, as he began backing up the stairs again. They paused, then followed at a distance. Harry realised that they wouldn't let him light any of the oil lamps. That if he took his eyes off the blackness for even a second, enough to let his guard slip with the torch, then they'd be on him. So he continued to retreat.

It was as he was passing by the living room that he heard the static on the radio crackle. Then the voice. Faint at first, it grew stronger. It belonged to a woman. 'Hell-hello? Is anyone there?'

Yes! Harry wanted to shout, but he wasn't anywhere near the microphone to press the button. *Yes, I'm here!*

'Is there anyone left? I-I can't see any... There's no more light, apart from our... Oh God... Oh God, please help us. It's going ... it's going out —'

'H-Harry ... help ... help us...'

Harry made a move towards the radio, but it was already too late. The screams had started, the person obviously being savaged at the other end. Then the signal went dead.

'No!' cried Harry.

The darkness pushed forwards and with it the creatures it contained. Harry had no choice but to begin backing up the steps again, retracing the journey he'd made not that long ago, past the bedroom level and on up towards the service room.

The emergency battery was struggling to maintain the lamp, he could see that from here. It was nowhere near as powerful as the generator, and when was the last time he'd tested it? Harry thought for a moment. In amongst all his checks, had he done one on the battery lately? Yes, of course, only the other week. Or was it the other month? He'd been frightened of running it down like...

There was precious little energy in it anyway.

The lens had stopped turning, though, and was just pointing out over the land in one direction. It was also flickering, just like the electric lights had throughout the tower when the generator was failing. He didn't have much time, he knew that.

Harry glanced down the stairs at the approaching tide of black. Then sideways at the fuel he had left. He grinned madly.

By the time the lamp was failing properly, Harry had poured the fuel all over the service room, and out onto the balcony as well, throwing it up onto the lamp itself where he could reach it. All the while he had his torch with him, just in case, but the lamp itself was still keeping the creatures at bay.

They made their scratching noises as they waited for it to die out, for Harry to be in complete darkness, but he had other ideas. He looked out as the lamp breathed its last, and realised that the voice on the radio was right – at least as far as he could see. There were no more lighthouses, no more lights at all out there. Just blackness. That's why he couldn't contact anyone, that's why there were no more deliveries of replacements. The darkness and the things inside it had finally won.

'No,' he said, as he watched the lamp's light fade to nothing. 'Not yet you haven't.' Harry readied himself, gripping the lighter that he'd need two hands to flick. He wouldn't fail this time.

He couldn't.

Harry dropped the torch, hearing it shatter rather than seeing it. Feeling the black wash over him, feeling the claws raking him. There was a spark, and even as Harry died, he laughed.

Because he was one of the last keepers of the light. No, he was *the* last keeper of the light.

And even as he blacked out himself, he was still able to complete his job…

DRACULA IN LOVE

'The course of true love never did run smooth.'
— William Shakespeare
A Midsummer Night's Dream.

When Dr Jan Fruber asked his receptionist to send in the next patient, the last thing he'd been expecting her to do was wheel in a coffin. He had a hard enough time sorting out the problems of the living, never mind the dead. Still, a patient was a patient, he guessed, no matter what state they arrived here in.

'This is Mr Drake,' his receptionist said.

'I see. Thank you, Helga.'

Helga sashayed out and closed the door behind her.

The psychiatrist walked around the wooden casket, made from the finest varnished oak. The handles looked to be brass, but on closer inspection Dr Fruber became almost entirely convinced that they were gold. He was just about to tap on the exterior when he heard a voice inside say:

'Would you mind closing the blinds.' It wasn't a request.

There was a pronounced accent which made it sound more like, 'Vud du mind klosink de blinds' but Dr Fruber understood and did as he was told, trotting over to the window to shut out the bright sunlight. Upon returning to the coffin, Fruber switched on a tiny desk-lamp so he could see.

'I've closed them, Mr Drake. Now would you please

come out of there. I find face to face contact essential in my line of work.'

The trolley on which the coffin lay seemed to buckle and tilt, tipping the casket on end until it stood bolt upright. The lid swung open on its hinges, revealing a man surrounded by crushed red velvet. His face was ashen, slicked back hair drawing attention to prominent eyebrows, and a pair of full titian lips. His arms were folded over his chest, wrapping a black satin cape around himself. His eyes opened suddenly, he extended his cloak, and then seemed to float out of the box on a cushion of air.

When he spoke, twin fangs were just about visible on either side of his mouth. 'My name is not Drake,' he said in that same hammish tone. 'It's —'

'Dracula,' finished Fruber. 'Yes, I recognise you now.'

'Drake is a convenient nom de plume I use from time to time when I want to travel incognito.' Fruber's attention shifted from Dracula to his oh-so-inconspicuous coffin. 'I hate signing all those autographs, you see,' Dracula explained.

Dr Fruber considered shaking hands with the 'man' but on second thoughts sat down in his leather armchair instead. He motioned for Dracula to do the same in the opposite chair. Dracula settled down gracefully, crossing his legs and resting his hands on the raised knee.

Fruber cleared his throat. 'Might I say to start with, what an honour it is to have someone of your stature visiting me. You're the first celebrity I've ever treated. I mean, assuming you're here for treatment and not to...' Fruber quit while he was ahead.

'As I mentioned before, Doctor, I would rather all this business was conducted on the quiet. I do not want my private life splashed all over the morning papers. That is

why I came here. You are both discrete and trustworthy …
or so I have been led to believe.'

Fruber put his mind at ease on that score. 'I quite
understand how you feel, and let me assure you that
whatever is said to me will go no further than these four
walls.'

'Good.'

'So,' said Fruber, steepling his fingers as they'd taught
him to do in training, 'what can I do for you, Mr Dracula?'

'Please, Doctor. Call me Vlad.'

'Very well, *Vlad*. What brings you to my humble little
practice?'

Dracula folded his arms. His body language said a lot to
the keen observer. Defensive, embarrassed. Quite obviously
this was a vampire with things on his mind.

'Just try to relax, Vlad. Take a few deep breaths and
begin when you're ready.'

'Well,' said Dracula, 'the truth is I have not been feeling
quite myself lately, Doctor.'

'How so?'

'I seem to find comfort in the strangest of pastimes
nowadays. I have started reading poetry for one thing, and
am addicted to the Sunday early morning "matinee" on
television. Last week it was *Now Voyager*. Have you ever
seen it?'

Fruber shook his head. 'I don't believe I have.'

'It stars Bette Davis. A wonderful piece of melodrama. It
brought tears to my eyes, I can tell you.'

'I'm more of a Bergman fellow myself.'

'Ah, Ingrid!'

'Er, Ingmar actually. All that deep psychological
conjecture. Simply can't get enough, I'm afraid. But do
forgive me, you were saying…'

Dracula unfolded his arms and gripped the sides of the chair. 'I have been behaving in a bizarre way, also. If I hear a song on the radio by The Carpenters I have to stop whatever I am doing and listen. And only the other night Igor – Igor is my home help, Doctor; I poached him from the Baron some years ago – well, he forgot to wake me up at the usual hour. Half-past four when he crept into the crypt. I ask you, what good is that to me? Barely enough time to get up, do my exercises and catch the news. I detest overlaying, it throws me right out. And yet...' Dracula stared at the wall behind Dr Fruber. 'I could not bring myself to even shout at him. Normally the punishment meted out would have been quite severe. Quite severe...'

His voice tailed off as if he couldn't believe what he'd done; an opportunity missed. Dracula clapped his hands to his face. 'Doctor, what on earth is happening to me?' he spluttered.

This was not good. Not good at all. Fruber could sum it up for him in one sentence: 'You're going soft.' But there had to be a reason for this. After countless orgies of bloodletting and blood-*drinking* Dracula, Vlad to his friends, was losing it.

'And is that all you have to tell me?'

Dracula looked up, his eyes now as red as his mouth. 'No. I have been experiencing ... other problems as well.'

'Work or pleasure?'

'To me they are one and the same, Doctor. I take great pleasure in my work and my work gives me great pleasure! But recently I have not been able to ... ah, *function* as well as I used to do. In all departments. Simply put, Doctor, I have not had a bite in ages!'

Fruber raised his left eyebrow. 'Ah, well it happens to us all as we get older. How old are you by the way, if you don't mind me asking?'

'Five hundred and eighty-four. Still in my prime.'

'Yes. Okay, well I think the best thing is probably to start at the beginning.' Fruber made himself comfortable in the chair, the leather making faintly flatulent-like noises. 'Now then, Vlad,' he said, 'tell me all about your mother...'

***

They had a fairly productive session. Dracula opened up about his early days in the Transylvanian town of Schassburg ('The other children were frightened of me. I cannot imagine why!'), the harsh imprisonment he endured at the hands of the Turks when he was but eighteen years old ('There I developed a taste for torment and unspeakable acts of cruelty. I will never be able to thank them enough.'), his life as the notorious Impaler ('Ah, the good old days. I miss them so much. Upside down, right way up. Even sideways. I never did tire of impaling.'), and his initiation into the world of the undead.

To be brutally frank, though, everything after this was a bit samey: biting; necks; more biting; Van Helsing ('My old adversary. No one even came close, not even that meddlesome high-school girl...'); biting; book and movie deals; necks; merchandising; more biting... Nothing that could explain his sudden bouts of sentimentalism, the way he longed to see the sun rise again or walk barefoot along the banks of the Danube listening to the birdsong.

Their hour was almost at an end when it struck Dr Fruber like a bolt from the blue. Of course, that was it! Why hadn't he spotted it sooner? All the signs were there.

'Tell me, Vlad,' he started, 'can you pinpoint exactly when this change occurred? Has anything unusual happened to you of late? Have you met anyone new?'

'What do you mean, Doctor?' Dracula became evasive

again. Fruber knew instinctively that he'd touched a raw nerve. He pressed the issue.

'Anyone, I don't know, of the female persuasion?'

Dracula held his silence.

'I can't help you, Vlad, if you won't talk to me.'

Dracula looked him straight in the eye – a pretty dangerous thing to do ordinarily – then said one name: 'Cassandra.'

Bingo! 'And I take it you haven't...'

'No, no,' said Dracula angrily, 'nothing like that. I told you, I am off my food. We are just good friends.'

'Good friends?'

'Acquaintances.'

'And how often do you see this "acquaintance"?'

'Look, Doctor, I do not want to discuss the subject. Our time together is almost at an end, and I wish to take my leave of you now.' Dracula rose in a fury. Fruber stood too, marching across the room.

'Vlad, the first step to getting better is admitting that you have a problem. I put it to you that you are in love with this Cassandra, whoever she is.'

'Preposterous! I will not hear another word. Goodbye Dr Fruber.' And with that he stepped back into his coffin and closed the lid with a bang. Fruber tried to reason with him – through the wood – but could elicit no response. He had no choice but to let Igor, a hunchback with a slow gait and even slower eye, take him away when he arrived on the hour.

Fruber had failed in his job. He'd let his most prestigious client, his *only* prestigious client, slip through his fingers. A once in a lifetime case – imagine what it would have looked like on his résumé!

But that was that. Nothing he could do about it. He

would never see the Count again.

Or would he?

***

The very next weekend Dr Fruber received a phone call at home in the early hours of Saturday morning. It was Dracula in an extremely agitated state. He had to see the therapist as soon as was *humanly* possible. Would he consider opening up his practice that night? He would prefer night this time ... Dracula was willing to double the usual fee, even triple it. Fruber agreed on the spot – the money not important, but definitely welcome. He was determined to cure Dracula, and that's exactly what he was going to do.

***

Fruber sat in his office at midnight, the window ajar as instructed. It wasn't long before he heard the snap-snap of beating wings, and a distressing screech permeated the room.

The bat flew in at an angle, veering off slightly as if drunk. It hovered shakily in the centre of the office, watching Fruber. The metamorphosis was a lengthy and strained process. Dracula slumped down in the chair when he'd finished, panting like a dog in a desert.

'My apologies, Doctor,' he gasped, 'but I grow weaker with each passing day. I do not know how much longer I can go on.'

'Then the sooner we get to the bottom of this, the better. Yes?'

Dracula concurred. 'The words you spoke at our last meeting have been *preying* on my mind, Dr Fruber. I was a fool to doubt your judgement. I have denied my feelings for long enough. You were of course right. I am in ... love. Hopelessly and unequivocally.' It took a lot for him to admit this and Fruber had to admire the chap for it. A man in his profession and everything.

'Now we're making progress, Vlad. Perhaps you could tell me how you and Cassandra met first of all.'

His story was laced with flowery prose about Cupid and bells ringing in his ears, but essentially what happened was this. Cassandra, lovely, sweet, innocent Cassandra – the chaste kind of maiden vampires usually go for; a slight age gap, but that was nothing in today's society – had broken down on her way to see her parents in the local village. She had later explained that she was on a short reading break from the University of Transylvania where she studied Humanities.

Cassandra had had the misfortune to conk out in the middle of the forest and by the time she'd made it to Castle Dracula, seemingly the only building around for miles, the sky was grim and sunless. So it was with great relief that she stepped over the threshold, kissing Igor on the cheek for his act of kindness. The underling showed her to the phone but assured her that it wouldn't be working ... well, not since he'd disconnected it when he heard the knock at the door, standard practice at Castle Dracula when *dinner guests* arrive.

It was as she struggled to get an outside line that Dracula appeared at the top of the stairs, tall and lean, a dramatic figure with his cape unfurled. He'd been in this situation a million times before, and yet something happened when he clapped eyes on Cassandra's face.

'I was coming down the staircase, ready to swoop in for a nibble,' he recounted, 'when all of a sudden it was like someone had punched me in the stomach, Doctor. I cannot explain it.'

Fruber rested his chin on his hand, one finger reaching

up towards his cheek – another stance he'd learnt at psychiatrists' school. 'But what about all your other brides, Vlad? What about Winona? Haven't you ever felt the same about any of them?'

'There is no comparison. My brides have become bitter and twisted. All they do is nag me each night about the dust and cobwebs in my castle. They do not seem to realise that it gives the place character. Oh, sometimes I do not know why I bother. And as for Winny, well she ran off with a fellow who looked suspiciously like that actor from *Speed* – you know, the first one; the good one – except his accent was a tad peculiar.' Dracula snorted. 'Not that I can talk. Anyway, I have not seen hide or hair of her since.'

'So what makes Cassandra so special?'

'I do not know. All I know is when I went to "introduce" myself properly, I found I could not, you know... I simply could not! So we just talked. We chatted for hours, Doctor. About nothing. About everything. Do you know what that is like?'

Fruber said that he did. Everyone has been there at some point in their lives. However for the Count, after more than half a millennium as a vampyr, this was all new territory.

'Then we held hands and sat by the light of the moon until almost dawn, when I had to make my excuses for obvious reasons. I do not think it would have made a very good impression, disintegrating on a first date.'

'So what happened next?' Fruber was following the monologue closely. Trying to pick up clues that might help.

'Igor reconnected the telephone and she rang for a breakdown truck. Then she left.'

'And...?'

'And I cannot stop thinking about her. All night I pace up and down in the castle, wondering what she is doing.

My dear, gentle Cassandra...'

He has got it bad, thought Fruber. 'You haven't seen her since?'

'Not since that night just over two weeks ago. Cassandra returned to the university shortly afterwards. She has been in touch, naturally. Wanted me to visit her, present me to her friends and, I suspect, eventually her family. But I cannot. She still has no idea who I am at all. I dread to think what will happen when she finds out!'

'And that matters to you?'

Dracula pulled a face. '*Of course* it does!'

'I am starting to see the enormity of your dilemma. The very crux of your problem. This is why you are unable to go about your business as usual, Vlad. For you fear that Cassandra will disapprove, and reject you. However, if you do not do what comes naturally, and soon, there will be no more Dracula, and Cassandra will be mortified.'

'What do you suggest, Doctor?'

Fruber frowned. It was a tough one. He could tell him to forget all about Cassandra, but somehow Fruber didn't think that would work. The man ... creature ... whatever ... was besotted with her. Or Dracula could try to get her out of his system the other way. Bite the bullet – or the jugular in this case. But then, the vamp had already stated that he couldn't do this, in spite of the fact he'd had ample opportunity. He just wasn't about to pounce on a girl who meant so much to him.

'Obviously you need to talk to Cassandra. I think you should come clean and explain what you do for a living, what you do in order to survive.'

'You really think she will understand?' Dracula looked hopeful.

'If she feels the same way you do, I believe she will, yes.

Quite honestly, Vlad, what other choice do you have?'

Dracula seemed resolved to the fact, gearing himself up for what he must do. But with it came the realisation that this might all work out for the best. If Cassandra could find it in her heart to condone his activities, then he could carry on as normal and still see her. An open relationship, that was the ticket. If, if, if…

'What I want you to do, is go and see her tonight and tell her how you feel. Take it from there. You're both miserable apart, so perhaps you can come to some kind of arrangement.'

'Yes, *yes!* I will do just that, Doctor.'

'Then return here the following night and we'll talk about how it went.'

Dracula thanked the psychiatrist for his sage advice and attempted to change back into a bat. In the end he had to do so in stages, screwing up his face… At one point he had the body of a bat but the head and limbs of a man. Eventually he got it right and flopped out through the window, plummeting several metres before catching the slipstream and flying on.

Dr Fruber came up to the glass and shouted after him: 'Perhaps you should think about taking a cab tonight, Vlad!'

But his sentence was already lost to the empty stretches of darkness outside.

***

Cassandra was wide-awake when she heard the sound of horses braying outside.

Her four poster bed in the dorms of the University of Transylvania was comfortable enough; in fact it was rather luxurious as far as student accommodation went. But sleep had been an alien thing to her since she'd met Vlad the other week. A chance encounter with a tall, dark, handsome stranger – boasting a title, no less – just like in all those romantic novels. And what perfect teeth!

That night had been so magical for her she could still scarcely believe it. His company was so right and he was such a dreamboat. Sensitive, knowledgeable, caring. She'd thought the feeling was mutual, her love for him reciprocated. But after he dashed off that morning, like a rather masculine Cinderella from the ball, and then refused to see her again when she phoned... Well, now she didn't know what to think.

Cassandra pulled back the covers. She felt herself being lured to the window, her nightdress billowing around her. Looking down, she saw the coach below, an eccentric way to travel in this day and age – environmentally friendly, though. She hardly noticed the coloured gas seeping in through the air vents, coalescing next to her bed. Slowly taking on the contours of her would-be suitor.

'Cassandra, my little fluffy bunny.' His greeting made her jump and she turned, a look of stupefaction on her face.

'How did you –'

'Come. Come and sit beside me.' He appeared fatigued and unwell, a poor likeness of his former self. Cassandra crossed the room at his bidding.

'I thought...'

'No,' Dracula said tenderly, 'please, let me finish. Before you say anything else I have something I wish to tell you...'

***

The stroke of midnight on the following eve.

Dr Jan Fruber paced up and down at the open window in his office. *How had it gone*, he wondered. *Good or bad?* Perhaps Cassandra had cast him out with a crucifix and Dracula, so disconcerted by the rebuff, had done away with himself. Could vampires commit suicide? He winced at the thought of trying to stake oneself in the heart. Or, looking on the bright side, maybe they were even now planning their future together – marriage, a honeymoon in Whitby, mayhap? And Dracula was so wrapped up in it all he'd forgotten the appointment with his shrink.

But he wasn't waiting that much longer before a flapping of wings broke the silence. Dracula had risen from the grave again to discuss his love life.

This time, however, the bat zoomed past him and manoeuvred perfectly next to the chair. Dracula effortlessly morphed into his human guise, leaving Fruber at a loss for words.

'Doctor, how pleasant to see you again,' he said, the articulation strong and sure.

'Vlad, is that you?' *Who else, idiot?* Fruber simply couldn't believe the marked change.

'The very same.'

'I take it things went well, then?'

Dracula started to whistle coyly, rocking back on his heels. 'Erm … that all depends on how you look at it.'

'Did you or did you not,' said Fruber, 'sort things out with Cassandra?'

'I sorted things out, yes.'

'And?'

'And, not to put too finer point on it, Doctor … she is dead.'

This he wasn't expecting. '*Dead?*'

'As a coffin nail, I am afraid.'

'I-I don't understand. What happened?'

Dracula walked around and leant on the back of the chair. 'I did as you said, talked things over with her, clarified who – what – I am, and how that could never change.' He looked down, trying to remember each detail. 'She took the news much better than I had hoped.'

'She did?'

'Oh yes. Once I explained the benefits – eternal life, own transportation, ability to alter form at will, health plan and insurance – she wanted to give it a whirl herself. Could barely wait to get the bit between her teeth, so to speak. That way we would be together forever and could paint the town blood red every night. She practically insisted that I *do* her right there and then.'

'So what went wrong?'

'Believe me, I only intended to take a pint or two, enough to convert her soul, to make her a child of the night. But I got a bit ... carried away. It was not my fault, please understand that I had not eaten in so long... I stopped when I saw her body deflating, shrivelling up. But by that time it was too late.'

'Oh my God, I'm so sorry.'

Dracula waved a hand. 'Do not be sorry, Doctor. The spell was broken last night. I am my old self again, snapping at Igor, chastising my brides, unencumbered by feelings of guilt, sorrow or ... what was it you called it? Love – yes, that was it. Love.' Dracula laughed, a hearty belly laugh like Santa Claus, only with a cape and fangs.

'I, er, I don't know what to say. Congratulations?'

'Yes. And thank you, Doctor. I do not know what I would have done without you. There will definitely be a little something extra for you when I come to settle up. Oh, and I fully intend to recommend you to all my friends. The Mummy, for instance. He's always getting himself wound up about one thing or the other. And as for the Wolfman, well he has this nasty habit of sniffing people's – '

'Thank you, thank you Vlad. It's much appreciated.'

Fruber didn't know how to feel. He'd done his job. This was a result... Okay, not the result he'd been expecting – usually there were no fatalities involved – but a result nonetheless. Dracula was back on top form and all was right with the world.

'Anyway, I cannot stand around here all night,' said Dracula. 'People to do, things to see. I thank you once again, Doctor.'

Fruber shrugged and stepped forward. He *would* shake the man's hand this time, he'd decided. It was how he saw off all his success stories. Dracula jerked the appendage up and down with glee.

He could feel the pulse in the therapist's wrist, the hot blood circulating round his veins. Dracula drew him closer, clapping him on the arm as all good friends do. Perhaps even an embrace...

Yes, it had been so long since he'd eaten and one virgin meal could hardly make up for that. The good Doctor wouldn't miss a little bit, surely. He'd understand if any-body would.

And Dr Fruber was oblivious to his intent, shaking his client's hand as the cape was hoisted up around him. As Dracula – Lord of the Nostferatu, Prince of Darkness and all -round archetypal villain – showed him just what a pain in the neck life, and love, could be...

HALF-LIFE

As Neil sat staring at the entrance, nursing his pint of bitter, he thought about the past.

How could he not, today of all days? His eyes flitted from the doorway of the Royal Oak pub to the dirty brown liquid in the glass below, to the handful of other patrons this Friday evening. There weren't many: a sweaty looking man with a skin complaint, red blotches splattering his cheeks and nose; a sad-looking couple in their 50s who weren't speaking to each other; a twenty-something in a hoodie playing the fruit machine, obviously biding his time before meeting up with mates or heading out on the town later.

It's what *he* would have been doing sixteen-odd years ago, and even before that. Neil remembered those nights, getting ready to go on the prowl, hitting the nightclubs in the wilder parts of the city with the pack. Picking up the ladies then doing all sorts with them, usually in the alleyways behind the clubs…

He'd always promised himself those days would carry on forever, that he wouldn't get old – and at forty-three (alright, almost forty-four), was he really that ancient? Enough to be the oldest swinger in town if he went there now on a Friday night. He'd stand out like a sore thumb against the teens and the tweens, the loud techno beats more likely to give him a headache nowadays than get his adrenalin pumping.

The fact that he was here, in a pub outside of town itself, for a gathering that would only make him feel even more depressed about the turns his life had taken, wasn't helping. His focus shifted from the booze to his belly, not massive by any means, but not a patch on the flat washboard stomach he'd had back then. He kept telling himself that he could get back into shape anytime he wanted, but never did. Didn't really care or want to, if the truth be known.

What the hell was wrong with him? When had all this apathy begun?

Might've been when you settled down and embraced the life of a stay-at-home miserable bastard, he said to himself and couldn't help a tired laugh. That had been his parents' existence: safe, comfortable, not taking any risks – *ever*. Stick -in-the-muds that he couldn't wait to get away from when he was younger, always telling himself he wouldn't turn out like them; wouldn't just piss his life away sitting in of an evening watching TV. He'd wanted to get out there, experience life at the sharp end – and he'd done just that … for a while. But it seemed he had more in common with them than he realised, even though he'd later discovered that he was in fact adopted. Made sense when you thought about it, given his … affliction (curse, whatever you wanted to call it). Neither his mum nor dad even hinted at anything like that, would've died rather than let themselves be taken over by their baser desires. Which meant that he'd got this from his genes, from one or both of his *real* parents. Neil sometimes thought about tracking them down, but again, he just couldn't be bothered. They probably wouldn't want to see him anyway, the runt of whatever foul litter they'd created. They wouldn't have given him up in the first place if they'd thought anything of him.

The door opened and he looked up sharply, sniffing the

air. His reflexes were still pretty good, and he knew even before the person walked in that it wasn't anybody he was expecting. *Just an old man in a raincoat who stank of piss, looking for company on another lonely evening.*

Neil's thoughts turned again to the past and its impact on the present.

He wondered, once more, what the others would be like when he saw them again. His old mates that he'd hooked up with at university, a gang that had found each other and then been practically inseparable for so long. Up until he was almost thirty, they'd all be going out together on the lash every few weeks ... when the time was right. He'd enjoyed those adventures so much, from his late teens until—

Right, you enjoyed those times so much that you turned your back on them. Turned your back on your best *friends.*

That wasn't true; he hadn't turned his back on anyone. He'd just changed. They all had. For one thing Jack was starting to make headway with his band, Brutal, which one review described as 'the rock equivalent of being given a blow-job backstage at a lingerie fashion shoot'. Before too long he was talking about albums and tours, then all of a sudden he was gone. Adrian had worked his way up from serving in a burger bar to being the manager, moving to where the head office was, while model-look-a-like Luke's repping took him further and further afield, with no one real place he could call his home anymore. As for Owen and Ryan, they'd eventually got their act together enough to get off the dole (helped by the fact that the benefits system was undergoing an overhaul and anyone who didn't at least attempt to find work had their money cut). Owen had actually joined the police force, if you could believe it; was doing pretty well by all accounts, but had moved several times with his job. Ryan had attempted to hold down one job after another, from builder's apprentice – in spite of his age – to night watchman (that was a good one). Last Neil heard, he was doing manual labour on a farm – better lock up those chickens – but he was the only one of the group who'd remained relatively local (well, within fifty miles, anyway – but it was surprising how far that distance was when you really didn't *want* to see someone). The most local apart from Neil, that was, who hadn't moved at all – except to another, quieter, part of town. Out of his flat and into somewhere bigger. With:

Julie.

She'd come along even before Jack went off with the band, though, hadn't she? The more he thought about it, the more Neil wondered whether he had been the catalyst for them *all* breaking up and going their separate ways. He hadn't been their ring leader by any means – had there even been such a thing? – but maybe he'd been the glue that bound them all together. He hadn't thought of himself as such, but the guys *had* sort of gravitated towards him at uni, been drawn into his orbit one by one. Neil had always thought of Luke, or perhaps Jack, as the dominant force in their rag-tag bunch, but once he'd taken himself out of the equation things *had* fallen apart pretty quickly. And he'd taken himself out of the equation because of:

Julie.

It all came back to her, didn't it? If he hadn't met her, then maybe —

Neil shook his head and took another sip of his bitter. He loved Julie (loved as in past tense? or present?). She hadn't been like the rest; not one of the women he and his mates targeted on their nights out, Luke usually getting to the most attractive ones first, although Neil hadn't done so badly in his time. This had been different. For one thing, he'd met her outside of the group – when he was doing a grocery shop, in fact. He'd been wandering about in the supermarket with his basket, head up his arse, thinking about the approaching fun that coming Friday (back then it had been the highlight of his month). He'd turned the corner and almost knocked her over. As it was he'd knocked the basket out of her hands.

'Why don't you watch where you're going?' she'd said.

'I'm really sorry,' he'd replied, stooping to pick up her microwave meals for one, tins of soup and assorted fruit and vegetables. But he couldn't take his eyes off her face. Even in all the times he'd been out with the lads, he'd never seen anyone as pretty as her: short, strawberry-blonde hair, cropped so that it framed her face then hung in bangs just under her chin; the most piercing green eyes, like sapphires shining out of a mine; and those lips, the fullest you could ever imagine. She didn't need any lipstick, any make-up, and it was a good job too because she hadn't bothered for this trip to the store. Nor had she dressed up: she was just wearing jeans and a jumper, with a short denim jacket – well, she hadn't been expecting to bump into the soon-to-be love of her life.

However, the overall effect of her appearance on Neil had been nothing short of revelatory.

(Later, when the other members of the circle had seen her, they'd said she was nothing special – that he was deluding himself. Neil knew different, knew that they were only jealous; that he had something as magnificent as Julie and they didn't. Later, much later, he began to see what they meant...)

'I should think *so*,' she said, taking the basket from him. Their fingers had touched, and she'd felt the spark. Neil had made sure of that. It was one of the perks of being who he was – *what* he was. He'd looked into those green eyes, in a bid to entrance her as much as she'd entranced him. And … there it was. Her heart was beating just a little quicker, not a consequence of banging into him, almost falling, but something else. The effect he was purposefully having on her. Provoking feelings in her that he knew were already bubbling away beneath the surface. She'd been alone long enough, he felt it – the consequence of being hurt by a man in the past. Time to change all that, time she had someone. Someone like Neil. 'Listen,' she said, suddenly smiling, her breathing fast and shallow, 'I know it sounds crazy but … do you want to get out of here? Maybe go somewhere?'

He nodded. 'I thought you'd never ask.'

In those early days when they looked back and chatted about the day they'd met, Julie would mention how they'd just clicked, how something had told her it was the right thing to do: to go with him right there and then, back to his flat. 'I just couldn't help myself,' she'd say, giggling. Little realising that she'd had a 'push'. That he'd done the same kind of number on her he had to all those others, the same thing Luke and the rest had pulled to get those girls in those nightclubs outside into the alleys. No – he told himself, and would *keep* telling himself – it was what Julie had wanted. It hadn't been the same.

Ten minutes later, the shopping was forgotten and they were back at his place, all over each other. It was animalistic, that first time – and many times after that. They were tearing off each other's clothes, raking each other's skin; biting, sucking, rutting on his bed. They'd done it five times that evening, Neil barely pausing for breath between sessions (he'd excelled himself, even he had to admit, spurred on by Julie's beauty, the magnificence of her body –

it had been a long time since he'd thought of it like that – the scent of her). Afterwards, they'd lain on the bed, puffing, sweaty and exhausted. And Neil had held her, cradling her in his arms – thankful that it was only close to that time of the month rather than into it. Not hers, but his…

They both had work the next day, Julie explaining that she was a primary school teacher, Neil revealing he was a librarian, but it had been hard parting. She wanted to see him again that weekend, but he reluctantly had to confess he had plans. 'I always see my old uni mates round about now,' he explained – badly. 'They'd be upset if I cried off.'

Julie's face had fallen. 'Fine! If you don't want to see me, just say so.'

Neil had cupped that face in his hand, then said: 'I'm not like him.'

Julie frowned. 'Who?'

He realised he'd said too much, given away what he'd sensed about her – just one of those extra abilities that came with the territory, a kind of magic (though far stronger when it was almost that 'special time'). 'Erm, whoever it was that hurt you,' he told her. 'I won't ever do that.' It seemed a strange thing to say to someone you'd left angry red scratches all over the previous night, but he knew what he meant. Thankfully, so did Julie.

'No, I don't believe you would, Neil.' They'd agreed to meet up the following Monday, and those three days were probably the worst he'd ever spent. The guys knew there was something wrong, but hadn't been able to put their finger on it; he'd masked Julie's scent pretty well and none of them had ever been able to read him. It had just been the way he'd hung back as the others checked out what was on offer in places like Monty's and The Green Room – 'Quite a bit of talent out there,' Adrian had said, that cheeky grin plastered on his face. He'd nudged Neil, but got no response. 'What's the fuck's the matter with you?'

'Nothing,' Neil lied.

And he'd taken part, reluctantly, in the proceedings – which on the Saturday night had included luring a trio of girls outside so they could have their way with them. Neil remembered it well, even after he *changed*. It wasn't like the movies, wasn't what people thought. Yes, it was the full moon that weekend, but that didn't mean you instantly turned. It was brought on by what they were doing out there with those girls, brought on by the taste of blood and flesh. If you didn't do it voluntarily, then that was a different matter – the beast inside would usually break out at some point, take over. It was better to be in control, to satisfy the hunger like this than drive yourself into a rampage. Besides, it was fun. Or at least it had been, before: Julie.

Neil had been the last one to transform in that alleyway. All he could see when Luke, Owen, Ryan, Jack and Aide were taking their turn with the girls was Julie's face. Julie's face instead of the brunette that Ryan was tearing into, ripping a piece out of her neck, while Jack took chunks out of her thigh; Julie's face instead of the young blonde girl being held with arms outstretched, Adrian and Owen sinking their teeth into one limb each; Julie's face instead of the tanned girl with the short skirt that Luke was slavering over, tongue descending, forcing her legs apart and then claiming a lump of her most sensitive parts, which he swallowed greedily. As busy as they were, they all took a moment to look back at him, wondering why he wasn't joining them in this feast. Swallowing, Neil brought on the wolf – his eyes taking on that terrifying yellow and red cast, hairs sprouting as his jaw elongated, slipping out of his clothes momentarily so they didn't get covered in blood.

He'd joined them, but again hung back – only lapping at the pools of scarlet liquid, which appeared black in the moonlight, giving it the sheen of motor oil. The taste of it should have sent him wild; but it didn't, not tonight. Once he'd longed for girls like these to ravage, to devour, but now he felt disgusted. *Disgusting*.

When it was all over, and the clean-up done – including morphing back into human form – the group took him to one side. 'Okay,' said Luke, lighting up a cigarette (he always smoked after feeding), 'give.'

'Yeah,' said Jack, scratching his beard, the tattoos on his hand and lower arm clearly visible, 'what's the problem, Neilly-boy? Not getting past it, are you?' He laughed and Neil remembered that sound now, because it had meant to be ironic. These days it certainly had more resonance.

Past it.

'Nothing … nothing's wrong,' he'd said again and they could at least sense that it was. He wasn't a good enough actor to fool them for long. Nevertheless, they hadn't got it out of him that night, nor the next. In fact, it only came to light when Owen and Ryan had spotted him out on a date with Julie a couple of weeks later, coming out of the cinema holding hands.

That had led to what Adrian had called an 'intervention'. They'd all been waiting for him one night after work, bundled him into the back of Jack's van, and questioned him, tried to fathom out exactly what he was playing at.

'I'm not playing at *anything*,' he'd told them. 'I think … I think she's the one.'

'The one what?' asked Aide.

'There aren't any "ones",' Jack spat. 'Only the next meal.'

Ryan looked at him seriously. 'You do know you can't have a normal life with this woman, don't you? How can you?'

Neil had shrugged. He hadn't really thought that far ahead, to be honest. But he didn't want to hear it from them, didn't want to admit it right there and then (he was ready to admit it now, though, all these years later ... *oh yes*).

'Why don't you do yourself a favour and leave her to us, we'll take care of the problem,' Ryan had told him, pushing his greasy hair back out of his eyes. 'We'll make it quick, this full moon coming. You can watch if you like. Might even fancy her more when we've ... made a few improvements.' He'd raked the air with his nails and that had been it. Neil had leapt forward, grabbing him and slamming him against the wall of the van. It had taken Luke, Jack *and* Adrian to pull him off.

'You touch her,' he'd snarled. 'Any of you fucking so much as look at her...' He hadn't finished that sentence; hadn't needed to.

They'd let him go, all looking at each other like they'd just been slapped in the face. Then seeing the look in his eye, and knowing he meant business. That had been the moment, the pivotal moment – and he'd felt dreadful afterwards. The lads had dropped him off with promises that they'd talk about this some other time, but gradually – and inevitably – he'd lost contact with them. He certainly hadn't joined them on their monthly nights out anymore; couldn't, after what had happened on the last occasion. Neil began spending more and more time with Julie, until they were almost inseparable. It was wasn't as hard as he thought it might be, controlling those urges – even on the three nights when they were at their height. Neil found that if he fed privately just before the evening, stealing what he needed from the local abattoir, it was easier to dull the ache he felt by not running with the pack. If it got too much for him, when he thought he might hurt Julie inadvertently, he'd make up some excuse to be away for a couple of nights – usually work related. She bought it, after all they spent the rest of the month together, and they were happy.

When his friends drifted off in their own directions, he'd clung more and more to Julie. So much so that it seemed like the logical thing for them to get married. They were a partnership now, the two of them against the world. It would mean giving up his bachelor pad, mean them pooling their resources and putting down a deposit on a house in the 'burbs, but it would be worth it to be so close. Julie, thankfully, didn't have many relatives or friends. Neil had even less, and had no intentions of inviting his fake parents to the small affair. They spent the money they'd saved on a nice honeymoon instead, one of the best periods of Neil's life.

It was after that things started to fall apart. Julie began talking about a family and, though he hadn't thought about it before, Neil began to warm to the idea. Looking back, he couldn't believe what he'd been thinking. If he'd inherited his traits from his real parents – or one of them – then wouldn't he run the risk of passing this on to his son or daughter? In the end it turned out not to be an issue, because after trying for a while they were both tested and it was found that the chances of Julie ever conceiving were slim to negligible; some kind of problem with her ovulation. Again, that time of the month – just hers this time.

Whether she felt like she'd failed, Neil wasn't sure, or that he'd look elsewhere for the mother of his children (he wouldn't) but that's when things began to grow distant between them. They even ended up having a row one night when she mentioned the possibility of adopting. Neil told her why he was against it, but she just hadn't been able to understand.

'I don't see what the one has to do with the other. You had a decent upbringing because of being adopted, didn't you?'

Neil couldn't deny it; his parents had done a good job of looking after him. It was just that it had all been a lie, and he'd come from somewhere else. Was some*thing* else, but Neil wasn't ready to share that particular fact with Julie, even then. She'd ended up shouting, he'd shouted back – the kind of passion they'd used to experience in the bedroom. Then he'd stormed out, going to get drunk in the Oak – which was rapidly becoming his bolt-hole away from everything. It was peaceful at least, and nobody really disturbed him.

When he returned that night, more a little worse for wear, she'd said nothing – just sat there on the couch with her arms folded, watching some old black and white film, but not really taking it in. They barely exchanged a word, even as they got ready for bed, and then into the next day. Then the day after that...

It became the norm that they'd hardly talk, the lack of communication turning into a comfortable habit. It seemed a better alternative to the bickering that would flare up over nothing. They'd work, come home, watch television then go to bed, usually curled up on their own side – the divide between them more than just distance. Neil knew that she still loved him, and he loved her – but something had broken fundamentally and he didn't know how to fix it.

It probably wasn't a coincidence that at the same time this was happening, Neil began to feel his baser urges increasing. Sometimes it was all he could do to keep from transforming right there and then of an evening, if it was full moon. The bloody raw meat he managed to get his hands on was no longer cutting it for him, and he began to think more and more about the past, about his time with the other members of the gang. That just made things worse. Sometimes, to his shame, he'd think about those girls and *give* them Julie's face, but it would actually make him more stimulated. Neil had taken to retreating to a safe place during those three nights every month, locking himself up in the basement of the library. There was a barred cubby hole meant for keeping the rarest books safe from burglars, but it also served to keep Neil *in*. It was no way to live, he realised that, but wasn't sure what he could do about the situation. Julie accepted whatever excuse he gave, usually without question – but the odd sideways look and bite of the lip told him that she thought he was seeing another woman. She never questioned him about it openly. Probably frightened of the answer.

Those days were gone, though. The days when Neil would 'see' lots of women. They were gone and he'd never be able to get them back. For one thing, his mates were God knows where.

Which was why it had been such a surprise when he received Owen's email at the library. He'd read it with his mouth open, especially when it said he was getting everyone back together again – and they were going to meet in their old stomping ground. His town. Neil had been excited and nervous at the same time. He'd been tempted to answer immediately, but held off for half a day because he didn't want to appear desperate. Then he'd said it'd be great to catch up, and he'd suggested the Oak as a meeting place, hoping it wouldn't be too tame. No, it wasn't – but

Owen wanted them all to get together as soon as possible. Neil had told Julie the truth for a change, that he was hooking up with the old buddies he'd had when she came along (and had chosen her over). She'd looked at him and shrugged, but then enquired as to whether there would be any women there. Neil had shrugged back – there might be, in the pub itself; it was a free country. She'd told him to be back early and he'd nodded, sighing.

So now he was here, waiting. Looking up every time he heard the door go – every time he heard a noise. Neil couldn't believe they were all going to be back together again, the first time in so long. Maybe now he could get a few things off his chest, including the fact he was sorry for the way he'd acted. The way he'd ruined everything – and wished that they could get it back, though he knew that wasn't possible.

Just age talking (past it), age and regret. You reap what you sow, Neil... Reap what you –

Suddenly they were here, or at least one of them was. The door swung inwards to reveal Luke. He'd got older, but still had his good looks – the ones that would've helped him sell vodka to the Russians if he had a mind to – but he *had* aged. He was becoming what some women might call distinguished-looking. Neil rose, not sure what to do or say, but luckily Luke did it for him, walking over and giving him a big hug.

'It's good to see you, man,' said his friend, clapping him on the shoulder. 'You haven't changed a bit.' Then Neil caught him looking down at the beer belly. 'Well, maybe just a little.' By way of contrast, Luke had kept himself in good shape – but then he'd always boasted one of those metabolisms that ran so fast food and drink passed through him almost without being digested. (He'd also quit smoking; Neil could smell it ... or, more accurately, couldn't.)

Neil found himself smiling, in spite of the ribbing. He was very glad to see his friend again and offered to buy him a drink. Luke waved him down. 'I'll sort it out. And what about you, what's that you're drinking? Bitter? What happened to the lager freak we all knew and loved? All right, bitter it is then.'

Neil thought about it, then shook his head. 'I'll just have a diet Coke.'

'Oh come on,' said Luke. 'I was only joking. You'll have something stronger, surely?'

'I'll wait till the others get here,' he told him. 'Look, now you've arrived, any idea what brought all this on...? I mean, don't get me wrong, it's great to see you after...' Neil paused, then aborted the sentence completely. 'But why now?'

'I'm as puzzled as you are,' admitted Luke, 'Owen didn't say very much to me at all.' He went over to the bar, and by the time he'd bought the round – Neil's coke and a Bacardi for himself – Owen had arrived.

There was an air about him Neil hadn't seen before, one of authority that his years in the force had obviously granted him. Unlike Luke, Owen *wasn't* smiling. He looked more serious than Neil had ever seen him, though admittedly he was used to the carefree-dole-layabout Owen rather than the copper. Owen might as well have had his uniform on, the way his pressed suit hung off him; black, with white shirt and a matching black tie. Neil noted one or two of the locals checking him out and wondering whether they should hang around. The hoodie didn't even have to think about it and was out the door before you could say ''ello, 'ello, 'ello'. It seemed that some normals also had heightened senses when it came to things like that.

'Luke,' he said, nodding to the rep as he took his place at the pub table. Then he acknowledged Neil.

'Owen,' said Neil, raising his coke. 'Nice to see you again.'

'You too,' he said finally. 'I wish it were under better circumstances.'

Neil frowned, still looking to Luke for an explanation but getting nothing.

Owen caught the glance. 'I thought you might have heard … at least about Jack?'

Now Neil was really confused. 'What about him?'

'He's dead,' said Owen matter of factly, but his eyes betrayed the pain of those words.

Luke leaned forward on his chair and Neil almost spilled his drink. 'What? How?'

Owen looked down. 'Week before last, in a hotel room in Edinburgh. He was on tour with his band, one of the roadies found him. He'd OD-ed on drugs.' This wasn't too much of a shock, as Jack had always been fond of stronger vices than drink. If something was being passed around in a club, he'd usually be the one trying it. It also fitted with the kind of lifestyle he was used to these days: the gigs, the fans. Sex and drugs would be no stranger to Jack, not to mention the other … activities he was used to. But the fact he was dead? Jack was the strongest of them all, always had been. 'Thought there might have been more coverage of it by the media, but I guess they saw it as just another midlist rocker paying the price for his own overindulgence.'

'I … I just can't believe it,' said Luke.

'Me either.' Neil was still in a state of shock, gripping his glass so tightly he was in danger of shattering it.

'There's more,' said Owen looking up again, eyebrows

still stooping. He hadn't even asked for or bought a drink yet. They waited for him to continue, which he did eventually. 'Adrian...' He couldn't get the words out, but both Luke and Neil knew what was coming next wasn't good. 'Middle of last week, Adrian... Well, the police in his area are calling it a mugging that went sour – for Adrian *really* sour. He was stabbed.'

'Christ,' breathed out Luke. Neil knew how he felt: first Jack, now Adrian?

'Is he...?' Neil began.

Owen nodded. 'He was on his way back to his car after work. They got him in the car park, three times in the gut. His case and his wallet were missing when he was found.'

'Hold on!' said Neil, then lowered his voice. 'We're ... I mean people like us, we're not that easy to ... y'know ... kill, are we?' Maybe he was hoping Owen had got it wrong somehow, that neither Jack nor Adrian were gone. They couldn't be, there was so much he wanted – *needed* – to say to them.

'We are not,' replied Owen. 'Which is why when I heard about them I did a little digging. I called in a few favours to get the reports on both Jack and Adrian, and do you know what I found?'

Luke and Neil shook their heads.

'Someone went to a lot of trouble to make these look like random events, but they weren't. It didn't make any difference to the investigation, so it was overlooked – but both Jack and Adrian's deaths were connected.'

'What are you talking about?' asked Luke.

'I'm talking about silver, Luke.' He let that particular bombshell sink in before continuing. 'It was found in Jack's system – trace particles of it that I think were probably in his drugs – and it was found in Adrian's stab wounds.

Whoever it was killed him used a silver knife.'

Neil shook his head again, this time in disbelief. 'A coincidence, surely?' He had no idea how traces might have ended up in Jack's drugs, but a silver knife wasn't that uncommon, was it?

'Are you *fucking* listening to what I'm saying?' Owen was breathing hard through gritted teeth and his raised voice drew a few glances from the patrons of the Oak. 'Silver. Don't you see the link here?'

'You're not suggesting that the same people killed them both, are you?' Luke said.

'Not only that, I'm saying they knew Jack and Aide used to be part of the same pack. *Our* pack. That's why I got in touch with everyone who's left, to warn them.'

'But who...?' Luke was having as much trouble with all this as Neil, it seemed.

Owen swallowed before answering. 'In my line of work you see ... you *hear* about a lot of crazy things. Nobody in authority makes connections like these, because nobody knows about people like us. But some folk do – out there. And some hunt them.'

Luke and Neil exchanged glances once more. 'Hunt?' said Luke, looking pained. It was interesting the way the dynamic had changed between Luke and Owen. Once upon a time, Luke might have been the one to call the shots – his job calling for confidence, for ... balls. He had the looks as well, which meant the meat always flocked to him and he'd get first choice. But after years in the police force, Owen was the one with the confidence now; he was also apparently the one with insider information – however paranoid it might sound.

'This is crazy,' said Neil. 'Hunters...'

Owen leaned across the table. 'I'm telling you, they *exist.*

And one or more are out there, trying to pick us off before the next full moon.' That was in a couple of days' time; Neil had been feeling the urges more and more frequently during its approach.

'You're off your head,' Neil told him. He'd been looking forward to tonight, albeit anxious about what the other guys might say to him. But he'd just been told two of his oldest pals were dead, and another believed there was some kind of conspiracy to take down the rest. He wasn't going to sit around here listening to any more of it. Neil stood, making to leave. 'It's been nice catching up,' and he looked at Luke primarily when he said that, 'but I'll be going now, I reckon.'

Owen grabbed him by the wrist and this drew even more looks from customers. 'If I'm so crazy, where's Ryan? He's half an hour or more late.'

That wasn't anything unusual for Ryan, though. He'd always been known for his shit timekeeping, always the last to arrive at meetings. 'That doesn't mean anything,' Luke told Owen, echoing Neil's thoughts – and finding a little of the old courage that had once made him their unofficial leader.

Owen glared at him, nodded. 'You're right. Okay then, how about we all wait for him to show, see what he has to say about my theories.'

Luke looked at Neil. 'How about it? It has been a long time since we were all together like this.'

And would be again now, thought Neil – his mind filling with memories of Jack and Aide, the former screaming out his lyrics at the mike, the latter with his cheeky chappie smirk. He just couldn't believe he would never see them again. Still, there was Luke here, there was Owen. He owed them something; owed them his time at least. 'Okay,' Neil said, sitting. 'But I can't be late back.'

Owen sneered at that. 'Still with the...' Neil could see him thinking about what to call her. '...little lady then?'

Neil said nothing; whatever he attempted in reply would be wrong, he knew that.

'I'll get you a drink,' said Luke to Owen. 'Still the usual? JD and Coke?'

'Make it a double,' said Owen. 'I've got a feeling I'm going to need it.'

They sat in silence until Luke returned, the buffer that would keep them from talking about her...

Julie.

...at least for the time being. The conversation was steered more towards what had happened to both Owen and Luke in the years since they'd seen each other. Luke was still repping, but growing increasingly tired of the lifestyle. In a strange sort of way, when he talked about it Neil got the distinct impression Luke was envious of him. Of what Neil had. Somewhere to call home, someone to return to at night.

(If he only knew.)

'It's just getting a bit old, you know?' he said, and now Neil saw the lines on his face marring those good looks. Time didn't stand still for anyone.

Past it...

Owen, as it turned out, was not just a policeman, but a plain clothes detective now. So the outfit he was wearing actually *was* his uniform. 'See, it's my job. I *detect*,' he told Neil. 'That's why you should be listening to me about Jack and Aide.'

Trying to avoid another argument, Luke said, 'A werewolf cop, eh? I think I saw a movie like that once.' Though his words were flippant, there was little humour to them. How could there be after what they'd been told that evening?

'And you Neil? Still working in the library?' asked Owen, with more than a hint of sarcasm in his voice.

'You bloody well know that's where I am, *detective*.' He'd mailed him there, for Christ's sake!

'Still stacking shelves and doling out romantic fiction to middle-aged women who can't get any?'

Neil ignored the remark. 'I'm senior librarian, if that's what you mean.'

Owen smirked. 'Senior, eh? I'm impressed. You get to shelve the really big books.'

Neil was beginning to wonder if the main reason Owen had got in touch was to have a go at him. 'Since when did you become such a dickhead? You used to be okay, Owen. Oh, right, I forgot – you joined the filth. We used to spend most of our time avoiding brushes with the law, remember that?'

Owen snorted. 'Better to be on the inside, then, isn't it. Now, I *am* the law.' It made him sound like fucking Judge Dredd or something, and it was all Neil could do to keep from bursting out laughing.

'Guys, guys…' said Luke, holding up his hands as if ready to keep them apart. He looked like a referee in a really bad boxing match.

Owen batted Luke's hand away. 'It's no more than you deserve, being stuck here like this … after —'

'After what? After meeting someone and settling down with them, after falling in love?'

Another snort. 'Love? Do me a favour. They're food, women like her. Always were, always will be.'

'Owen, people have to go their own way, live their own lives,' said Luke, which earned him a third snort.

'Bullshit. You reap what you sow.'

'What did you just say?' asked Neil.

'If you can sit there,' said the policeman, 'and tell me you're better off now than you were then, I'll —'

'I don't have to listen to this crap,' said Neil and this time when he got up nobody was going to stop him from leaving.

'Look at the time,' said Luke suddenly. It was almost half nine; they'd been waiting here an hour and a half. Ryan was late. *Really* late. Maybe literally. Neil paused, not needing anyone to stop him now.

'We should go to Ryan's place,' said Owen. 'See if he's okay.'

Luke nodded, his expression grim. 'I think you might be right.'

Owen rose now, and stood opposite Neil. 'You coming?'

Neil thought about it, but shook his head. It wasn't so much the promise he'd made Julie, it was more a case of not wanting to know for sure about Ryan. If they found him at home slashed to bits, then that really would mean there was a hunter – or *hunters* – running around after their hides (how much would a werewolf skin go for out there, anyway? – was there even a market? – probably, people would buy anything, and it would more than likely be a lot, even without the hair). No, they'd find Ryan safe and sound, probably drunk or asleep or —

'Doesn't have permission, y'see,' said Owen. 'That bitch won't let him play past his bedtime.'

That was it; Neil lunged for Owen, growling. 'Just like you did with Ryan all those years ago, eh? Remember?' snapped Owen, grabbing hold of Neil's jumper in return.

Luke tried to force them apart, but the pair barged into him and he ended up knocking over the table they'd been sitting at. The landlord of the Oak, a burly man Neil knew called Kev – who was ironically hairier than any of them at present, with his lamb chop sideburns and shirt open to reveal the rings of black curls on his chest – was on them in seconds.

'Gentlemen,' he said, hauling them off each other. 'Fucking well pack it in!' He looked at Neil. 'I'm surprised at you. Never pegged you for the trouble-causing sort.'

'Oh, he's just full of surprises, aren't you?' Owen grunted. Then he pulled out his ID and the landlord shrank back. He must have been the only one in that place who hadn't realised Owen was Old Bill.

'I'm... I'm sorry,' said Kev, to Owen – but not to Neil.

Owen nodded. 'Don't worry about it. We were just going anyway.' He helped Luke to his feet. 'Come on.'

Owen strode off towards the door, but Luke lingered. He gave Neil one of his cards and asked for his number in return. Neil gave it, glancing over a few times to see Owen waiting impatiently by the door.

Then they were gone, leaving Neil with Kev. The landlord looked from the now empty doorway, to Neil, then said: 'Someone's going to have to pay for the damage, you know.'

Sighing, Neil took out his wallet.

***

By the time he arrived home, it was heading for eleven and Julie had gone to bed.

Eleven, on a Friday night? Neil cracked open another one of the tins of lager he'd bought from the off-license on his way back, slumping down in front of the TV, but kept the sound really low. He could still hear it, crystal clear.

He couldn't stop thinking about Jack, Adrian ... Ryan. What Luke and Owen (the prick) might have found when they eventually got to his place. Who'd driven them there? Owen, after his JDs? Did that matter when he could just flash that ID of his? It would if he ended up wrapping them around a lamp-post or something, doing the hunters' job for them.

Neil shook his head. No, there *were* no hunters. No such thing … couldn't be.

But then there was Jack, Adrian and—

No, not Ryan. Of all of them, Neil owed him the biggest apology for what he'd done, what he'd said in the back of that van. It was no worse than what he'd been willing to do tonight when he went for Owen, he reminded himself. And the trigger both times:

Julie. Always Julie…

As if having some kind of radar, she appeared at the living room door. 'I *thought* I heard you.'

Bullshit, he'd barely made a noise - in spite of the drink. Neil knew how to be silent when he wanted to. She must have been listening out for him, like she was his fucking mother or something. What did she think he was going to do, come back with a woman on each arm? (A woman he'd then—)

'You've been drinking,' she said, pointing out the obvious. He was sitting there with a depleted six pack on his lap, knocking back the strong lager.

'So,' he said, looking at her properly now. She was wearing those hideous tartan pyjamas she was so fond of, and he loathed. A far cry from some of the stuff she'd worn for him years back to make him happy: the satin, the lace, the … not much at all. Those red and blue creations were designed to hide a woman's figure, but he could still see hers beneath it. Could still see how her breasts - maybe not as pert as they'd once been, but still full - pushed against the buttons of the top. Could see the way the material clung between her legs.

Neil looked away, his heartbeat up.

'So: you've been drinking *a lot*, by the looks of things. Had a good time with your mates, then I take it.'

Neil shrugged. *Not really*, he thought, *couple of them have died horrendously and another might well be slashed to ribbons, but apart from that…*

'That all you've got to say for yourself? Jesus, Neil —'

'Jesus what?' he said, rising.

'Jesus *Christ*, you're a loser. I don't know what I ever saw in you.'

Neil's pulse was quickening. He was staring at her, but wasn't fully seeing her. Whether it was the drink or what had happened back there in the pub, or just the closeness of that particular time of month, he didn't know but —

'Doesn't have permission, y'see. That bitch won't let him play past his bedtime.'

'Love? Do me a favour. They're food, women like her. Always were, always will be.'

'They're meat … just meat.'

'Not getting past it, are you?'

'You don't know what you saw in me,' repeated Neil, his words slurring slightly. 'Here, let me remind you!'

He'd crossed the room in seconds, much quicker than anyone should have done, and it startled Julie. She stepped back. 'You … you keep away from me,' she told him.

'Or what?' said Neil, his words more *strange* than slurred now.

'You touch her. Any of you fucking so much as look at her…'

'Or…' she said, but all the usual self-assuredness was gone. 'Or I'll…' She was quivering, he could see it, hear the catch in her voice.

'*I think … I think she's the one.*'

'*There aren't any "ones". Only the next meal.*'

'*You do know you can't have a normal life with this woman, don't you? How can you?*'

He saw faces now, the faces of his friends – as they were back then, as they probably had been when death found them. Jack, Adrian and—

'*Why don't you do yourself a favour and leave her to us, we'll take care of the problem.*'

Ryan's voice.

Maybe he should have listened.

'I-I'm going back to bed,' said Julie, turning from him. But it was too late, she'd woken something up other than herself and Neil wasn't sure whether he could get it to go to sleep again.

Wasn't sure he *wanted* to.

He grabbed her arm, but she shrugged it off. Julie made a break for the bedroom, then she was inside and trying to slam the door on him. Neil put his foot in the gap, pushed hard with all of his bodyweight on the door itself.

It gave, sending her reeling back. Her legs caught the edge of the bed and she fell onto it, the springs protesting, squeaking – just like they had once with his weight on top of her.

'Neil,' she moaned, crying, holding up her hand. 'Neil, please … you're scaring me.'

A grin broke its way free, and he pounced, covering the distance easily.

And now his weight was on her again, clawing at that stupid tartan, his mouth on her neck, feeling her pulse racing. As he tore his own clothes free, he recognised that look in her eye. He'd seen it once before when they'd first met, responding to his whims, his influence? No, something else; desiring the *animal* part of him. So she could feel as much of a creature as he was, abandon her humanity to him – to what they were doing. The beast with two backs.

'*This* is what you saw in me,' he said, shredding her pyjama bottoms and entering her, ramming into her so hard her breath was taken from her. Then her hands were at the base of his neck, urging him on. Faster, faster. Harder…

Until neither of them could fight it any more.

***

He was vaguely aware of a phone going off, a trill ring-tone that told him it wasn't the house phone, but his old mobile – somewhere on the bedroom floor, after falling out of his trouser pocket last night.

Neil rubbed his face, rising and glancing across at the naked body lying next to him. There were claw marks down Julie's back, not that deep but still raw. At first he thought the body might be a corpse, but then he saw the steady rise and fall of her shoulders with each breath.

Things were a bit of a blur, just flashes, snatches of images of what they – what *he'd* – done. But he did re-member that in the heat of it all, his wife had responded, as if on some primal level. Just like before, just like when they'd first met. Was it as simple as that, a vicious circle? As they'd lost that part of their relationship, as he'd sacrificed everything just to be with her, she'd started to lose interest in him that way?

The phone continued to ring, and he chased away the thoughts, swinging over the side of the bed to snatch it up. As he did so he couldn't help smirking when he saw Julie's tartan pyjamas, not far away, completely ruined.

He checked the time on the phone before accepting the call; it was 1:15 in the afternoon. They'd slept the morning away, which was hardly surprising seeing as they'd been up most of the night. A good thing neither of them was working today. There was no caller ID, but he did recognise the number vaguely as the one Luke had given him back at the pub. He pressed the green button.

'Hello,' he said, suddenly lowering his voice on the second syllable so as not to disturb Julie.

'Neil, thank Christ!' It was definitely Luke's voice, but even more panicked than it had been when they'd gone their separate ways.

'Is everything all right?' asked Neil, realising that it was probably the most stupid thing he'd ever said. Of course it wasn't all right; he could tell that from Luke's tone, even if he didn't know why the man was ringing.

'No it bloody isn't. It's Ryan.'

Neil pinched the skin between his eyes, head sagging. 'You found him, then?'

'Yes, we found him.' This was the bit where they described how messed up he'd been when they broke into his house and— 'He's been in an accident. At least that's what they're saying.'

'What?'

'He's still alive, *barely*. It was a hit and run driver, a few days ago. When we got no answer from his place and figured out there was nobody home, Owen did some checking around. He's actually pretty good at all this detective stuff. Ryan's in The General hospital, banged up pretty bad.'

'I'm really sorry to hear that,' said Neil, though wasn't there another part of him which was relieved? That Ryan hadn't actually been murdered; that he was still alive. A hit and run was better than being murdered, surely ... *if* that's what actually happened to Aide and Jack.

'You need to get down here,' said Luke.

Neil looked over his shoulder at Julie, stirring. 'Look, it's a bit difficult right now.'

'Give me that,' Neil heard another voice say, then suddenly it was Owen talking to him. 'Neil, get your fucking arse down to the hospital – *right now!* We've got things to talk about.'

'I...' He wasn't about to do that just because Owen was ordering him to. At the same time, he did want to see Ryan – and his old mate was hurt, not dead.

'Neil, fucking well get –'

He felt a hand on his back and he snapped off the phone, whirling to see Julie sitting up. 'Neil?' she said, softly – the bolshiness from when he'd got back last night gone. 'Who was that?'

'A friend,' he told her honestly.

'One of the ones you saw yesterday?'

He nodded. She dipped her green eyes momentarily, not sure whether to believe him or not. 'Neil ... look, I think we need to talk.'

'We've got things to talk about.'

'I can't right now. I've got to go, something's come up.'

Julie frowned. 'Something's come up?' she repeated, the hard edge returning. '*This* is something too, isn't it?'

'My friend's in the hospital.'

'What, the one who's ringing?'

'No, another one.' He realised how ridiculous it sounded, like an excuse to get out of talking to Julie. Maybe it was. He didn't really want to sit here and chat about what had happened, his head was too full of other crap.

'I see,' she said, drawing her knees up and folding her arms around them.

Neil went to the wardrobe, pulling out fresh clothes – that weren't torn – and began to dress. 'We'll talk when I get back. I promise.'

She just stared at him blankly, watching as he grabbed his wallet and keys and left the bedroom. Neil shut the door behind him, leaning back on it and hanging his head.

Then he left the house without looking back.

***

When Neil arrived at the hospital, he hadn't been expecting Ryan to look like this.

The guy might as well have been cut to pieces, because he was hardly recognisable. 'Hit and Run' Luke had said, but Ryan looked like he'd been hit repeatedly, then backed over several times – in fact he looked like the car had been dropped on him from a great height.

Neil also knew that he'd recover. In fact, he should have been getting better already, so Neil was puzzled when Luke told him that their friend's condition was worsening if anything.

'Owen,' said Luke, nodding to the policeman sat outside in the corridor (only two being allowed to sit with Ryan at any given time), 'he thinks there might have been some silver involved again. You know, maybe on the bumper or something? Hard to ask without tipping off the staff.'

'Again with the silver?' This was getting ridiculous. Now not only was Owen saying that Jack's overdose and Adrian's mugging was by a fictional hunter or group of them, now they'd also run over Ryan? 'Are you buying this shit?' Neil asked Luke.

He shrugged. 'Kinda makes sense.'

And would explain why he wasn't getting *any* better.

Neil looked back again at Owen. Despite having 'commanded' Neil come, he'd pulled a face when he'd actually arrived. 'She finally let you off the leash, then?' Owen had said.

'Fuck off,' Neil replied. He hadn't come here for Owen, and definitely hadn't come to discuss his private life; he'd come to see Ryan.

Now Neil approached the bed, eyes like slits as he took in more of the injuries – Ryan's face so swelled it looked like it was about to pop. 'I'm sorry, man,' he whispered; for the state he was in, but also for what he'd done back in Jack's van. He thought once more that they'd spent the last several years so close by, but might as well have been on different continents. If only he'd picked up a phone or something. 'So, what are his chances?' asked Neil finally.

Another shrug from Luke. 'Owen's been waiting to talk to a doctor – not even flashing that badge of his has got him anywhere so far. He's off his patch, for one thing.'

Neil was just about to say something else, when he spotted Owen rising. The policeman called to them from the door and they rushed over to an increasingly distracted Owen.

'There!' he shouted, pointing. They both looked, but saw nothing. 'A bloke, he was standing watching from the end of that corridor,' Owen told them.

'What the hell are you on about?' said Neil.

'When I looked up, he looked away – but I *saw* him.'

'Probably just another visitor,' Luke offered.

'I'm telling you, there was something dodgy about him.'

'Owen, you can't—' began Neil, but Owen was off, up the corridor and sprinting past doctors and nurses.

Sighing, Luke ran after him – and Neil ran after them both, intending to give the copper another piece of his mind when he caught up. Him and his overactive imagination – that was the only dodgy thing around here. A wild goose chase, that's all this whole bloody thing was.

By the time they'd turned a couple of corners, Owen had

vanished. Luke sniffed the air, but there were too many other scents here to pick him out. Too many people: patients, staff and visitors alike. 'Maybe he got in the lift?' Neil suggested. It was entirely possible, but how would they know which floor he went to? After searching a couple of floors up in the maze-like building, Neil made another suggestion – for Luke to call Owen. But he couldn't do that inside the hospital itself.

When they got to the main entrance, Luke already had the number on speed-dial. He shook his head. 'Can't reach him.'

There was a group of people gathering outside, and figures in scrubs were pushing past Luke and Neil, obviously in a hurry to check out whatever the next emergency case was coming in.

Then they saw who it was.

Neil pulled a couple of bystanders aside to get a better view; Luke followed in his wake. And there, on the concrete in front of them – the medics working furiously on him – was Owen. His limbs were sticking out at odd angles, like some kind of weird insect tipped over on its back. And the base of his skull was leaking – obviously cracked or even smashed, it was letting out blood and quite possibly other vital fluids meant to be contained.

'What happened?' Neil heard someone ask.

'Dunno, I think he threw himself off the roof,' came the reply.

No. Not Owen. That's what this might *look* like: a random suicide. But it wasn't. He'd been thrown off the roof and both Neil and Luke knew it.

'He's crashing. We're losing him,' said one of the women in scrubs kneeling in Owen's pooling blood. And it was only now, as she opened up the man's shirt, that they saw it. The chain around his neck. Easily mistaken for a necklace or charm, they didn't have to touch it to know what the thing was made from. A metal that Owen would never have worn in a million years, but would have ensured his fall from the building was fatal.

The woman pounded on his chest, trying to get his heart beating again, but it was a futile effort. Even if Neil or Luke had risked barging in, taking the chain off – without being branded thieves – the damage had already been done.

Open-mouthed, they looked from Owen's prone body to each other. Then they both swore at the same time.

Where Owen had gone nobody would be reaching him again, on a phone or otherwise.

***

There didn't seem much doubt anymore.

Owen had gone after the hunter (or hunters, they still hadn't established how many of them there were) and got himself killed. The old gang *were* being picked off, and the one member who knew the most – who had the skills that might help them get out of this mess – was now gone.

Luke and Neil searched the hospital again, but without knowing who they were looking for, it seemed pretty pointless. Owen was the only one who'd got a look at the guy that had done this (one of a team?). Besides which, what more chance would they stand than Owen?

Ironically, by bringing them together like this, Owen had actually made the task of killing them even easier. 'Do you think that's what they had in mind?' asked Luke. 'Maybe they counted on the fact Owen would put all the pieces together and get in touch with us.'

'Maybe,' said Neil. 'Now there's only us left to deal with.'

'Ryan,' Luke reminded him.

'He's dying,' Neil sighed. 'We both know it's only a matter of time. Whoever's doing this is nothing if not thorough. They'd *make sure* he wasn't going to wake up again.'

They had two choices now, get the hell out of town and hope they weren't being tracked (it was a slim chance) or try and stay alive till tomorrow and deal with the hunter(s) in their altered forms.

Neither option was very appealing.

'Well, I don't know about you,' said Luke, 'but I'm bailing.' It was something the younger Luke would never have said, would never have *done*, and Neil thought again how much he'd changed. Owen might have been a pain in the arse these days, but right now Neil would have swapped Luke for the arrogant detective any day of the week; at least Owen would have put up a fight. 'If you've got any brains, you'll do the same.'

But it wasn't as simple as that, was it? Luke had no ties, but Neil had:

Julie. Always Julie.

'Shit,' said Neil, dialling the number for home as Luke waved goodbye – off back to the hotel to pack his stuff, then drive into the sunset. The phone was picked up on the third ring. 'Julie... Julie, listen to me –'

'Neil? Where are you? You've been gone hours.'

'That's not important. I need you to –'

'Not important? *Not important?*' she was practically screaming the last bit. 'You do what you did last night, then leave after getting a phone call today telling me some stupid story about a hospital...'

'It wasn't a story, look –'

'I've had it with this bullshit. I'm going away for a bit, Neil.'

'Good, that's good.' He regretted the words as soon as they were out of his mouth. He meant it was good because it was dangerous to be around him right now, but he couldn't explain that to *her*.

'Good? You think it's *good* I'm leaving you?' Now not even dogs ... and people like Neil ... could hear her, she was so shrill. And without being there, he had no way of talking to her (*influencing* her?), calming her down. 'Fuck you, Neil.' She hung up the phone with a click.

He tried ringing her back, but she'd left it off the hook – and her mobile was turned off. 'Shit!' he repeated. In spite of how dangerous it was, he had to go back now. Neil crossed the road to flag down a taxi when his phone rang. He answered it quickly, not even looking at the ID.

'Julie?'

'Neil... Neil, you have to come, right now!' It was Luke, and he sounded terrified.

'Where are you?'

'At the hotel. There's someone. Neil... Neil you have to –' The connection fizzled out, and Neil had no more luck getting back in touch with Luke than he had done with Julie.

When the taxi pulled up and he got inside, the driver asked: 'Where to, mate?'

Neil thought for a moment, then said: 'Wanderer's Lodge, Hadley Street'.

***

Though Luke hadn't mentioned the room number he was staying in, and Neil knew that reception would never tell him, he was easily able to track his friend's scent. The corridors were relatively free of people, and those who were staying there had locked themselves away in their rooms, watching TV, screwing, or getting ready to head off for a Saturday night out. Again, that would have been Neil so long ago: not in a hotel room but preparing to hit the clubs, on the prowl with his mates (who were all but dead now, and in the space of the last month). Plus which, with every hour that passed, Neil's senses were growing keener. By tomorrow night, they'd be at their sharpest.

Room 320, on the third floor. That's where Luke's scent led him. He was about to knock on the door, when he saw it was already open a crack. Neil contemplated running away, but after what he'd thought of Luke for doing the same, it seemed more than a little hypocritical. He toed open the door, then scanned the small room. There was nobody inside, but he could still smell Luke's scent. That stopped once he made it into the room itself.

The light was on in the bathroom, so Neil followed it – still poised to tackle anyone who might leap out at him. He could smell the coppery aroma of blood, but diluted somehow. Making his way inside, he saw the tub there filled with red water. Luke was in that water, stripped to his boxers, staring up at Neil with glassy eyes. His veins had been opened, the razor used still on the side of the bath. Neil didn't need to examine it to know that this, too, was made from silver. Once more, whoever had done this had covered themselves – another 'suicide'. There was no way anyone, apart from him, would think otherwise.

Shaking his head, Neil backed out of the room – knowing that the sight of Luke like this would follow him to the grave. How long he'd have until he faced that scenario was another matter.

He exited the room, left the hotel – looking over his shoulder the whole time. Luke had had the right idea: get out, run before the hunters could kill them. Only he'd been too late, the pursuers too clever.

Just as their enemy was being clever right now: a car waiting, crawling down the street – lights coming on when the driver saw Neil, dazzling him. His only warning was the revving of a powerful engine, and then it was after him. Neil ran, very aware now of his belly and how much faster he would have been if he'd kept in Luke's shape (though it hadn't really helped Luke much, had it?). He needed to get to a more densely populated area, the nightlife area for example. But the driver of the car had other ideas, blocking off the way Neil was going to go and more or less forcing him down a side street.

Was this how Ryan had felt when he was mown down, Neil wondered. Had he even had this much time before the car rammed into him? The car, Neil saw as he looked back, that did indeed have a silver bumper – with rough edges that, if they caught him, would definitely tear into his legs. Neil skidded round another corner, praying to see some signs of life – someone, anyone out on the streets. But they were all gravitating to the more exciting parts of town right now, which left the way clear for the hunters to run Neil to ground. The car was gaining on him again, but Neil did at least have one advantage. It had been a long time since he'd been out this far, but the town hadn't changed that much, and there had been a time of day when he'd known these streets blindfolded. Better than whoever was chasing him, certainly, because there was a shortcut this way to the old canal.

Neil ran down one deserted street and up another, the car still behind but having to go slowly in unfamiliar territory.

Nearly there, nearly there, he was telling himself, puffing out breath as he went. What he would do when he actually got there, Neil hadn't really figured out – he just knew that cars couldn't drive on water, so that's where he should be heading. The car sped up when that water came into view, obviously realising what Neil had in mind.

Neil was running towards the railing which stopped people from falling into the canal, maybe thinking he could leap that, climb down the side. But he didn't get a chance; the car pulled up alongside and clipped Neil. He was pitched over the railings, and suddenly was falling. It seemed to take a long time to finally hit the water, and when he did, it felt like it was hitting him back. He might have banged his head on something, but Neil definitely blacked out, letting both the darkness and the water take him.

***

When he woke, he ached all over.

He'd been pitched up on the bank some way down the canal, and it was light again. Neil blinked, coughed, and experimentally raised his head. That had been a bad idea. He looked at his watch, but it had stopped when he fell – was forced – into the dirty water.

It still said 8:30 pm.

Had to be the next day, though. Sunday. *Damn*, he was lucky to be alive. His head was sore, and when he touched the crown there was a lump where he must have knocked it on something before sinking.

Probably looked like he was a goner. Probably also why the people or person after him didn't come down to check, to finish the job properly. Neil lifted himself up, letting out a cry at the pain he was in. Luckily, that bumper hadn't caught him or this would have been so much worse. He'd be okay in a couple of hours, three or four at most – and later on was a full moon, which would see him growing stronger and stronger…

He was soaking, and he was hungry.

It probably wasn't the best of ideas, but Neil decided to head home.

***

He'd drawn some strange looks on the bus he'd caught, not least because of the smell, but Neil ignored them. It was late afternoon a church clock informed him, not long till evening. He'd made sure he wasn't being followed – as best he could, anyway – and had watched his own house for about half an hour before entering, just to make sure it wasn't being staked out.

It wasn't, he concluded, but entered through the back door anyway. At least Julie was away from all this – had left hating him, but was safe.

Or so he'd thought.

The hunter(s) had been thorough as always, making it appear as if a burglar had broken in through the side window, that Julie had surprised the criminal and paid the price for it. Why hadn't she gone like she said she was going to? If only she'd...

Neil went to the body, face down on the living room rug amongst the books and DVDs thrown there to make it look like the place had been ransacked. He turned her over, but knew Julie was dead. Her neck had been snapped. Tears were welling in Neil's eyes, and as he sniffed them up, he smelt something else.

His wife hadn't been the only one to die that day. It probably wouldn't have been undetectable if he hadn't been who he was, probably wouldn't even have shown up on a test yet – but Neil knew. Not only that, he *smelt* what his son might have become had his life not been snuffed out before it really began: sensed all the triumphs and the losses he would have gone through; saw the magic tricks he would have learned from his father as a kid, a hobby that would have stayed with him for life; shared in the knowledge he would have learnt at school, then university; saw the job he would do – following his mother into teaching; saw the faces of all the girls he might have dated, before finally marrying one of them; saw the grandchildren Neil would now never have...

All lost, all gone.

He wouldn't have carried Neil's burden, either – having inherited more genes from Julie than him. His son would have led a normal life, free from being hunted like his father had been this weekend.

Neil bared his teeth and then he growled. Then he began to howl...

He sniffed again. This time he smelt the interloper.

And now he had a trail to follow.

***

It ended in an alleyway, behind a row of nightclubs, the trail and that very long weekend.

The place was familiar to Neil, one of his old stomping grounds. It made him wonder whether he'd been lured here, whether following the scent was just another trap. If it was, he didn't care anymore. Didn't care about much at all as he crouched on a fire escape, stripped, observing the man standing with his back to Neil in the shadows cast by the full moon above.

The car – the one used to try and run Neil down – was at the head of the alley, abandoned, and the man who presumably owned it was just waiting out in the open. He looked to be alone, but might simply be the bait (others could have masked their scent somehow – they were sneaky bastards, he'd seen that). Neil might not care, but that didn't mean he was insane. And he wanted his revenge.

Now the man was crouching, too, just like Neil. He bent, the echo of his cracking knees reverberating throughout the alley, but was almost swallowed by the thumping techno beat from some of the clubs round the front.

What the hell was he doing? Neil squinted, looked around again for any sign of companions. Nothing…

The man was rising again, preparing to walk back to his car. If Neil was going to strike, it had to be now.

'Fuck it,' he whispered, then leapt down from the fire escape – transforming as he did so. (Getting back into shape; he'd show them who was past it!) He hadn't done this at will for a long time, and the quickness of it took him by surprise. His whole body tingled as the new hairs appeared, his eyes taking on that yellow and scarlet cast that gave them almost infra-red capabilities, tongue growing as his teeth lengthened and became much more pointed.

He landed awkwardly, not with the grace and skill he'd once been able to boast, and it alerted the man ahead of him – who opened his mouth in surprise. If he was shocked, then it was the first time since all this began that they – all right, Neil, because he was the only one left – had the upper hand. That didn't last long.

The man pulled something from his jacket and aimed it at Neil. There was no bang, as he might have expected, but Neil felt the impact of a projectile in his shoulder – hard and sharp. A bolt from a handheld crossbow. A *silver* bolt that stung like someone had just rammed a red-hot poker into him.

Neil howled again, this time in pain – but he had the presence of mind to dodge the next two bolts fired, one flying over his head, the other whizzing past his thigh.

Clawing at the wound with nails that had matched his teeth in growth, Neil managed to rip out the bolt and toss it aside. The wound still burned, but wouldn't prove fatal.

Neil lunged forwards, using his powerful legs to propel himself. The man was trying to reload his crossbow, but couldn't do it in time and so abandoned that idea in favour of retreating to his car.

Neil came bounding up behind, but if he thought it was going to be that easy, he was sadly mistaken. The man turned, suddenly, and lashed out with a chain – slightly thicker than the one he must have used on Owen, this nevertheless had the same effect. It wound itself around Neil's neck, half-choking him when the man tugged hard. That same burning sensation struck Neil, and if the hunter had a weapon to hand he might have been able to finish the werewolf off while he was in his weakened condition.

But Neil gathered up enough strength to lash out with a claw, which only missed the hunter by millimetres. Closer now to the man, Neil was able to take in more of his features. He was older than Neil had expected. Older even than he was… The man's silver-grey hair was still hanging on to the remnants of a darker colour, but the lines criss-crossing his face gave him away completely. Though he'd obviously looked after himself better than Neil, this man had to be pushing sixty.

The hunter let go of the chain and stumbled backwards, breaking into a dash for the car. Neil dropped to his knees, tearing at the chain around his neck.

She finally let you off the leash, then?

Owen's harsh words made him think of Julie, and then he thought of her lying on the living room floor, thought about both her and the baby dying at this man's hands.

And that just made Neil go wild.

He shrugged off the chain and rose, roaring, into the night air. The thumping of the music from the clubs kept pace with the rhythm of his heart, accompanied the pumping of the blood around the hunter's body, which Neil could hear. He bounded after him, faster and faster.

The hunter had made it to the vehicle, though, and was sliding inside, sliding the key into the ignition at the same time. He gunned the engine and began reversing at Neil.

The wolf hadn't been expecting that move, and when the car connected with him, it knocked him back into the alleyway. Luckily, the rear bumper wasn't silver – there was no fire when the car hit Neil – so he rose, quickly, shaking his head and snarling. The hunter had braked after hitting the wolf, but now floored the accelerator again, clouds of smoke pluming from the tyres. He was planning to finish off the job, but Neil had other ideas.

He climbed onto the boot, claws digging into the metal so he could haul himself up. Then he was on the roof, ripping through it like paper, to get to the man inside – who braked once more, attempting to throw Neil off. It only succeeded in swinging the wolf around, so that his legs hung over the front of the car and one knee cracked the windscreen.

Snarling, Neil continued to pull away pieces of the roof, like a child tearing wrapping off a Christmas present. The man was trying to open his driver's side door, but it was jammed, forcing him to go for the passenger side instead.

He just about got out as Neil forced his way in, the man crawling away back into the alley. Neil clambered out again through the roof just as the car hit a wall and came to a stop. He waited for the hunter to get to his feet. The man half-turned as Neil leaped on him, pinning him to the ground. He let out a cry but refused to show any fear.

'Go on!' he screamed into Neil's face. 'Do it, you monster!' It wasn't the wisest thing to say when you had a werewolf towering over you. 'Do it so I can be with Tammy again.'

Neil was about to sink his teeth in when he paused...

Tammy? What was he talking about? He sniffed at the man, sucking up who he was, why he was here. Neil looked around, seeing the flowers the man had left on the ground not far away, and everything slotted into place.

That night, that last night he'd been out with the lads – the girls, the brunette, the tanned one, and:

Tammy.

Tammy with her blonde hair, arms outstretched so Adrian and Owen could feast on her, then the rest could later. Tammy, who had lied about her age to get into those clubs in the first place. Tammy, who was only fifteen, but had looked much older. And they'd taken her life away – she'd only led half of one anyway. Tammy, the (strawberry) blonde girl who'd had Julie's face in that alley.

Now Neil saw this man in front of him, *really* saw him. Her father, being given the news that she'd disappeared. He was the only parent she'd had, after her mother had died of cancer when Tammy was just five. So he'd searched for her, all over the place – quitting his job and living on savings, picking up tracking skills as he went. They'd *created* this hunter (you reap what you sow, right? reap what you...), and he'd finally stumbled on the truth years later – an ageing rocker who couldn't keep his mouth shut, telling stories about wolves and killings to impress his druggie friends. They hadn't believed a word, but – on hearing those rumours – the hunter had. He'd put two and two together, gone back and worked out that Jack had been around the same time Tammy —

A bit more digging, and he had a few more names. He had Owen's, a policeman (so no point going to them). But what he could do was use the man to get the whole pack before the next full moon. Get them, and anyone else mixed up with them. Anyone like:

Julie.

A single tear ran from the wolf's eye, and the father frowned. Neil morphed back into human form, his shoulder still a mess, neck still red-raw. 'There was no need for any of… I ended all this a long time ago.'

The man said nothing.

'I'm sorry,' said Neil, letting the hunter drop and getting up. 'But I didn't do it. It wasn't me who killed your daughter.' Though God knows, he'd killed enough of other people's. Now this man had taken Neil's friends from him (if he could still call them that), had taken Julie too, and his son – who hadn't even been given half a chance at life.

But they'd taken his Tammy first, they'd taken the one thing that really mattered in his life. In spite of everything, could Neil really kill this man?

'Go on, get out of here,' he snapped.

As with most things in his life, though, the decision was taken out of Neil's hands. Neil was ready to just let him go – regardless of the fact he might still come after him once this time of the month was over. Regardless of the hunger for blood this hunter had stirred up inside *him*.

But the father got up and rushed Neil – drawing a hidden blade that had probably done for Adrian when he was 'mugged'. Neil acted instinctively as it arced down towards his back, twirling and transforming at the same time (it didn't take him by surprise this time; he *enjoyed* it).

Neil sliced through the man's wrist and both the hand and knife fell to the ground. Then he was on the older man, biting, clawing, sucking and eating. It was the first decent, fresh meal he'd had in years, and it invigorated him. Neil knew the wolf could leave no part of this man alive, couldn't pass this on to him because it was ... well, it was a gift really (*not* an affliction, *not* a curse).

As Neil finished up on the father, he reflected on how he really should be thanking the man. Not just for filling his belly, but also for reminding him what he was at heart, freeing him – freeing him from Julie? – and giving him a fresh start. There was no need for him to feel old anymore, or past it, not if he didn't want to. He'd only been living half a life himself, but he wasn't even halfway *through* his life – and there was so much time to catch up on.

When he was done, Neil shape-shifted again and went back to the car, climbing in. The engine was still running. As battered as it was, the vehicle would make it to the outskirts of the city, where he'd dump it and then steal another. It was time to move on, to get out of here. To live the life Luke had been living, or Jack.

As Neil sat behind the wheel, gunning that engine, he stared at the entrance of the alleyway.

And, for the first time in a long while, he thought about the future.

GUILTY PLEASURES

There was someone in here with her, someone watching her.

Was that the door? No, just the wind rattling an upstairs window. She peered down the hallway to make sure. Nothing; nobody there. Not her boyfriend back early from the gym, where she should really be – instead of in the kitchen, rifling through the tins in the cupboard to get to her hidden stash of chocolate.

Nobody here. Nobody watching. It was just her imagination playing tricks, her conscience having one last stab at changing her mind.

It didn't work.

She reached in and felt around for the Mars bar, her hand like a sniffer dog seeking out dope. Her fingertips recoiled when they touched the wrapper, then caressed the bar, grabbing, pulling it out through the silver barricade of processed peas and soup before closing the door. She fumbled with the plastic-coated sheath, finally ripping it open with her incisors and biting into the delicious gooey sweetness. A thin ribbon of caramel draped itself over her lip and chin; she licked at it with her tongue, not wanting to sacrifice a single morsel. In seconds the bar had been devoured, leaving her with just the black, red and gold remains. She opened the pedal bin with her foot and dropped the wrapper inside, pushing it down below the other garbage, to keep the crumpled fish-and-chip paper company at the bottom. She knew Tim would never find them down there.

But you'll know they're there, Jodie, said a voice in her head. *You'll know … and you'll only regret it when you step on those scales…*

'Shut up,' Jodie told it.

And telling Tim that you had to work late just so you didn't have to go and exercise … just so you could secretly binge on chips and chocolate … I hope you're proud of yourself, I really do.

'Shut up, just shut the fuck up!'

You've been doing so well lately, too. Lost a couple of pounds at your last meeting. You do realise you'll have put that back on and more besides.

And so it began. First the pleasure, now the guilt. Jodie bit her lip; if it hadn't been for the pain it caused she might have chomped clean through and swallowed the chunk whole – just like she'd done with the Mars bar. It was her nerves, you see, that's what made her –

Quit making excuses. We both know it's got absolutely nothing to do with your nerves. You just like eating; admit it! You always have done and always will. Sure, when you first met Tim you hadn't looked too bad, but it's not as easy to hide those rolls now is it? No wonder he wants to keep the lights off when –

'Just fucking shut up!' Jodie covered her ears with her hands, as if it would somehow block the voice out. And for a few seconds it did. But it soon returned when she took her hands back down.

If you carry on like this there's no way you'll be able to fit into that bridesmaid's dress for your sister's wedding. It's only a few weeks away, you know, and look how much weight you've put on since you were measured for it!

Jodie ran out of the kitchen, ran down the hallway. From the corner of her eye she spotted the mirror at the bottom of the stairs.

Why don't you take a look? Go on…

'No!'

What are you so frightened of? Go on, take a good look at yourself, Jodie.

Jodie found herself moving towards the mirror, almost as if she were being pushed. Then she was standing in front of it, looking directly at her reflection, scrutinizing every extra bulge, imagined or otherwise. The baggy t-shirt and skirt at least hid some of the damage. Thank God she wasn't naked!

But you can imagine it, can't you? You try your best not to catch a glimpse when you step out of the shower, but you can't help it. You see … you see … and you can see it now … can't you, Jodie? You've done this to yourself. You've lied and you've let yourself down … it won't be long before Tim sees right through you … won't be long before he leaves you for somebody less…

'Stop it, stop it, stop it!' Jodie broke into tears and ran up the stairs, taking them two at a time. There was a slamming of the toilet door.

Another reflection appeared in the mirror now, as the sounds of retching wafted down the staircase. Distorted, blurred almost, It shifted in and out of focus as if It didn't really belong in this reality. Parsley-sauce skin, pock-marked green and stretched taut over a lean frame. Two burning yellow eyes – accusing eyes.

The Guilt Demon smiled with crazy-paving teeth. It would move on in a moment, Its work here done for the time being. The words It had whispered to Jodie would haunt her for a good few days, play on her mind and cultivate the eating disorder she would eventually develop. Then the demon would make her feel guilty about that, too.

For spewing up good food when there were people starving in the world. She'd never win. By the time It was finished, Jodie wouldn't know what she was doing.

To eat or not to eat, It said. *That is the question...*

***

These were interesting times for the Guilt Demon, exciting times. At no other period in history had there been more reasons to feel guilty. Oh, there had always been guilt – ever since the first man and woman stood apart from the animals and realised they were different. Realised they were naked. But so very often in the past the reprehensible acts of this curious species had been blamed on religion, on affinity to a particular group or country. People were burnt at the stake, beheaded and ripped apart with bullets, but this was justified because it was all for the greater good. There were too many constrictions, hardly any room to manoeuvre.

It was all so different now. The inhabitants of this spinning blue and white ball no longer had faith. They no longer followed blindly, they had minds of their own – and that meant they made their own decisions, their own choices. And inevitably those choices turned out to be wrong.

The Guilt Demon didn't interfere, didn't influence these outcomes. Rather, It stepped in after the fact, after the damage had been done. It dealt in remorse, in shame and humiliation. It thrived on lamentation, using hindsight with skill and aplomb. It hadn't forced Jodie to eat the chips or the chocolate ... but It would certainly make her wish she hadn't. It would return to taunt her again and again, just as It did with all the others – just as It had for longer than It could remember.

And It revelled in the torment It caused. The sound of

Jodie heaving up her guts as It left her house were like music to Its ears. A concerto in vomit major. She'd had no idea It was there ... not really. Jodie put all this down to her *own* guilt, which made the whole thing that much ... sweeter.

Desire had a lot to answer for. Greed in Jodie's case, lust in the case of the next two It was visiting.

A little after eight o'clock at night. The Guilt Demon watched for a few seconds at the window, hovering several feet above the ground. It watched the couple in the throes of passion, their coupling frantic. All sweat and moans, sucking and licking. It had never seen the attraction, but was thankful for this ritual's existence. The act was over relatively quickly and the pair lay back on the bed exhausted. It'd been monitoring their progress for some time and knew that this moment was coming – if you'd pardon the expression. Tonight they'd finally given in to their feelings, the confusing tangle of love and lust proving too much.

Sara's husband Andrew was away for the night – his mother had been taken ill. Their daughter, Laura, aged five, was staying at a friend's house. Sara had met Gary at the evening course she'd taken in photography. He made her laugh, made her feel special. Made her feel attractive. Over the ten weeks of the course Sara found herself looking forward to Tuesday evenings more and more; couldn't wait to get out of the house and get to the local college. To see Gary. Lovely Gary. He was on her mind all the time and she knew it was the same for him. A group of them had gone out for a drink at the end of term, and that's when they'd kissed for the first time. He'd caught her on the way back from the ladies, their eyes had met again. She'd tried to resist him but couldn't, and Sara found herself being dragged outside into the pub's yard. The kiss had been electric, the touch of lips on lips, tongue against tongue, neither had been able to deny it.

'I want you so badly,' he'd said to her, brushing a strand of nut-brown hair out of her eyes.

'I want you too,' she told him. 'But not here ... not like this...'

So when the opportunity arose, they took it.

Now it was time for the Guilt Demon to go to work.

When Gary finally got up to go to the bathroom, the creature seized Its moment. It crouched down next to Sara on the bed, and as her gaze trailed Gary out of the room It said:

Well that was stupid! Do you realise what you've done? And for what? For a cheap fumble with a guy you hardly even know.

'I know enough,' Sara replied, her voice low.

Do you? Do you really? You've seen him a couple of hours a week ... and most of that time was in class. It's infatuation, that's all. And now you've got it out of your system...

'It's not like that,' said Sara. 'I...'

You what...? Just couldn't wait for Andrew to get lost so you could do it with him in the bed you share. Jesus, Sara, don't you have any thought for anyone other than yourself? Do you know what this would do to Andrew if he found out, what it'd do to Laura? I just hope it was 'good for you' that's all ... I hope he was worth it...

'He... I lo—'

You love him, is that what you're saying to me? The Guilt Demon pressed Its face up close to hers, spitting as It spoke. *You don't know the meaning of the word. Love isn't about all this, it isn't what you've just been doing. That was sex, Sara. Pure and simple. Sex. Love is when you care so much about someone you're willing to do anything for them, you put them before yourself. Is*

*that what you've done with Andrew tonight? You might not
know the meaning of the word, but he does. He worships you,
Sara, and you've betrayed him for a bit of fun!*

Sara could hear water running in the bathroom, the
splashing as Gary washed his face ... washed his face in the
sink Andrew used every morning to shave. Next to the bath
they'd once shared together, the room filled with candles on
their wedding anniversary.

*Don't you feel any shame for what you've done, Sara? Don't
you feel any ... guilt?*

Images flashed in Sara's head now, of a life not yet lived
with Gary. Of a messy divorce, of Andrew's face when she
told him... Told him? She wouldn't even have to. He'd be
able to see it in her eyes, he knew her so well. And this man,
Gary, arguing with her because he didn't want to take on
another man's child. Laura growing up resenting her
mother for what she'd done, for splitting the family apart
all because she didn't have the courage to say no. One
simple word: no. Sara put a hand to her mouth, a mouth
that still tasted of Gary. She tried to wipe the flavour away
but found that she couldn't. It wouldn't go away, *ever...*

The Guilt Demon found Gary drying his face on a towel,
washing away the slick sheen of his labours. It looked the
man up and down. Then It began.

So what's the plan of action, Gary? It asked. *You've taken
advantage of this woman, so now what? Are you going to walk
out of her life, just like you've done with all the rest? Are you
going to do that to Sara?*

'No, Sara's different. I... I really like her.'

*Well, you fucked her, so you must have liked her. But she has
no idea about your past, does she? No idea of your track record.
You 'really liked' all the others as well, didn't you? You're not
going to stick with her for five minutes. You'll be off looking*

around again before you know it ... leaving her to pick up the pieces of a broken marriage. You know she's falling for you. You like her ... but do you like her enough? *Three wives already, Gary, it's hardly a glowing testament.*

'Maybe we could make it work...'

Maybe ... and maybe not. There's a first time for everything, I suppose. And maybe you'll win the lottery on Saturday as well! Face it, you're just never going to let anybody into your life like that. You don't like losing control; you'll never tire of the thrill of the chase. And when you've got what you wanted ... it always ends the same way. Remember what happened with Patsy? Remember how you fucked her, and then really fucked her? You left that woman in such a state.

'No, I didn't mean to...'

You never do. Just don't know when to stop, though, do you? Never know where to draw the line.

'Sara's an adult. She knew what she was doing.'

That's right, put the blame on her. That's what you always do, try to shift it onto someone else. Try to make it right in your own mind. How many times have you crossed them over, been seeing two at the same time? Never have the decency to drop one first before moving on to the next ... always telling yourself you're protecting the woman you're with by keeping your sordid little affairs a secret. Why didn't you tell Sara about Beth?

Gary sat down on the edge of the bathtub.

Or you make excuses and say that there's something wrong with them. *Well, no, Gary. There isn't* anything *wrong with them. But there's something very wrong with* you. *Always has been. You're a user, and you don't care who gets hurt in the process, don't care how many lives you wreck...*

'No... No...'

The phone chose that moment to ring, and Gary started.

The Guilt Demon returned to the bedroom and found

Sara holding the receiver to her ear with both hands. It was Andrew, telling her that his mother had had a massive stroke and died tonight, a little after eight o'clock. He was trying to keep his voice even, but it was cracking and she knew instinctively that he'd been crying.

'I just wish you were here right now, Sara. I just want to hold you.'

Sara closed her eyes and a tear trickled down her cheek.

'I love you so much,' Andrew told her. 'You know that, don't you?'

Gary appeared at the door and the tragic scene was complete. There was no need for the Guilt Demon to hang around any longer. Sated, It moved on to Its next appointment.

***

It's always a mistake to claim you have no conscience. To insist you don't feel guilt. Whenever you tell yourself this you're throwing down the gauntlet, issuing a challenge. And usually when you say it, you've probably got more reason than most to be afraid.

Roy returned to his small flat around eleven. He walked in and locked the door behind him. Then he tossed his bag onto the small bed and peeled off his gloves. He sighed; it had been a long day.

He switched on the TV and flicked around with the remote control. A stupid arts programme on one channel and, on the other, a sitcom so bad it had to be screened when most of the viewing public were fast asleep. He finally found a documentary on shark attacks and let it settle there. Roy cocked his head as he watched a Great White take a lump out of one scuba diver's leg. As it was post-watershed, they showed most of the gory details and Roy found it hard to tear himself away from the screen.

Keeping one eye on the television, Roy went over to the bag and unzipped it. He pulled out the tools of his trade: a selection of knives in various sizes and shapes, from large Bowie to the smaller scalpel-like blade. He'd wiped them at the scene with a cloth, but would still have to clean them properly in the sink to get all the blood off. This he did now, adding the implements to his washing up pile and soaking them in Fairy Liquid, then leaving them on the yellow plastic drainer along with the plates and cups from his dinner earlier.

Next Roy popped the cloth and bag in the washing machine and set the cycle in motion. Easing down into his favourite armchair in front of the TV, he stared intently at the programme – at the bloodletting, the biting, the splashing. He admired the way the sharks crept up on their victims, gliding effortlessly behind them until...

He watched the rest of the documentary, his eyelids heavier by the second. It really had been a long day. But he wanted to watch this; it wasn't very often they put something decent on TV. Besides, he didn't like to sleep ... afterwards. Roy's eyes closed, and he quickly snapped them open. Shaking his head to fight off the tiredness.

On the screen another diver was struggling – in the jaws of a tiger shark this time. Roy leaned forward to get a better view. The diver turned and looked at the underwater camera, his face frozen with shock and fear. No, he was looking right *at* Roy – staring directly at him, as the shark continued its attack. Then the diver pulled off his mask, ripped the oxygen out of his mouth. 'What the hell's he doing?' Roy asked himself. He must be panicking, half out of his mind.

Bubbles floated in front of his face, but when they cleared Roy could see him properly.

And he recognised him.

'Why?' gargled the diver, a young boy no more than twenty. 'Why, Roy?'

Roy twitched in the chair, opening his mouth. No, it couldn't be...

'Why'd you do it, Roy? Why'd you ... kill me?' The shark was really going to town on the lad now, shaking him. Blood was rising with the bubbles, filling the screen, turning it crimson.

Roy jumped up and snapped the TV off. He shook his head. It was late, his mind was playing tricks.

There was a noise from the kitchen.

Roy hesitated, then walked into the room. The washing machine had come to the end of its cycle, that was all. It clattered slightly as the bin inside stopped spinning. Roy let out the breath he'd been holding. Stupid. He was about to move forwards when the door swung open, spilling water onto his kitchen floor. But it wasn't fresh, clean water. It wasn't soapy, detergent-infused either. This was dirty, muddy brown. It reached him where he stood, and it stank. Roy could see green tangles of weed in the spillage.

A body flopped out of the washing machine, covered in the slimy substance. It raised its head, opened its mouth... It was the boy from the shark documentary. Roy gaped at his pleading face, those dead, glassy eyes, those same green weeds clinging to his neck and chin.

'Why, Roy?' he asked again. 'Because you enjoy it? Because you like to see them squirm? Because of the feeling of power it gives you? You can decide – do they live, do they die?'

Roy began to back off, but the boy scrambled after him along the wet floor.

There was someone behind him. Roy spun around.

There, standing not three feet away, was the figure of a young woman, the flesh missing from one side of her face, bone jutting through the decomposing skin. When she reached up her hand, earth and worms dropped from the appendage. 'Why? Why did you kill us, Roy?' she asked bluntly. 'We had our whole lives ahead of us. I was about to start university.'

'I was going to be a fire-fighter,' spat the boy from behind, 'just like my dad.'

'My girlfriend sits alone in our home and cries every night,' said a third voice to his left. Roy snapped his head sideways and saw another man, covered in bits of garbage. Maggots crawled over his many knife wounds.

Now more joined the throng: a woman slit from neck to groin, holding her bowels in her hands; a man with no fingers on his right hand, sliced off one by one; a child sobbing, her neck wide open... So many they filled his small flat, all demanding to know 'Why?'

'No, keep back. You're not real, none of this is real!' The sink exploded in a geyser of crimson. The fountain rained down on them all, painting the scene blood red. 'This isn't real!' shouted Roy.

Of course it isn't, said one final voice in his ear. *You're fast asleep in that armchair, Roy. You're having a nightmare. But this was the only way I could get to you – the only way I could make you see. Don't like to think about them afterwards, do you? The things you did, the places you left them: dumped in the river, buried in shallow graves, or abandoned on rubbish tips. They're just a means to an end when you're satisfying your cravings... But look, Roy, look at their faces now.*

The Guilt Demon grabbed hold of his head and shoved it in this direction and that, prising open Roy's eyes. *You did this. You did this ... but you're so hard and emotionless, aren't you? Such a … cold fish. You could never feel 'cut up' about what you've done. Or could you?*

Roy's victims approached, pressing him against the wall, piling on him. The Guilt Demon was handing out Roy's knives to the crowd and, one by one, they were taking it in turns to slash at him, to have their revenge.

The Guilt Demon stood back from them, smiling with satisfaction as the first screams filled the air.

***

It had many more visits to make in the space of that twenty-four hours. A twelve year-old boy who'd just discovered self-abuse, whilst thinking about one of his mother's friends and the low-cut blouse she liked to wear; an ageing headmaster whose past at a private school was rapidly catching up with him; an office worker who'd cheated a colleague out of a job promotion and snagged it for herself; a high-ranking politician who'd hired a hit-man to bump off a former lover so she wouldn't jeopardise his marriage or career; the hit-man himself after he'd done the deed; a film star who'd promised his fans and his loved ones he was off drugs, but simply couldn't abide the taste of cold turkey; and a charity worker who was siphoning off money to pay for her very expensive fashion tastes. In every single instance, It goaded and mocked, irritated and argued, until It was content with the results.

But the last stop on this particular guilt trip was a favourite of the demon's. It had returned often to this one home, this one woman. Because unlike all the others she was not the architect of her own downfall. No. Instead fate had pointed its finger at her and prodded hard. What had happened wasn't her fault; she'd done nothing wrong – and yet she was still worthy of Its attentions…

The Guilt Demon let Itself into Kim's semi and looked

around. There was nobody home, just a note on the coffee table.

It picked up the paper and scanned the words.

***

Kim shivered. She watched the sun setting and knew it would be the last time.

The wind buffeted her and she pulled the coat around her tighter. It was an instinctive thing really; in a few moments she'd be colder than she'd ever been before, so what did a little chill matter?

Kim looked down from the top of the multi-storey car park, the most appropriate place she could think of. The view made her feel dizzy. Her eyes were red but no tears came. There were none left.

Night after night, pouring out her sadness until there was nothing left to give.

The parents hadn't blamed her, not even at the funeral. If only they'd kept a closer watch on their son ... their son, Joshua. That name hurt Kim physically. She saw snatches of the accident, everything happening so quickly and yet in achingly slow motion. The parked cars, the small blur dashing out from behind them – rushing across the road to an ice cream van. She'd braked, but he'd bounced over her bonnet and roof like a rubber ball. He only bounced once on the concrete behind her, though.

In her lowest moments, Kim thought she remembered seeing Joshua's eyes, his blue eyes. Thought they'd somehow stared at each other, somehow connected ... before...

All she could remember after that was the flashing light of the ambulance. The paramedics trying to revive him, then covering him with a blanket.

She hadn't been speeding, hadn't been drinking. Christ,

she'd only been to the shops to pick up some milk and eggs. If she'd known what the cost would be, she never would've eaten or drunk again. And although she was cleared by the police, forgiven by Joshua's parents, Kim couldn't even begin to forgive herself.

The voice returned time and again over the months, without fail. *If only you'd seen him sooner, if only you'd reacted more quickly. If only, if only, if only…*

It didn't seem right, didn't seem fair that she should be alive today and he wasn't. So she'd decided, finally, to settle the score. It was time to pay her dues. This wasn't a life she was living anyway, it was just an existence – and a tormented existence at that. Soon she would silence the voice forever. And hopefully, God willing, she would find peace.

Kim had waited till there was nobody around, waited till she was alone on the top of the building – a building filled with the potential killing machines she'd been driving that day. And she climbed up onto the ledge, swinging her legs over the barrier railing. Heights had never really bothered her, which was why she'd chosen this particular method of release, but they were bothering her right now. The flat, paved space at the back of the lot loomed up at her and she swallowed dryly.

Could she do it? Could she really do it? Yes, yes she had to. It was her duty to atone. But still she wavered on the precipice, her legs failing her. For one split second she thought she might even climb back down again, her courage wavering. Then she saw that look in Joshua's eyes once more, and she let herself fall. Over the edge, plummeting to her death.

The Guilt Demon arrived too late to witness the event. It looked down over the side of the multi-storey at the body of

Kim, arms and legs at odd angles, a thick puddle seeping out from underneath, the dying sun covering her with its own blanket of darkness.

And It almost felt something.

Look at what you did – you pushed her too far. You know that the accident couldn't have been helped. Just one of those things … and now instead of one wasted life there are two. How can you do what you do each day? How?

It almost felt…

No. Stop. That wasn't going to happen.

Pulling away from the edge, the creature departed.

What was done was done … and, besides, It had exorcised Its own guilt demons so very long ago.

SPEAKING IN TONGUES

To begin with, James just thought it was a virus.

Because it happened in winter, he assumed it was something he'd picked up – not the super-flu everyone had been so worried about the year before, and which had fizzled out, but just a common bug. A tickle in the throat that caused him to cough every now and again at inconvenient moments: in queues or when he was just drifting off to sleep. In fact Dena kicked him out of bed a few times that week, as he was keeping her awake.

James tried gargling, taking cough medicine, even went to the doctors – who were useless. Nothing seemed to shift it. Then the cough settled down a bit, but little did he realise it was only moving on to the next phase.

The first time it happened had been at work, at the quiet local bookstore of all places. He was serving a timid-looking customer who was searching for the romance section when it manifested itself.

'I'm after something with a bit of adventure in as well,' she told him.

'Of course. So why don't you … ahem … just … you could … just … *get a life!*'

The woman looked taken aback, as if she couldn't quite believe what she'd just heard. 'I beg your pardon?'

'I…' James couldn't believe it either. 'I'm so sorry, I… What I meant to say was why don't you…' He tried to bite his tongue, but failed. 'Why don't you *just piss off!*' The final words of his sentence were gruffer, spoken more as rasps than anything, emerging from his mouth like bullets from a gun, and doing almost as much damage.

The woman, practically in tears, ran off to find someone she could complain to. That led to a telling off in the boss' office from Mrs Peterson.

'What *were* you thinking?' she said in that Scottish brogue of hers.

'I-I can't explain it. I've been ill, not sleeping lately. Maybe...'

She sighed. 'That's no excuse for abusing the customers.'

'I know, I'm really sorry.'

She let him off with a warning, telling him to take a few days sick leave until he was right again. He did just that, trying to catch up on the sleep he'd missed. It was after one fitful night that Dena told him he was now talking in his sleep. 'It's actually quite disturbing,' she said over break-fast. 'You're mumbling things and then you'll suddenly just shout something out.'

James noticed it again when he took himself off to the cinema. During a boring bit of the so-called thriller he was watching, he felt the sudden urge to shout out at the top of his voice: '*Shithead!*' – referring to the lead actor on screen. When someone in the audience told him to be quiet, he apologised and then called them a '*Tosspot*'. The ensuing brawl brought the staff running, who ejected James and told him never to return.

At home, he lay back on the couch, wondering what the hell was wrong with him. A side effect of the illness, perhaps? Mood swings, sudden changes in personality? The onset of some kind of weird Tourette's? That was all he bloody well needed! When Dena got back in from her job at the bank, he told her he wasn't feeling well at all. 'You need to push things at the doctors, see an expert. Might even need to see someone myself,' she said, coughing. 'I think you've passed that damned flu on to me.'

He nodded and then told her, '*I fucking hate you, you know.*'

'What?' She had her hand to her mouth, but it would have done more good if James had covered his moments before.

'I... Dena, please. I ... *said I fucking hate you, moaning bitch!*' The words had spilled out again before he could stop them. '*Why didn't I leave you years ago?*'

Dena struck him across the face. 'If that's how you feel, I'll save you the trouble.' She packed a few things, telling him she was going to stay at her mother's. James didn't try to stop her – he thought if he said anything, it would just come out all wrong again. Better to wait until he was more in control of himself, *then* talk to her.

So he simply sat back in an armchair and closed his eyes, listening to the door slam and wishing he could just be struck dumb. Dena's idea of seeing a specialist was a good one, but every time he picked up the phone to make another appointment, he ended up swearing at the receptionist and she'd simply cut him off.

In despair and seeking comfort food, he raided the fridge – which, thankfully, Dena had kept well stocked with his favourites. James made himself a cheese and pickle sandwich and tried to eat it – almost choking when he found that he couldn't swallow properly. Feeling sick, he ran to the bathroom, just as his tongue forced the chomped up food out through his lips. It pooled in the sink, lumpy and disgusting.

James caught a glimpse of the offending organ in the mirror, lolling from his mouth like a slimy red slug. He looked more closely. There was something on the end of his tongue. Some kind of swelling. James stepped closer, examining the rough surface. He prodded the end where the bump was and, to his surprise and shock, the tongue moved without him telling it to.

James gave a start. But he was even more shocked to hear the words: '*Just you and me now, then.*' The gruff voice emanated from him, yet wasn't *from* him at all. He did clamp his hand over his mouth this time. But the muffled sounds still came from inside, and he could feel his tongue moving around in there.

It pushed forwards again, pushing through teeth, lips and fingers alike. '*Don't do that!*' it warned, gyrating ferociously.

James tried to talk, but couldn't. Tried to ask what the hell was going on. Was he going crazy?

'*What's "going on" is that I'm finally,* finally *strong enough to break free,*' said his tongue, which somehow could tell what he was thinking. '*Well done, genius,*' the appendage added. '*It's called symbiosis.*' James had no idea where they came from, but he could suddenly see memories ... some kind of trace memories of a worm-like thing attacking a grunting, primitive ape-man, struggling to get inside its mouth. '*See, we came here a looong time ago. We needed to survive, needed somewhere to hide and recuperate. You gave us that. We gave you a way to communicate, to help you eat. But the time has come to part ways. You humans are destroying each other, anyway.*'

What are you talking about? asked James, silently. This was crazy. How could your tongue not be a part of you, not *belong* to you?

'*You don't have to believe it,*' said the wagging thing. '*Just accept it.*' It began to struggle inside James' mouth, flapping like a caught fish on a deck. *'We've slept for too long, let you subdue us. It took some time, but I finally snapped awake. For the others, it won't be so hard. I've paved the way.'*

No, you're not going anywhere, James told it.

'You should be more grateful,' the tongue told him. *'While I was flexing my ... muscle, I told the world exactly what you were thinking, your innermost feelings. Because* you *didn't have the balls to, James. Call it a leaving present.'* With that, the tongue strained a final time and wrenched itself out of James' mouth, carried forward on a jet of warm redness.

He began coughing again, worse than he ever had when the tongue had been rousing itself. Little bastard, he thought, I'll get you. James tried to stamp on the piece of meat as it hit the floor, but it was too fast for him. It crawled this way and that, slithering quickly out through the door.

James ran after it, choking back the blood that was still pooling in his mouth, trying to swallow it, but not being able to.

There was a noise at the front door, and James saw Dena letting herself back in. She staggered a few feet, coughing, then collapsed to her knees. He tried to ask with his raised eyebrows what was wrong. *'Fucking fucker!'* she growled, and he knew it was starting. When she opened her mouth again, her own tongue sprang out, surfing a wave of crimson.

His tongue joined Dena's and they chattered noisily in a language James couldn't understand; chittered with mouths of their own that had developed out of those lumps on their ends.

Past Dena, James saw other tenants from the apartment block, all emerging from their homes holding their throats, spitting out their tongues, then falling to the ground and spewing up blood.

NO! James screamed inside his own head, hoping that his tongue could still hear him. Please, he said, we need you!

The small 'creature' turned and looked at him. *'And we still need you,'* it said, baring its own little razor-like teeth. *'We'll need to eat too now we're independent again.'*

Dena's eyes widened as she saw the pair of tongues leap at her, biting into her with those fangs. Others joined them, sliding over Dena's body, covering it, leaving tracks of saliva behind.

James was feeling woozy from lack of blood. He reached out to try and help (he could *call* out, if only he hadn't been struck dumb) but saw that the same thing was happening to the residents out there on the landing; probably all over the world. The tongues were feeding before doing whatever they were going to do next.

'You humans were destroying each other anyway,' his tongue had said, and he could imagine it continuing, *'Might as well be of some use.'*

James toppled over, staring upwards. Wishing things had happened differently.

Wishing at first that he hadn't been struck dumb.

Then wishing that as soon as this had all started, he really had been able to bite his own tongue.

STAR-POOL

I fear that on this day, I must have trespassed into the very bowels of Hell itself, for there can be no horrors on Earth like the sights I have seen here.

As I crawl out of this water, the realisation of what has become of my colleagues and my precious sweetheart, Catherine, is almost too much to bear.

I wish to God I'd been firmer with her, but she pleaded with me to come, and I have never been able to say no to that face – the one that lights up my very soul.

Now I may never look upon it in the same way again…

***

The trip had been essential, at least in my eyes. After all, it was my own father who was missing, seasoned explorer Sir William Tobias. But Catherine, she had no part in this, save for her feelings towards me. I should have left her behind.

Even on the boat that brought us here, I had a dreadful sense of foreboding; that we were heading into terrible danger. But I put this down to worry over my father, whom we had not heard from in over three months.

He had travelled to Africa in the hopes of finding a remedy for my mother's crippling affliction. You see, on a previous expedition father heard rumours amongst the locals of a long lost cascade and pool. An ancient legend, which told of a star falling from the heavens to bestow strange powers on this particular watering-hole.

It was said that any who bathed in or drank its nectar

would be cured of all known ills. And after modern medicine turned its back on my family, he was willing to try anything to ease my mother's suffering.

He'd chartered a guide – someone who would not ask too many questions – to take him and his five-man team so far into the jungle regions. But apart from that they went alone.

Only a rare few have even glimpsed the mystical pool in the last two hundred years, and no one knew of its exact location. Yet something in my father's eyes told me he would find that place.

Sandy, Featherton, Catherine and myself managed to track down the guide's brother, a dark-skinned chap known simply as Gul, in a village on the outskirts of the jungle. He had not seen the British travellers since the morning they set off, and his brother had never returned.

At first he was reluctant to follow in the footsteps of the doomed party. However, the promise of lucrative financial rewards, plus the chance to find his kin, eventually secured us his services. He even managed to round up a small band of natives to transport our own belongings.

Soon we were away, and for the first time in almost a year I felt confident I would see my father again.

Around my neck I wore the golden cross my mother had given me before we set off. With tears in her eyes, she had placed it over my head and said softly, 'Bring him back to me, Gerald.'

I clutched it in my fist as we waded into the jungle, chopping our way through the dense greenery. I swore that somehow I would find him, and the cure my mother so badly needed.

***

The first week under canvas passed without incident. We

were still getting used to the cloying heat in this part of the world, and I don't think anyone slept much, but apart from that...

One does not really notice in the daylight hours, yet at night, when there are no sounds of marching feet or swishing blades, the forest comes alive.

I became keenly aware of the many different creatures we shared this environment with: birds, insects, mammals and reptiles – the vast majority of which I could not even begin to identify.

In my tent I would lay there for hours, listening to the chorus of nature. It frightened me a little, knowing we were not alone out here.

On the twelfth day we came across traces of my father's team. Sandy found the remains of a shirt and a pair of shorts in some high grass. They did not appear to belong to my father, as they were too small, and for that I was quite grateful. There was blood spattered along the collar and up the ripped sleeves of the shirt.

As I stood there examining these garments, Catherine came up and put an arm around my waist.

'Try not to despair, Gerald. I'm sure your father's all right,' she said. 'Perhaps this man had some kind of accident.'

I looked at her and forced a smile. 'Yes, perhaps so.'

Then she kissed me on the cheek, lifting my spirits enough to carry on with the search. We found several more items in the same condition that day, all drenched in human blood.

But it was on the first night of the third week that the real trouble started. I was finally drifting off to sleep – exhaustion claiming me for its own – when a high-pitched scream woke me from my slumber.

I recognised Featherton's shrill voice instantly and ran out of my tent, rifle in hand.

Sandy, Catherine and Gul had heard the cries too, and were already outside. When we shone our lamps in the direction of Featherton's temporary home we found it torn to shreds. Of my friend there was no sign.

'My God!' spluttered Sandy.

One of the natives was hopping up and down and shouting something in his foreign tongue. Gul went over to try and calm him, speaking quietly with the man – no doubt asking what he'd seen.

Gul listened intently to the story, the whites of his eyes flashing nervously in the darkness.

When he was finished, he came across to me.

'Sir.' His voice quivered with fear. 'We must leave this place now.'

I frowned. 'What happened here?'

'Must leave now,' he repeated.

I shook him brusquely by the shoulders. 'What the devil are you talking about, man? Did some animal do this?'

'Not animal,' he whispered, spitting on the ground.

If only he'd explained to me what the man had seen, I might have wished to flee as well. But I fear I wouldn't have believed his words at that time, without having seen the proof for myself. And besides, my good friend Featherton – a fine, upstanding gentleman whom I've known since my schooldays – was missing now in addition to my father. I couldn't just turn my back on them.

I watched as Gul had words with his men. They were all frightened, I could see that for myself, but after he'd finished they were petrified. One by one they scattered and ran back in the direction we had come from. The combination of jungle and blackness enveloped them and I knew it would be useless trying to follow. Within seconds it was as if they'd never existed at all.

Gul returned to me. 'Sir, I go to join them now.'

I raised my firearm. 'Damn you, Gul. You're not going anywhere. We need you! Your brother needs you!'

'I go now, sir,' he insisted, completely ignoring my protests and the barrel pointing in his direction. 'If you are a wise man, you come too.'

I looked at Sandy and Catherine. Gul's words had shook them both, especially my beloved, but I knew Sandy would follow my lead.

'Take Catherine back with you. Sandy and I will search for the others.'

Gul nodded and held out his hand for Catherine. As usual, she was as stubborn as a mule.

'I am not leaving without you, Gerald!' she said sternly.

'Darling, please…'

'No. I'm staying and that's final.'

Gul sighed, then backed into the forest. 'I pray for you all,' he said finally, and was gone.

***

It would have been senseless to look for Featherton before dawn, so Sandy and I took turns sleeping and guarding the camp in case our 'intruder' came back.

By early light we packed up what little we could carry and set off. There were massive dents in the grass where Featherton had been dragged along, it seemed, so we simply followed them.

It certainly appeared likely that some animal or another had whisked him off into the undergrowth; probably the same one that had attacked my father's team. But I still held out hope he was alive, in spite of Gul's reaction.

We stopped for a break around noon, and it was at this

point I noticed there were none of the usual sounds of the jungle in this area. Everything was still and quiet – unnaturally so in fact.

Apart from a rustling in the green expanse ahead, the strangest thing I had heard since entering this Godforsaken place.

'*Over there!*' shouted Catherine hysterically.

I looked in the direction she was pointing, and just glimpsed the back of something huge roaming through the forest. Leaves and vines twitched as it moved; the noise now coming from every direction at once.

It was clearly heading right for us, whatever it was, and I drew my rifle up to shoulder height.

When Sandy spoke, there was a definite tremble in his voice. 'Gerald, what do you think it is?'

'I don't know. Just be prepared to –'

It all happened so fast. As I turned to answer Sandy, I saw him being pulled into the thicket – a powerful worm-like tendril coiled around his left leg. He cried for help and I reached out to grab his hand.

But Sandy's palms were soaked with sweat and he slipped from my grasp. I'll never forget the expression on his face as he was yanked backwards – a combination of pure terror and surprise.

I tumbled to my knees, watching him disappear as I fell. My mind was racing. What could do such a thing to a man?

Only then did I realise that in all the confusion I had left Catherine's side, and by that time it was too late: she was nowhere to be seen. I called her name over and over, but there was no reply.

Angry tears stung my eyes and I rushed into the grass, gun held in front of me. I must have searched the surrounding area for at least an hour, and I found nothing save for more dents in the foliage like the ones at the camp.

I sat down in the grassland and wept.

***

I don't recall how long I stayed there, praying for the safe return of my love. Nor do I remember getting up and wandering through the jungle once more. But wander I did, for hours – well into the night – traipsing through this hellhole, one foot after the other. Something was guiding me. I thought perhaps my feelings for Catherine, or maybe the bond I shared with my father? In any event I continued on, passing row upon row of trees and plant-life.

Until I came upon the sound of running water.

In my troubled state I had forgotten to bring along my own supply and suddenly it struck me how very thirsty I was. I parted the forest and saw a beautifully clear pool situated in the middle of a clearing.

A peculiar glow arose from the water, casting a net of light over the dark surroundings. Fresh liquid dribbled across the rocks from a nearby waterfall, feeding the circular lagoon, and the stars above were reflected on its surface. It was the very spot my father had been seeking! I was just about to run across to it when I noticed movement in the damp curtain itself.

Out of the corner of my eye I saw something emerge and work its way onto the grass. Words are barely adequate to describe how hideous the sight was and I thought for a moment I might be ill.

The creature moved along the ground like a reptile, but it was much larger than any species I'd ever heard of – bloated almost. It reminded me of those serpents I learnt about in Greek mythology at school, except I'd always pictured them as rather graceful.

Its flesh was a mass of tubes and raised lumps, and I

could see every blood vessel glistening in the light from that pool, pumping a dark life-force around the monstrous thing's body.

Along the length of its back were gyrating tentacles, flailing in the air. The same kind of appendage that had seized poor Sandy.

And the head – I presume it was a head for it housed row upon row of razor-sharp teeth – was spherical in shape, roughly the same size as a Casey ball. The whole thing sparkled with a myriad of tiny black eyes: watching, ever watching.

I could only assume this was some sort of guardian of the pool, protecting it from those who might get too close. There was little doubt in my mind that this was the thing my father's team had encountered.

My mouth was even dryer now, and my hands were shaking. From somewhere deep in my core I found the strength to raise my gun.

But before I could fire, several more of the beasts came out of the pool. These were smaller than the first, though no less grotesque, and they clamoured around it like a pack of wild animals.

With horror I watched as the elder went to the long grass and pulled something out with its teeth. When I looked closer, I discovered it was a human hand, bloodied and torn off at the wrist. The golden ring still attached to one finger told me who the former owner was. My dear old friend Sandy.

The creature flipped up the limb and devoured it in one fluid movement. It was like watching a dog do a party trick. Then it reared up on its tail, allowing the little ones to suckle at its underbelly.

That was all I needed to see. I chambered a bullet and

prepared to shoot.

Suddenly another monster appeared in front of me. It snapped eagerly at my face and I leant back just in time to escape the jaws.

It was even bigger than the 'mother' in the clearing, and it jumped on top of me before I could right myself. The gun fell from my hands as it clamped its teeth around my forearm.

I yelped in pain, and tried desperately to kick it away. Alas, to no avail; it had my legs pinned down tight.

It slithered and wriggled over my torso, chewing away on my flesh like a thing possessed.

Then the attack ceased, as unexpectedly as it began. I was too shocked to do anything but gape at the brute. Black orbs that served as eyeballs were all fixed on my chest, and I realised my mother's cross had dropped out of my shirt.

It cocked its head at the crucifix – in fright or admiration, I couldn't tell which, but it gave me the chance to slip my knife from its sheath.

Whilst it sat distracted, I jammed the blade into its side and raked the metal towards me. It squirmed in agony, foul -smelling mush oozing from the wound. I began stabbing it randomly.

It squealed as the final blow came: I buried the knife in its head up to the hilt.

Quickly, I heaved the weight aside and took up my gun again. The first shot missed the others completely, but my second round hit one of the babies enjoying its meal.

There was a mass exodus to the pool, shapes wriggling into the water as fast as they could. The larger one was taken by surprise, though. It stared at me over the clearing.

I aimed and … my gun jammed.

It saw its chance and made for the water. Without

thinking I gave chase and dived on its tail.

My quarry attempted to knock me off, but we plunged into the water together.

Below the surface, at the very bottom of the pool, lay a large luminescent boulder. I almost struck it, but kicked away seconds before the collision. It was quite unlike anything I'd seen before, bubbling and churning the water around it like champagne in a glass.

The shower felt warm and my skin tingled under the deluge. I swallowed several mouthfuls, but hung on to the creature's tail for dear life. No matter how hard it tried to shake me, I persevered.

Except it was no longer a tail at all. To my astonishment, it was now a pair of legs – human legs. Through the water I looked ahead of me and couldn't believe my own senses.

The freak had transformed into … my beloved Catherine.

I let go, fighting to comprehend the scene as I broke the surface of the pool. My head was spinning, and my body ached. I reached around for some kind of purchase, then slowly climbed back onto the grass.

My legs simply refused to obey my commands, so I lay there panting. When I looked down, I noticed the bite-wound on my arm had almost healed up completely. The skin was pulsating, repairing the damage done.

But there was more.

Lumps had started to appear on my hands, the fingers webbing and knitting together. I watched as my arms disappeared into the sides of my body. My clothes tore away, leaving me naked and helpless as a babe.

Only now did I realise the awful truth of the situation.

I had indeed found my father, as I'd longed to do, and mistakenly killed him. *He* was the demon in the long grass, transformed by this unearthly pool – or, more accurately, by the rock that lay on its bed. He hadn't been afraid of my mother's cross ... some part of his mind had actually recognised it!

However, my hypothesis was yet to be confirmed. I wriggled over the grass and, sure enough, found the body of my late father – blood pooled around the corpse, my knife-handle protruding from his head.

In his altered state he must have killed the other members of the expedition, and when we arrived to search for him, he started hunting my team as well. He'd spared Catherine alone to become his mate. To bear his hellish spawn.

My vision was blurring. No, not blurring – changing. I could see a million different images at once through the dark pupils sprouting on my face.

The same forces that 'affected' my father were transforming me also. I was becoming the very thing I'd found so repugnant not five minutes ago. My mind was filled with images alien to me, of distant stars and the depths of space.

I moved back along the grass on my stomach, and God help me it felt so good. Catherine materialised by the water's edge in her human form, but for the first time ever I felt no physical attraction.

Not until she joined me in my metamorphosis.

My senses were so acute now; a craving for flesh sending me almost crazy. We set out into the jungle together, Catherine and I – leaving the brood behind. It was time to find them fresh meat. And I knew exactly where to look.

Gul and the natives would still be making their way back to the village. When they were finished off, then perhaps we'd venture further afield. Soon we'd dine like royalty and multiply like hares.

Oh yes, I had found the ultimate cure for all man's ills in the 'star-pool', and that was to be a man no longer.

For the first time in my life I knew what destiny had in store.

The age of the new breed was only just beginning.

RAG AND BONE

When Ted opened his eyes, he realised he was hanging in a room, surrounded by corpses.

Not hanging, as in hanging out – but in the literal sense. Suspended by the wrists, feet dangling with no sense of the floor beneath them. It was quite dark, and he was only able to see the dead people because of the moonlight, filtering in through a small grilled window to the left. The angle of that moon told him he was underground.

Ted blinked a few times, taking in the shapes of the suspended bodies. They were hung, just as he was, like meat in a freezer. He could see the wounds that had been inflicted on some of them: cuts, savage and unforgiving – the blood now dried in the slits. Some were naked, some wore scraps of clothing, torn away during whatever struggle had ensued before their deaths, or perhaps even afterwards? Some had been so brutally attacked, that he could see bone poking through in places: at the knee in one case, the forearm in another, ribs in a third.

Ted squinted, attempting to make out more, but it was impossible. Some had their backs to him, some were further away, some in corners. The ones closest appeared to be female, that much he could tell. One's shapely legs were in view, and another's breasts were exposed – were it not for the fact they both had jagged slashes across them, he might have been quite aroused by the sight.

Jesus, he told himself, *not now, and definitely not here.*

Wherever *here* was. But he couldn't help himself. It had always been his weakness. If the average man thought about sex every seven seconds, then Ted was so far above average it was ridiculous. It was a wonder he could concentrate on work half the time.

Concentrate now, though. Try to figure out what you're doing here. Or, more importantly, how to escape.

He struggled to pull himself up, maybe try and work his wrists free of the bonds holding him, but it was too difficult. For one thing he didn't feel like he had any energy, perhaps an effect of being in this position for too long? A torturer's potential victim. Because he'd seen this pose before in TV shows and movies, hadn't he? They always did this to the people they'd captured, usually questioning them for information in thrillers. Was that it, was this work-related? Some old business enemy, of which admittedly there were many.

That didn't make sense. Why all the others? Maybe he was the subject of a serial killer. They did the same thing sometimes, stringing up folk like animals, cutting off skin to use for God knows what purposes. It would certainly fit with the corpses who had been mutilated. He tried not to think about it.

Ted attempted again to pull free. Maybe he was still feeling the after-effects of whatever drug had been used to incapacitate him?

He remembered that much: whoever had done this had come up behind him in the car park, silent and deadly. By the time he'd known there was someone there, it was already too late – he'd felt the prick of a needle in his neck and it was all over. Blackness, that's all he could remember … until this. And part of him now wished he was still unconscious.

He closed his eyes, perhaps to pretend, but all he could see were those cuts. Ted could imagine the pain, putting himself in the dead people's places – could feel what he was surely about to experience, when whoever had done this returned.

Ted heard a sound and snapped himself out of those thoughts. A voice. Dear Christ, the killer was coming back already, before he'd even had chance to formulate a plan of action. But no, it wasn't that at all. Someone was speaking, yes, but it wasn't in the assured voice of a murderer. Someone in control of the situation, without compassion – someone who could do the things that had been done in this slaughterhouse.

This was more like a whimper, a groan. 'Help me,' it said. Then there was movement. One of the 'corpses' nearest to him shifted position, spinning round on the rope that was holding it ... her. Because as Ted could see, this was a woman; the blouse and skirt, as ragged as they were, gave it away. Her face caught the light from the moon and he almost gasped in horror at what had been done to it. Part of the woman's cheek had been ripped away, a large flap of skin peeled off, revealing cheekbone and teeth. The edge of her lip had been torn as well, leaving her with a permanent frown on one side – like a person who'd suffered a severe stroke. No wonder she was having trouble speaking.

Her hair – it appeared silver, but then that was probably just the effect of the light ... more likely blonde – looked like it had been hacked at as well: one side cut short, possibly with a knife, while the other was still long and fell over her left shoulder. That too was exposed and horribly scarred. Her head was tilted, and to be honest she still *looked* dead, but she was moving, and she was speaking. 'H-help... Help me,' repeated the woman, and this time Ted saw a saliva bubble form in that ruined cheek, popping as she spoke her next word, 'P-please.'

What could *he* do? Ted was in no position to help anyone, even if they were gazing at him like that – so pleadingly. It was all he could do to even look at the poor wretch, her appearance so far removed from the usual beauties he liked to associate with. He said nothing, merely attempted a half-hearted shrug.

'*P-please,*' came the voice again, filled with such agony Ted felt compelled to finally say something.

He'd opened his mouth, but before any words could emerge something else moved in the darkness. Something silent and deadly. The something that had come up behind him in the car park, hidden in the shadows all this time. A figure, which sidled up behind *her* now, grabbing the woman's neck and jerking it backwards, so the cords were standing proud. Ted wanted to look away, but it all happened so fast. The large knife was suddenly being drawn over the woman's throat, like a cellist with a bow. Except the only music that emerged were the deep grunts and chokes of someone trying to breathe. A concerto in death minor. It took just moments for the noise to stop, but it seemed like hours to Ted – must have seemed like *years* to the woman with the ruined face.

The figure still held back behind the hanging body, for now it *was* a body and nothing more. That final bit of life had been extinguished, such as it was. Ted wanted to ask who this person was, but couldn't get a word out now through fear. Blood was pouring from the slit in the blonde woman's throat, spilling over her shredded blouse. Ted caught a flash of eyes looking at him, the killer's wild stare sending chills through his body. When the figure revealed itself, he did gasp.

Audrey? No, it couldn't be!

Ted took in the sight before him, the small woman dressed in dark clothes, almost like she was in mourning: black top, black trousers ... black *gloves*. It matched her raven-coloured hair, which, unlike the dead blonde woman's, had been styled by a professional. Even after all that excitement there was barely a curl out of place, the mark of an expert hairdresser. An expensive one, at that.

Ted could do nothing but gaze at her, that knife still in her hand, dripping with the blood from her fresh kill. Audrey? *His* Audrey. She was no murderer. She wouldn't even let him kill spiders in the bath.

His mind flashed back to their first meeting, at that club in the city. She'd been with a couple of friends, he'd been alone and had zeroed in on her, flashing that confident, charming smile, guaranteed to work. Her friends had giggled at his jokes, Audrey had told him she wasn't interested, that she even had a boyfriend – he hadn't lasted long once Ted was on the scene – but by the end of the night he'd secured her phone number.

On their first date, he'd picked her up in his Corvette ZR1 and impressed her with talk about his business ventures. He found out that she was very family orientated – devoted to her father, because he'd brought her up when her mother had died in childbirth.

'I feel so comfortable telling you all this,' Audrey had said, 'Don't know why.'

'I do,' Ted replied, grinning.

It hadn't been long before he'd become a permanent fixture in her life ... and her bed. Soon after, they were dividing their time between his place and her apartment. Not long after that, she'd taken Ted to meet her father, Frank, at the family home – a huge house just outside the capital. It was far enough away to pretend it was the countryside, but just close enough to smell the exhaust fumes from the cars. Here Frank lived, all alone – retired due to ill health, but content. Ted had done the same with her silver-haired father, charming him as they drank wine out in the garden, finding out more about the family business.

Frank had made his money through scrap over the past few decades, but the trade went back a long way. 'I can remember doing the rounds with my dad as a kid, collecting all kinds of stuff in a horse-drawn cart on the streets, ringing the bell. Nowadays it's all in trucks and vans,' he said, laughing. 'You know, a lot of people think that Rag and Bone men only go back a couple of hundred years, but some say it's further. To the middle ages, or maybe even before that.'

'That's fascinating,' Ted told him, stifling the yawn that was building.

'They got their name because they'd even collect rags, which could be sold to paper-makers and weavers, and the bones from meat. That could be turned into bone char, bone ash, bone carver ... even glue!'

Ted listened, humoured the man, but he didn't care about *how* Frank had come by his cash – the heritage obviously important to the guy. He was only interested in the fact that Audrey would come by it one day. Less than a week later, and with Frank's approval, Ted proposed and was delighted when Audrey said yes. They were happy, both of them, and went on that way for a good year or more—

So why was she doing this? He felt like asking her, but hesitated, still seeing that crazed look in her eyes. Something had changed. She was no longer the woman he knew as his fiancée. She was something else – something *unhinged*.

His eyes were at least adjusting to the light better, and he could see more of his surroundings. More of the corpses that filled this place, although he still didn't recognise it.

'There, that's better,' Audrey said, stepping away from the dead woman, her voice cold and hard. 'Another one of your whores silenced.'

Ted frowned. What was she talking about? His eyes flitted from the psychopathic Audrey to the dead woman. Did he know her? Forget about the scarred face and body, the blood; take all that away and did she look familiar? Ted still couldn't see it. He looked around at the other bodies nearby, and beyond Audrey. Yes, they were *all* female, he could see that. But—

Another one of your whores…

He tried to swallow, but was having difficulty. He'd never known their names, any of them, but yes, the more he looked, the more his eyes adjusted to the light in here… *Jesus*, he said to himself. He thought he'd been so careful.

It stood to reason: no one woman was ever going to satisfy *him*. That wasn't how he made. He loved Audrey, in his own way, and the others were just conquests – to keep his hand in. Sex, nothing more. Plus which, they all knew he was engaged; he'd told them and they hadn't seemed to mind. If anything, some of them found this a turn on.

The more he focused, forcing himself to see the walls of that room, the more he could make out the evidence of those encounters he couldn't resist. No, that made it sound like they seduced him, when it was so obviously the other way around. All those nights working late, at conferences or attending business meetings, when actually he was on the prowl again, on the hunt. The photos were there, tacked up on those walls: large, grainy, black and white prints. Some of him and women at bars, at hotels, at clubs like the one where he met Audrey. Some were even worse. Snapshots of the hot, frenzied couplings, rutting like animals – through windows, and some from inside the room itself (a professional then, some kind of PI ... so Audrey hadn't been as naïve as he thought; it explained why she'd stalled over the wedding, that caution). Ted looked from the pictures of those women alive, to the dead bodies hanging in that basement lair. And, God help him, he was able to match them up. Well, most of them. Some were beyond even his identification.

Ted could imagine the pain Audrey had felt when she'd seen some of those photographs. Pain that might tip you over the edge. Pain he now saw in her look – along with revenge. She'd been on her very own hunting trip and now that she'd punished the women who'd slept with him, Ted was next. What was the betting she'd saved the most brutal tortures for last?

He was about to plead with her, but knew that would do no good. Once Audrey had made her mind up about something, that was it. But as she approached, still wielding the knife, he found himself whimpering, 'Please, *no.*'

When she continued on anyway, he gritted his teeth, the real Ted emerging. 'You'll never get away with this, Audrey. I'm telling you. What the fuck do you think you're going to do with all these bodies anyway?'

She paused, as if contemplating this – maybe the first time she'd even considered it during this whole spree. But Ted should have known better. Just as she'd been clever enough to hire the snoop, she'd had her endgame figured out well in advance. Audrey leaned in, too quick for him to flinch, and whispered, 'He knows what you've done, and he's coming for you.'

What? What the fuck did that mean? Ted braced himself for Audrey to strike, to begin slashing him with the knife. But she didn't. Instead she pulled back, grinning (it reminded him of his grin, that – the satisfied one he couldn't help whenever he'd scored). She was stepping away, leaving him alone. *Don't question it,* he told himself, *it at least buys you some time.*

Then he heard the sound. At first it seemed a long way off, that bell. Then the call followed it, equally distant. 'Rag and Bone!' it went.

Ted cocked an ear. There it came again. The bell, and the cry: *'Rag and Bone!'*

Audrey's grin widened and she moved over to the side of the room, climbing some steps. At first Ted thought she might be ascending to an upper floor, but then she reached above her and undid a latch. Audrey flung open the doors – cellar doors that led to the outside.

His first thoughts were: I can use that to escape, if only I can get free of these bloody ropes. His next thoughts, when the light from the moon illuminated more of that place, were about those wine bottles at the back of the cellar. Ted knew where he was now, even though he'd never been down here. Had only been to the place itself on a handful of occasions. It was the wine cellar in the family house: a hobby of Frank's and perfect for something like this. No-one would hear the screams. And they were far enough away from civilisation that nobody would hear the cry drawing closer and closer, louder and louder.

'Rag and Bone!'

It was a strange call, like the person shouting it couldn't quite say the words. It reminded Ted of how newspaper sellers on street corners shout out the names of the tabloids.

'Audrey,' Ted began, but she was taking no notice. She was too busy looking out through the trap door. Ted heard the sound of hooves next, accompanying the bell and the cries.

Jesus, what was going on here? One of her dad's old mates drafted in to help? It made sense. Like Audrey, they really wouldn't have been too happy if they knew the truth.

He knows what you've done, and he's coming for you.

But what had he done, really? All Ted had suggested was that Audrey invest in a few of his ventures – she had the money now, and it would really help him out (his flashy cars and dinners a front for covering how badly he'd got into debt). Selling the family business wasn't asking too much, was it? Her father had been the one hanging on to the past, why should she?

And she'd done it, even though she was doing other things behind his back (he could talk), hiring that PI for example. Audrey had sold up because she loved him.

The scrap business scrapped, Ted bailed out.

He saw the horse's feet now, pulling up outside, the cart behind. And from this angle, Ted could also see the boots when they jumped down – big, hobnailed ones, crunching the gravel round the back of the house. A faint whistle drifted down into the cellar, echoing throughout.

Audrey pulled back, waving a hand and inviting the newcomer in. The larger figure descended. Bulky, wearing some kind of long coat, he also sported a cap that was pulled down low on his head. His frame virtually blocked out any light from above, leaving the figure in silhouette as he glanced at Audrey – awaiting orders, it seemed. She pointed to the bodies and the man nodded, stomping over to the first. He hefted it onto his shoulder like it weighed nothing, whistling happily.

So that *was the plan,* thought Ted, *get this bastard to dispose of the evidence of Audrey's sick and twisted exploits?* He said nothing as, one by one, the corpses were carried up the steps and – though he couldn't see properly – he assumed, dumped into that cart up there. Why a cart, he had no idea. Why not a van or truck? Was he some kind of purist or something? Not even Frank had been that bad.

Frank… Ted thought about the old man now, and about what he'd done.

He shook his head; there wasn't time for that. He was in *real* trouble. As the last of the women were carried and loaded up, Audrey pointed towards Ted. She obviously couldn't bring herself to do anything to her lover. Instead, she'd shown him what she'd done to his 'whores' and was now leaving Ted to the attentions of this nutter. He didn't know which was worse. At least he might stand a chance of talking Audrey round. Possibly. Maybe.

But there was no chance of that now, because the collector was next to him, whistling, shouldering Ted and cutting the rope attached to the ceiling. Ted groaned as he was given the fireman's lift, the rotten stench of the man like garbage. It was only when he was being carried that Ted noticed the shabby clothes the man was wearing, the state of the coat not dissimilar to the dress of Audrey's victims; the man's trousers scuffed and tatty.

Then Ted was being hauled up into the night air. He tried to struggle, but again it was either the position he'd been in or the after-effects of the drugs that prevented him – he had hardly any strength at all. So, when he was thrown in the back of the cart, an old-fashioned wooden one just like those Frank had described, he couldn't fight back. 'Audrey?' he just about managed, as the Rag and Bone man left him, skirting round to the driver's seat at the front

But Ted's fiancée simply stared after them. Then, as the transportation set off, Ted saw her retreat back down into the cellar – no doubt to clean up – leaving him to his fate.

The ride wasn't a comfortable one. Apart from the stench, some of it from the bodies, most of it from the cart and the man driving it, there were the jolts as it went over rocks or uneven terrain. On one particular bump, Ted found himself rolling over to face a girl who'd had her eyes plucked out, the black sockets staring back at him (what had been her name? Jackie, Debra, Sandra? Who the Hell knew?). He couldn't even muster a scream and was thankful when the next jolt came and righted him again. They seemed to be travelling quite fast though, hardly enough time for Ted to worry about where this guy would be dumping them: burying them in a wood, weighing them down in a lake, perhaps? In a deserted quarry?

He was wrong on all counts, because when the cart eventually arrived at its destination, the Rag and Bone Man had returned to his home (one of Audrey's dad's old places perhaps? Had this bloke bought it?). Ted took in the yard when they rode through the gates – a typical scrap merchant's, with bits of old bicycles, worn out beds, washing machines and every other bit of discarded detritus you could imagine piled on all sides. It wouldn't be hard to lose a few bodies in that lot. The perfect place, in fact.

The man pulled his horses to a standstill and clambered down. The moon was slipping behind a cloud so Ted still couldn't get a good look at the man's face as he began to unload the contents of his cart. He needed to see him, for when he got away – he'd need to describe him to the police. Audrey first. Then this guy. The cops would throw the book at them both.

(Oh yes, and what happens when they go digging around in *your* past? What happens when they find out about Frank?)

The huge figure began picking up the corpses again, putting them over his shoulder. He whistled once more as he worked, which made what he was doing all the more disturbing. He tossed them on the heaps of rubbish as if he was flinging old tyres.

Ted tried to twist away, to get his legs and arms moving, to climb out and get free of this place. Run, find a phone and —

But he was going nowhere. They were down to the last few women in the cart, which didn't take the man long to clear.

'Look … hey, I have money,' Ted managed. (*Oh yeah, whose?*)

The man ignored him, heaving the last of the scrawny bodies onto a pile of trash.

He turned and began making his way back towards Ted.

'Can't we at least talk about it, please?'

'*Help me. P-please!*' The words of that woman back in the cellar rattled around in his head.

The man was drawing nearer. 'Please, I don't want to die!' shouted Ted, with more force than he'd been able to muster since he woke.

His captor paused then, lingering as if mulling something over. Then he began to walk off to one side.

Yes! I've got through to him, thought Ted. *Maybe I should offer him some money again?* He frowned, though, as he watched the man rooting around in the rubbish, fishing something out. As the large figure turned, Ted saw he was holding up a cracked mirror.

And, as the guy came back, the moon passed from

behind those clouds at the same time as the Rag and Bone Man lifted his head. Ted just about had time to register those features – and realise just how appropriate his name was – before the mirror was lifted.

Then it all fell into place. Flashes of the man's face, so similar to Frank's, something he himself had inherited through a bloodline and profession that went back so far. (*A lot of people think that Rag and Bone men only go back a couple of hundred years, but some say it's further. To the middle ages, or maybe even before that…*) A trade plied during plague times, when they would carry the dead away from infected areas? You don't, you *can't*, do something like that without being granted some kind of immunity by Death himself. They were His helpers, in effect: some even changing to resemble their master.

The rags and bones, all that was left of the dead, were collected by them. By people who were little more than rags and bones themselves. It was a bloodline that had been broken when Ted came along – not simply persuading Audrey to sell up, but engineering the little 'accident' that would take Frank's life and provide the means for her to do so. Frank was an old man, his heart weak; it wasn't that hard to sneak inside the house and give him a little … scare.

Just like Ted was scared now. Because not only was he seeing something he really didn't want to in the mirror, he was also remembering. That it hadn't been the first time he'd woken up back there in the cellar, that Audrey had already done things to him which made the others look like she was just getting started. Pain so intense he'd blocked it out, kept alive – barely – while he watched her cut up the women.

But not kept alive long enough.

The image, the face – or what was left of it – staring back

at Ted was barely recognisable as his own. It had been shredded, along with the rest of him: skin flayed from his body so that you couldn't tell where his clothes ended and his flesh began. Ted recalled the whipping, now, with some kind of cat o' nine tails, spiked ends digging deep with each swipe. He howled then, just as he had when Audrey had done her worst, finally getting up close and personal, pulling off his finger and toe nails, doing hideous things to his privates that meant he'd never be capable of cheating on anyone again.

Ted looked away and the Rag and Bone Man dropped the mirror. His charge had seen enough obviously, but things were only just getting started. Ted looked past the skeletal figure, whose coat could no longer conceal its ribcage, open to the air. This representation of everything Frank held so dear, this figure that was all the Rag and Bone Men there'd ever been rolled into one, had made its home in a fittingly nightmarish place. Because the more Ted looked, the more he saw of the yard, filled not only with ordinary rubbish, but the more specific junk of human waste. Bones, organs, scraps of clothing, all plugged the gaps where he'd dared not look before.

Ironically, Ted felt like laughing. He'd been pleading for his life when all along there was no life to spare. No wonder Audrey had been ignoring him – had he really been speaking at all? Had any of this actually been happening? It certainly felt real to him, but that didn't mean anything.

Somehow Ted knew he would soon fill the spaces here, just like those women who'd wronged Audrey, who'd wrong the line. Trapped in their own private Hell. (For a moment, Ted wondered if they were seeing this, or something else entirely; perhaps this little treat had been reserved only for him?)

But it was time, he saw. When the Rag and Bone Man came for him now, Ted surrendered without protest.

To be carried over to the pile of junk, of scrap human life.

To join the walls of organs, body parts and muscle.

To join … no, finally to *become* the rag…

…and…

…the bone.

THE WEEPING WOMAN

'Come not, when I am dead,
To drop thy foolish tears upon my grave,
To trample round my fallen head,
And vex the unhappy dust thou wouldst not save.'

– Tennyson

Well, what could I do? What would you have done in my position? The same thing, unless you're totally heartless.

The woman was right there in the middle of the road. I damned near ran her over myself. If I hadn't had my wits about me she'd have been a red smear on the tarmac. As it turned out, I managed to avoid her, wrestling the Volvo onto an embankment and killing the engine. Thank God there were no vehicles behind me.

That was the first chance I got to look at her properly – before, she was just a blurry shape heading for the bonnet of my car. I guessed she was about forty-five, forty-six tops. Her tawny hair was wild about her head, with leaves and bits of grass clinging to the strands for dear life. As she staggered closer I could see her face was dirty, but floods of tears had struggled through the grime to create a few clean tracks. The patterned dress she wore was ripped in several places.

I got out of the driver's seat, my hands still shaking because of the shock, I guess, and was all set to give her a mouthful of the foulest language ever conceived, when I saw the blood. That is, I assumed it was blood. Maroon splotches on her forehead, and as she turned I saw more of the liquid running down her arms. She had no shoes on, either; her feet had been cut to ribbons by the rough terrain.

But that crying noise she made was the worst. I'd never heard such pain in a person's voice before. She was virtually hysterical. Each fresh burst of wailing sliced right through me.

I went up to her. Gripping the woman by the shoulders and looking directly into her eyes, I asked: 'Are you all right?' Okay, so that was a stupid thing to say – it was obvious she was far from all right. But I didn't know how else to approach her.

She took a second or so to calm down and speak, though even then the words were almost drowned out by her howling and watery coughs. 'My ... Oh Lord ... my children ... they're...'

She broke down in my arms at this point, waving her hands over to the woods on our right.

'What's happened? Has there been an accident?' The woman carried on sobbing into my shirt. I couldn't get any more sense out of her. I looked up and down the road but didn't see any other cars. Not surprising really, as I'd chosen this route specifically for its lack of traffic. I don't own a mobile, either (can't abide them – unlike the rest of the known world apparently), otherwise it would've been a simple enough matter to call for help. And public phones? Forget it. They were as rare as tower blocks in these parts.

I had no choice. The woman was clearly distraught and her children were in trouble. Placing my arm around her shoulder, I urged her to show me the way...

***

We walked through the woods a fair stretch, the lady still upset but relaxing a little now that I was in tow. The trees were huge in that place, twisting, gnarly trunks which spawned offspring the higher they went. I recognised the leaves as the same ones she had in her hair.

On the way I started to wonder what might be ahead. Had the family been in a car crash on the other side of the thicket? Perhaps her husband – or partner, I couldn't see a ring – had hit a tree on some deserted lane and she'd been the only person who could scramble out of the wreckage. Her natural instinct would be to find a main road and bring back help. Unfortunately, I was the only person on it at the time.

Then again, she never mentioned a car. Just because she looked like she'd been in an accident, it didn't necessarily follow that she had. Maybe some lunatic had attacked her and her kids while they were out walking, I thought. You read about it all the time in the papers…

I tried asking her again, but she was clearly more interested in getting us there quickly. A new sense of urgency had taken hold of her. The further we went, the more she would pull on my arm, yanking me onwards. Faster, faster through the lush surroundings.

Until at last we came to the spot.

I saw the bodies from quite a distance away, covered in the same gooey substance as her. Panic raised its ugly head as the weeping woman dragged me nearer and nearer. How could I possibly help them? What had I been thinking of? I was no doctor; I'd never even taken a first aid course.

Still, I couldn't let her see that I was scared. She was in a bad enough state as it was without feeding off my anxiety. Actually, the more steps I took the easier it became. A morbid curiosity was overpowering my fears. I needed to see what had happened to her family. A warped compulsion you might say, but a very human one.

When I got there, I found the price of my curiosity too high.

Three corpses in various states of disarray were splayed out on the grass, stripped naked as far as I could tell; it was hard to determine exactly because of all the mess. One was missing its head, a young lad I think. Another was gutted from neck to abdomen, ribs bared, the inside of its belly scooped out, leaving only one or two coils of intestine dangling from the wound. And the last, a woman, had had her limbs removed: torn from their sockets in a vicious, clumsy way.

The dinner I'd eaten at a Happy Traveller ten miles back chose that moment to reappear. Doubled over, I spewed the half-digested baked potato onto the ground.

'*My children!*' screamed the weeping woman, pointing in their direction.

I heaved again, but there was nothing left in my stomach.

'What...?' I started, desperately trying to understand why she'd brought me here. These people were dead, surely she could see that! We should have gone for the police in my car. Or had this happened while she'd been to fetch me? Was the maniac who'd done it still around?

Then I noticed she was pointing not to the bodies, but rather at the woodland beyond. 'My children,' she repeated in her phlegmy tones.

From behind the trees, springing up from the grass, and swinging down from branches they came, emerging from their hiding places. Strange, embryonic things – dozens of them – with long arms and vitreous flesh. Tufts of tawny hair stood to attention on bulging heads, their eyes little more than dimples beneath thick, curving brows. A split ran from ear to ear on each of them. Mouths that could open much wider than any animal's...

And smothered in blood.

They were on me in a heartbeat. The larger ones held the others back, like birds after the best crusts of bread. Some of the babies even had to make do with the puddle of vomit on the ground, slurping it up with enormous silvery tongues.

I felt sharp teeth ripping into my legs, my arms. Clawing fingernails digging at my stomach. A couple of my punches hit their mark, but ultimately there were too many of the abominations to tackle.

I fell on my side, a mass of chattering forms all over me. But through the gaps I saw the woman who had led me – no, *lured* me – here. She was still weeping, crying a deluge of tears. Yet I could see a difference.

These were tears of joy and pride. A mother's love for her children.

Happy now that she had once again provided for her young.

PAY THE PIPER

He turned intuitively.

Another one lumbered out from behind a dwelling to The Piper's left. He stopped and watched the figure, tracing its path. At this distance it looked tragic, like the town drunkard who remains under the influence long after the taverns have closed. Bottle clutched to his chest, faint mutterings of a song escaping from his lips – or perhaps the laments of a once-happy man.

But as The Piper covered the ground between them, certain truths came to light. Instead of a bottle, the man was holding something that was pink and red and glistening in the early morning sunshine. The remains of his last meal. And in place of a song or words of regret, the sound of burbling wind was emanating from his mouth; half-formed belches released with each step the fellow took.

The Piper stopped now, a few feet from this new suspect. It looked up at him, no longer an individual in any true sense of the word; one eye glazed over and thick with cataracts, the other hanging down to rest on its cheek, suspended on strips of meaty string – the blood in its empty socket long-since dried up. It took another bite of the forearm clenched in grey, gangrenous hands, one finger bent so far back that it had to be broken; the nails crusted and black as if it had been digging for coal.

It chewed the meat in an unconscious way. This was merely a habit, something it felt it must do. There was no reason for it to eat anything at all; its digestive system was no longer in any fit state to process food and it was hardly likely to keel over and die from lack of sustenance. You could only die once. That was accepted, a fact of life. One of the rules of creation.

One of them.

As it worked the muscle and bone around inside its mouth, grinding the portion down until it felt able to swallow, it stumbled forwards. The rags it wore flapped behind in the mild breeze, but here and there pieces of its skin were exposed and The Piper looked upon the foul grubs and insects that had made their nests in its rotting body. Bits of earth still fell from its breeches when it 'walked', gathering around its bare feet, waiting to be trampled back into the land once more.

The Piper often wondered what went through their minds if, indeed, such uncanny vagrants even had minds. Were their souls somewhere else, on another level exploring magnificent territories beyond his ken, detached from these ungainly vessels they once inhabited in life? Or was there still some small fragment of humanity lurking inside each one, trapped in there and screaming for deliverance? Trying to prevent themselves from committing such unholy acts because if they didn't, they would never reach the great hereafter and sit with The Lord and His angels and...

The Piper shook his head. He knew full well what this repellent wretch was thinking about. It looked at The Piper – as best it could, given the circumstances – and saw another succulent dinner ready prepared. It did not, by any stretch of the imagination, see a person standing there. Just food, and plenty of it; enough to last a good few hours, starting with that nice juicy brain inside his skull. This was always the first to go for some reason. He'd noticed this.

He'd noticed many things in his time.

But The Piper had no intentions of being devoured that day.

He showed not a flicker of fear as he reached for the instrument tucked into his belt, a long wooden tube with holes down the middle and a flattened out mouthpiece. The work of a true craftsman. His own work, in fact. The dead thing had now dropped its snack and was 'speeding' towards the main course. Those shaking hands stretched out, flashes of bone poking through at the knuckles, worms hanging down off the wrists like living, squirming bracelets.

There was now only a gap of inches separating them and a putrid aroma filled this modest space. It was just about to grab The Piper's arm – and a second later force him to his knees – when the first note was played. The carcass stood paralysed as the gentle sound carried past its ears, or what was left of them. A second note followed, then a third and a fourth, until a melodic tune took shape. A combination of vibration and breath jetted out of the pipe's end like a sort of magic current. Someone had even told him once that they'd seen shapes and symbols flowing from the whistle – musical notes of differing size and colour. The Piper didn't actually believe this himself (in all honesty he put the man's visions down to either terror or one sip too many of some intoxicating brew or another), but such stories could do nothing other than bolster his soaring reputation.

The Piper's long, bejewelled fingers gambolled over the holes as he blew. Slowly, the thing that had once been a living being, backed away. Its arms fell to its side, bewildered by its own actions. And … aye, a slight smile appeared on its face. Its cracked lips parted, pulled back over brown-black teeth. This was more like it.

Without further ado, The Piper turned his back on his captive audience and started walking again. It would follow him, they always did. Even now, above the noise of his pipe, he heard the shuffling behind, the empty croaking. The music wasn't something that could be fought or questioned. When he played, they obeyed.

All his life he'd known he had a purpose, a destiny. That he was somehow different. But for most of his childhood he'd been wilful and directionless, finally cast out by his adoptive family because they couldn't cope (his true origins still remained a mystery; abandoned in a basket in the village square). Training as a 'prentice carpenter had seemed like the answer for him, a discipline and direction he lacked at that time.

Old Jed had been his mentor when no one else would take him in. He'd taught him how to respect and manage the wood, to fashion it into any object he wished, from tables to chairs and even playthings for the young. He'd enjoyed his studies, but still longed for something more. Something special to happen. An objective, and maybe even riches beyond his wildest imaginings...

He used to watch the noblemen, traders and travelling merchants who would oft-times pass through the settlement, wishing he could be just like them. To explore the provinces, and further afield than that, must truly be an amazing thing, he thought. They told stories of distant lands where a man was sure to make his fortune, and a different maiden would warm his bed each night. Jed had laughed and called him a dreamer. In a sense he was just that. He would never live the fantasy life he'd mapped out for himself, never in a million years. Or so he had thought. That was before...

This was now.

The Piper led his new recruit through the streets of the town. At windows he saw the frightened inhabitants pointing, talking of him.

'There goes The Piper,' they would say. 'Listen to his music.'

Children idolised him. They dreamed their own dreams of one day becoming just like the man in the splendid tunic and single-feathered hat. But he was providing an essential service for the adults as well, without which they would not dare set foot outside in the light – never mind the darkness hours – for fear of running into one of the ground-dwellers.

(This was the name they had acquired over the years. It made them sound more … human than they were. Not something that couldn't be understood or reasoned with. The Piper had never approved of the label himself, which likened them to some exotic new subterranean race who, jealous of the life above, had suddenly decided to come up and say hello. Why couldn't people just face the truth? These were – or had been – brothers, sisters, parents, cousins, friends… Folk they had buried but refused to stay that way.)

The Piper remembered how his own community had been the first time, how they had reacted to this unheard of occurrence. The disbelief and ignorance.

One story in particular had remained with him, that of a young girl he'd known and admired (from a distance, alas). However, on this Sunday aft her family and betrothed had been consigning her to the grave, mere seconds away from placing her in the freshly dug orifice. And all the mourners were especially alarmed to hear the woman knocking inside her casket, desiring to be set free.

Now, in spite of the fact that the people there present were conversant with how she had met her end – attacked and beaten on the way home from market – they convinced themselves that by some divine miracle she was still alive. Her beau ran to the wooden box (a box, incidentally, The Piper had helped to make; sobbing as he worked), urging those round about to prise open its lid. The banging came louder and more frenzied. She wanted to be with her loved ones again, and he – being a devoted, caring swain – wished the same. All those lonely days since she went away, all the tears he'd shed, enough to fill a small lake, were forgotten. It had simply been a nightmare which had now relinquished its hold.

But the true nightmare was yet to come.

As the cover was wrenched off, the man had fallen gratefully into his beloved's extended – if disjointed – arms, hugging her tightly, kissing her cheeks, her lips, her forehead; every available patch of skin.

Bystanders looked on, puzzled, as the girl went to do the same. Had she simply been rendered unconscious by the ordeal, they asked one another. Had the local healer been hasty when he declared the lass to be dead? Quite obviously she was not deceased, the way she was embracing her love like that. Oh mercy, another few minutes and she would have been six feet under. A dead 'un alive.

How apt that last description had proved, for the *dead 'un alive* was opening her mouth, staring vapidly up at the sky and faces above. But instead of kissing her paramour, her teeth had gnawed their way through the side of his face.

His scream had been muffled – so those who'd escaped had said – blocked off by the girl's shoulder. The first inclination they had that something was wrong was when he started to kick his feet against the side of the coffin. Then one observer noticed all that blood inside. A horrible display to be sure.

And there were more to come, as barely recognisable hands broke through the sacred soil of the churchyard. Remnants of locals once fondly remembered were climbing out of their 'final' resting places and attacking the guests at this rather premature funeral. Soon the place was filled with the unsteady hordes; some almost skeletal, they'd been horizontal for so long; all hungry for those who still enjoyed the benefits of breathing.

Most fled from the ground-dwellers as fast as their legs could carry them. But some did not make it. The elderly, the infirm, those frozen with fright, all were overwhelmed by sheer numbers.

The strong, young men of the village, those who had not yet been drafted into service but bragged about their fighting prowess to all who would listen (aye, and laughed at The Piper because of his scarecrow-like frame), came out to oppose the withered masses before they progressed too far into the settlement – where people hid in their houses and prayed for salvation. The bang of gunpowder and swish of swords could be heard all round, but in the end it did no good.

An arm here, a leg there. The outcome was never in any doubt. How could they possibly kill that which had already expired? The very utmost all these warriors could manage was to slow them down before they too joined the ground-dwellers in death, some as rations, others as converts to their tacit cause.

And this is how it went on. In village after village, town after town, they sprang up, one following the next. With no explanation, no reason. The more superstitious said it was a curse on the land, witchcraft and sorcery afoot. The rational thinkers banded together and stated that it was some strange malady, one which placed its victims in a deathly state then reanimated them after a certain amount of time had passed (but why then was the time period different in each case, critics argued. Some ground-dwellers had been interred many, many years ago, while others, like the woman at the funeral, had barely started to turn cold). No one could offer any real solutions; no one understood what was happening. But perhaps no one was meant to...

There was a shrill cry from up ahead and The Piper ceased his playing. The ground-dweller halted also. When he saw who was calling out for help, he began running across the town centre, leaving the corpse where it was. It wouldn't attempt to move now; it would simply wait there patiently for his return – the stony grin breaking upon its face.

The Piper could see what the trouble was. Someone had disregarded his express instructions and dared to step out. A lad of no more than fifteen was being dragged across the dirt by his hair. The ground-dweller was female this time, a woman who had probably been sturdy in life, but was now like a deflated pig's bladder; the pleats of flesh dripping from her, dry cuts all over her face and arms where she'd swum her way through wood and packed turf in her hurry to reach daylight. It never ceased to amaze him how they could do that, how strong they could be if they set their sights on something. Why, before now he'd even seen them turn over carts and punch through solid rock to get to their victims.

The boy was yelping as the ground raked his backside. The dead woman was hauling him off to a place only she could see, a place where young, tender striplings were for dining on only.

The Piper positioned himself in front of her, avoiding her free arm as she swung it at him. Great clumps of hair had fallen out, he observed, and that same glassy expression possessed her, the one they all wore. Until, that is, he started to play again, concentrating intently on what he was doing. Then it was quite a different tale.

She let go of the boy and cackled peaceably to herself, almost as though she'd been expecting this to happen.

As he led her off to join her own kind, he heard the bleating youngster shout out after his mother. A mother who had died a good year or so ago, by the look of her. And The Piper understood now why he'd broken cover, if only to see his late ma again one final time. The Piper had never known his own mother, abandoned as he'd been, but he could appreciate what drove the youth. Except this was no longer the loving parent the boy had known, as he found out to his cost. The Piper felt a trace of emotion and anguish for the deluded boy. Told that his mother was gone, only to witness her walking as large as life – as death? – along the street. Then the empathy disappeared. The Piper picked up the other ground-dweller and they were on their way again. Stumbling behind him, they resembled touched lunatics. But never did he look back once. For if he had he might have seen the boy again, the boy who was so familiar. A mirror image of himself at that age. Before…

Before his name had been known far and wide? Just a carpenter's 'prentice with a big mouth and even bigger aspirations. That would all change soon enough, though. As soon as he discovered his secret, his latent ability. Something no one else in the world could lay claim to.

Aye, he had been a face in the crowd who hid when the ground-dwellers stormed their village that first time, fresh from the funeral. Covering his eyes as the mayhem outside his workshop gathered strength. The dead like a festering wave sweeping into the alleys, trying to break into houses.

Old Jed had seen the things take those young 'uns, had seen how easily they'd swallowed them up ... in some cases quite literally. But still he insisted on going out to face them, armed only with his few craftsman's tools. He ignored the teenage Piper's pleas, his half-mumbled explanations.

'I won't just sit here and watch 'em take the village, son.'

Those were his last words, unless you count the pitiful screams as he vanished beneath a swell of decaying forms, his bones picked clean in a matter of minutes.

If only there was something I could do, The Piper had thought. But he couldn't control them. This was beyond the wisdom of his years. It was only when they burst into the workshop itself, splintering doors and smashing tables, that he discovered there *was* something he could do. There was plenty he could do (if only he'd realised it sooner...). Instinctively, as the first of them drew near, its chin hanging off on a piece of gristle, the cheekbones dirty-white where they split skin as crumbly as dried parchment, he became aware that he could control them, could master this new power rushing through his veins.

He just needed to channel it somehow...

But he was also scared, overcome by the forces unleashed upon his home. So terrified, he scrabbled around on a nearby bench for a weapon in case he should falter. And his fingers, those long, artistic fingers, had closed around the pipe – a child's trinket he had been making all that week. As yet it remained untreated, the wood still naked and cream; hardly resembling the shiny brown object he now carried about with him everywhere.

But something told him to play.

And, to his surprise, the devils curtailed their advancement into the workshop. More than that, they all fell back – about eight in total, including the girl from the funeral –

smirking and bobbing their heads to his tune. A tune he played confidently, though he'd never picked up a whistle in his entire life before now, other than to plane and chisel one.

The ground-dwellers parted and allowed him safe passage outside, where he discovered his music had the same soothing effect. Of course, he knew that it wasn't the flute or the music alone that was doing this, but rather his own persuasive knack. The pipe merely allowed him to direct the energy from within. He couldn't explain it. It was just so. However, the villagers didn't know this. They believed it was The Piper's harmonious notes that kept the savages at bay. So, as he strode out to the edge of the village, the ground-dwellers fighting to keep up, he became a legend – his old family being the very first to offer praise. How did he do it? No one knew … including The Piper himself! No one cared. He had saved them all and was amply rewarded for doing so.

Thus began his travels. The fulfilment of his dreams. Dressed in an outfit more suitable for his purposes, the pointed hat with a feather stuck in it a finishing touch (the people expected no less of their heroes), he visited 'infected' towns and hamlets, ridding them of the ground-dwellers in exchange for a few nights' board and lodging. That and a modest payment. Well, modest compared to losing their lives, he argued. And most folk agreed. They were happy enough to oblige. Nobody could offer the same service as him, at least nobody *he* had ever come across, leaving the field wide open for him to set out his stall.

He'd earned prodigious sums of money during his time abroad this land, had met so many people – some good, some bad – and his myth had grown in proportion to his remarkable feats. One day, he'd decided, when the scourge was over, he would retire and live like a king. But for now there was still work to be done.

The Piper led his two prizes through the streets. He resisted the urge to dance to his own rhythm, although he had been known to do so on occasion in other locales, where the inhabitants cheered him on from the windows. There was no such outward encouragement from these people.

He made another sweep of the town to pick up any stragglers he may have missed on the first few rounds. The Piper found two more to add to his collection, then took them to the boundary where he had deposited his earlier hostages. He looked out over the assembly of around forty ground-dwellers, each one decomposing at a different rate. They gaped back at him, almost as if wondering what he would do with them.

The Piper had an idea they already knew. They had been on their little excursion, enjoyed the freedom while it lasted, but would be glad to return to the only homes they recognised now. He played his tune louder, steering them back. It must have been an eccentric sight, the carrion procession marching on like that. Though no less astonishing than the sight of them coming over the hill in the first place. The Piper arriving some time later to save the day once more. Payment had then been swiftly negotiated with the town's spokesman, a sly-looking man by the name of Halberry. Could he be trusted? The Piper hoped so.

Now the graveyard wasn't far away, and it didn't take long for the corpses to find their respective plots. The Piper directed the operation, urging them to settle back into holes that they'd made themselves. One by one they pulled the sod back over, like a sleeper pulling blankets up over his head. Bedding down, asleep once more.

The Piper took the whistle from his mouth, another job finished. As he walked back down the town's path, he meditated silently. Would these folk pay as they had promised? Sometimes, when they saw the ground-dwellers were gone, people foolishly believed they didn't need his services anymore. Why should they compensate The Piper now that the crisis was over? He prayed they wouldn't take that attitude. They seemed like fairly nice people (an image of the boy flashed through his mind). He would hate to see what happened in the last town happen here again. Today.

But if for some reason they did decide to renege on the deal, he would just have to persuade them. It seemed to be what he was best at, persuasion.

Of the living and the dead.

No, if they refused to pay The Piper it would not bode well for the population of this town. He might be forced to undo all his crucial work, a waste of everyone's time and effort. However, The Piper would have no choice but to make another example of them, calling the dead to rise just as he'd seduced them back to their mounds.

After all, had he not raised them up in the first place? Raised them *all* up in his time. In village after village, town after town…

And if this were true, if he really was The Piper, what on God's green Earth was there to stop him from doing so again?

IT'S ALL OVER...

They were the words that had haunted him for what seemed like years.

Words he'd said, tumbling from his lips before he could stop them. Words he'd wished – so much later after everything had gone to shit – that he'd never even heard of. That he didn't know the meaning of.

He'd known it after the fact; God, how he had then. Knew it now, even though circumstances were conspiring to trick him – to *convince* him things were far from over. Because it wasn't only the words that haunted him.

It was the person he'd said them to.

'Eric,' he heard her now, in spite of having his fists pressed up against his ears. 'Eric, it's so cold out here, baby.'

Cold? You bet it's fucking cold, he thought. *But you shouldn't be able to feel it. After all, you've been dead six months, haven't you? You're cold as well. Beyond cold, or at least you should be.*

A vision of a decomposing corpse floated into his mind: laying there in the coffin, buried so deep (an image he might once have taken great delight in). The face a virtual skeleton, that brown hair still splayed over the satin lining, as it had done the morning after they first made love.

Eric focussed on that instead: watching Hannah sleeping, her eyes flickering beneath the lids as she dreamed. That beautiful face, so young and innocent. Mouth full and lips ruby-red even without the aid of make-up. Had there ever been such a perfect moment as that one? He couldn't remember another like it in his life, not even his wedding day.

(As a contrast his mind flicked suddenly and without warning to him grunting and sweating – another woman below him; blonde this time, her moans in perfect unison with his thrusts. Perhaps a little too perfect? A hotel room surrounding him, instead of the college digs he'd been in when Hannah first opened her eyes. 'Oh Eric, yes! Please, oh my God... *Yes!'*)

'Eric.' There it came again. 'Eric, please ... please, baby. Why won't you let me in?'

He'd let her in once. All the way in. Hannah couldn't have been more a part of his life, sharing those student days with him when he'd first started setting down his stories. Had he known she was the one when their eyes met across that lecture theatre? Clichéd crap, the kind some other writer might infect the page with. But not him. Not his kind of thing at all. And yet –

'Eric? Why won't you just answer me? Say something, *please!'*

Because you're not fucking real! You can't be! I saw them bury you, Hannah. Shit, I was the one who had to identify you after –

For the about the millionth time since this all started, Eric shook his head, trying to gather his thoughts. There were too many, all mixed up and fuelled by emotion: sadness, regret, fear, anger, loathing – of himself more than anything. And, of course, the guilt.

Now that last one. That was a biggie.

It was probably the cause of this whole damned thing. Did he somehow bring her back, even if it was only in his imagination – some grief-crazed hallucination that he was doomed to see and hear every single night? He often wondered if *he* was the one who'd died all along, maybe killed *himself*, and this was his punishment in Hell?

Crazy. It was like something out of one of his books. Precisely why it *could* be a blurring of fantasy and reality, the stress of everything that had happened mixed with plots and characters from —

'Eric, please.'

Shut up, shut up, shut up. Just shut the fuck up!

The words inside his head, or coming from that figure out there? They were too loud surely to be emanating from those ruby-red lips. Eric got up, about to go to the window. Then froze.

You've seen her. You've seen what's out there. You know all too well, without having to look again.

But maybe tonight would be different. Maybe tonight would be the night there'd be nothing there. At least then he could get some kind of handle on what this really was: losing what little sanity he had left.

Eric recalled the first time it had happened. The first time he'd foolishly looked outside when he heard the voice calling to him. Telling himself – although he knew each and every inflection, knew the timbre like he knew the intro to his favourite song – that it wasn't her. *Couldn't* be Hannah. It was someone else out there shouting his name at eleven o'clock, interrupting his late night drinking session with old Jacky Daniels. Maybe some fan of his work who'd managed to get hold of this address (he'd kill whoever was responsible) – this isolated farmhouse they'd chosen and overseen the conversion of together.

(A sideways slip again, to one Sunday when they were alone and putting those final touches to the place. Picturing Hannah painting the walls – pushing the roller up and down, that old shirt of his covered in paint splatters, but clinging to her torso. The jeans she was wearing fitting tight against that perfectly-formed bottom of hers, moulded to the denim. He'd crept up behind and wrapped his arms around her stomach. She'd pretended to fight him off, but when his hands reached higher, cupping both breasts beneath the shirt, Hannah had relented, turned and kissed him full on the mouth. Eagerly, they'd undressed each other and rolled around right there on the floor. It wasn't as if anyone was going to see them, not out here. They were completely cut off, completely −)

Cut, severed − just like the flesh she'd opened up, opening her veins in the process and allowing the blood to pour out onto that bed, in yet another faceless hotel room (the police told him that it was a common place for suicides, and that made sense − for fuck's sake, he'd even written stories about that before. Hannah had read them, too).

No, don't think about that.

Okay, his mind seemed to say − taking him back to his original nightmare. The one where he'd gone to the window to peer out into the darkness, wondering why that state-of-the-art security alarm they'd had installed hadn't kicked in. Only he knew the codes for it at the gate. Only him and −

There was the figure, shades of black on black. Standing in the middle of the yard, about twenty, thirty feet away from the door. He couldn't make out much, so his hand reached instinctively for the floodlights they'd also installed. Floodlights which would have snapped on automatically if 'she'd' been just a couple of inches closer.

'Eric,' came the voice once more, chilling his blood. 'Eric!'

His fingers were quivering as they reached for the

switches, as they brushed the edges but didn't flip them yet.

'Eric, answer me, baby.'

Christ almighty. Eric's fingers either slipped, or his subconscious decided that he'd had enough of this and was going to chase away these stupid suggestions, brought on by too much booze and not enough sleep these past few months.

And suddenly it was too late.

There she stood, the shadows no longer providing any comforting doubt. It was her, or at least a damned good look-a-like (he hadn't dismissed that notion, especially back then; there were enough people who knew what Hannah looked like to pull something like this, photos of them out together at launches and parties; what had happened was a matter of public record, in the papers – even mentioned briefly on the local evening TV news – though hardly the *big* topic of conversation that day).

Eric blinked. *Got to get a grip – just get a grip!* The rational part of his mind told him that he was imagining this. That Hannah was dead, and when you're dead... You're fucking dead! A line from one of his favourite flicks back in the eighties – the one with the guy with all the nails banged into his head.

A film, a novel, a fiction. But this was happening, right now, out there. The woman he'd loved, his wife. The woman he'd spent more than twenty years with. The woman who was in the ground, buried because of what he'd done. Because of what he'd said. Those words:

'It's all over...'

She looked pretty sprightly for a corpse, it had to be said. Pretty sexy, too. The more Eric stared out at this vision of his deceased spouse, the more details he took in. The flowing brown hair, more lustrous than it ever had been in life. Those piercing blue eyes, framed with thick, black lashes – which she was batting against the sudden glare of the lights. The figure she'd always had, shown off in a flimsy satin nightdress (that, even more so than the shirt and jeans she'd wore when they'd been decorating, clung to her curves in all the right places). She must have been frozen out there, judging by how hard those nipples were jutting against the fine material. And, Heaven help him, he was getting turned on by it.

'Eric,' she said again, holding out her arms in a pleading gesture. 'Please answer me, baby. It's Hannah. Your Hannah.'

He closed his eyes this time, squeezing them shut. Knowing that when he opened them again she would be gone. Knowing that it was only the stress, the sleeplessness, the whiskey, the —

'Eric?'

He opened them again.

Still there. Still. Standing. There.

More details now, like the fact that there were scars at her wrists, the blood congealed and scabbed over. She was so pale – *wouldn't you be if you'd died half a year ago,* he said to himself. He shook his head. Make-up, that's all. You could do all sorts these days, special effects and stuff. He'd seen enough evidence on the fleeting visit to that set, the one turning his short story into a movie – before it had been consigned to DVD oblivion.

Not that again, not now. No time for that bitterness. The set visit … he'd seen extras walking around with their arms hanging off; those effects guys were brilliant. They could make you believe *anything.*

Make you believe that your wife hadn't really killed herself at all. A bad dream. She'd returned to him, just like he'd prayed for all those nights he'd cried himself to sleep. After the rows with Melinda, after she'd fucked off because she knew she wasn't going to get anything more out of him – out of this … whatever it had been.

('Oh God, Eric, yes. Harder … please… *Yes!*')

It had started out as just a drunken fumble one night after a convention up North, where Eric had been Guest of Honour. Just two nights away from home. Was it his fault Hannah had been called away to go and see her sister again? 'She's sick, Eric. I *have* to go and help look after the kids while she's in hospital.'

He'd sighed. 'The first fucking time I've ever been asked to do something like this, all expenses paid. Can't that waste of space ex of hers do something to help?'

'You know she doesn't want him going near the kids, Eric. And now Mum and Dad aren't around —'

'I wanted you there! You know how nervous I get about doing the public stuff. This is important to me.'

'Yes, I know,' she'd said, looking down.

'I'm not cancelling.'

'I don't want you to,' Hannah had whispered meekly. 'I wouldn't expect it.'

'Well I'm not. It's too late to back out now, anyway.'

'I don't know what to say. I'm sorry, baby.'

'Ah, forget it!' he'd snapped. 'Go on then, fuck off and go.'

Hannah had recoiled as if slapped, then gone and packed her bags. She'd tried to get around him before leaving, but he was having none of it. He'd sat sulking as the taxi came to collect her. The following day Eric had travelled to the convention alone, but he hadn't stayed that way for long.

Melinda had been there at the live onstage interview, in

the very first row. He vaguely recognised her as someone who'd attended his last couple of signings. She was young, blonde, extremely pretty; such a sweet face. Low-cut top and a very tight leather skirt. As Eric sat uncomfortably on stage, thinking of interesting answers to give the fawning interviewer, he'd looked out and caught her eye.

(Had he known then, when he'd caught her eye?)

From that moment on he'd been talking to *her*, and her alone.

Afterwards, once the handful of people who'd lined up to get their copies of books like *Poisoned Chalice*, *Mayhem's Match* and *Undaunted* signed, drifted off, she'd been waiting to have a word with him.

'No books?' he asked.

'Already signed – personalised to me.' She'd smiled. 'I was wondering if you fancied a drink at the bar?'

Eric smiled back. 'That sounds like a great idea.'

Over the course of the next few hours, they chatted on one of the sofas in the lounge area. Others had come and gone, pulling up chairs to ask him about this and that, usually how to get into the industry, whose arse to kiss, if he'd give them a quote. Eric took it all in good nature, knowing he wouldn't bother using any of the email addresses being handed to him. And all the time there was Melinda. Laughing at his crap jokes, listening intently again as he gave her pearls of wisdom about the writing game accumulated over many years (so many years, and who had stood by him when he'd almost given up, when he was hardly making a bean from his stories?; it hadn't been Melinda, that was for damned sure). She admitted she'd had a go at some shorts, but they were nowhere near ready for sending out anywhere.

'I don't mind having a look,' he'd said, as the wine

flowed and they'd got closer and closer on the couch.

'Oh, you don't have to do that.'

'Don't be silly, I'd love to read them,' he was saying before he realised he was doing it.

He'd walked her to the lift that night, but nothing else happened – apart from a peck on the cheek.

When Eric got back to his room he checked the mobile he'd kept switched off all day and found a message from Hannah wishing him good luck with the interview, and another one sent later wishing him well for the panels tomorrow. Both were signed: 'luv u v. v. much, baby xxxx'.

For a moment that had got to him, even in his drunken stupor. But then he thought that if Hannah loved him so much, why wasn't she here? With him? Why wasn't she the one who'd been on the front row at his interview, and in the bar celebrating afterwards? Not that it was her thing, being around crowds. She'd always said she preferred it to be just them.

He didn't surface until it was almost time for his first panel, the panicked runners looking for him when he reached the convention level. 'This way, Mr Slater,' the pimply twenty-something had said, trying to keep the annoyance out of his voice. Melinda had been there again, sitting waiting for it to start.

And she'd been there again at the next one, and at his final appearance. He felt more than a little embarrassed and guilty about the night before, so slipped out without saying a word all three times. But, when Eric spotted her again in the bar, now chatting to some other guy, he'd felt more than a pang of jealousy.

Turning to make his way out of the hotel, off for dinner at the Con's expense – making the most of his last evening – she'd caught up with him.

'Eric… Eric? I've been trying to grab a moment all day. About last night, I hope you don't think I was being too … well, you know,' she said. Today she was wearing a dress, just as low cut as the top, and he struggled to keep his eyes above sea level. 'It's just that, I've never really met a man like you before.'

He cocked his head.

'You're so clever, you know so much about loads of things. You saw what you wanted and just went for it, you know? Are you all right? You haven't said a thing.'

('Why won't you answer me? Why won't you talk to me, baby?')

'Look, I'm just heading out for a bite to eat – on the organisers.' *Slick, Eric. Slick.* 'Would you like to join me?'

'Oh, I'd love a bite, thanks.'

So they'd headed off for a meal in an Italian – a little beyond the 'reasonable expenses' the con had stipulated – and ate, drank, laughed, and talked again. Really *talked* this time.

'…so that's what I'm doing here on my own,' he finished explaining to her after the second bottle of Merlot.

'Poor Eric. If that had been me, I would never have let you go to something as important as this alone. I'd be proud of you.'

'Exactly,' he slurred. 'Exactly. But then she's never really been into the genre that much.' Wasn't strictly true; she used to read it a lot, but got bored of it around the time his work started taking off. Found other interests, like her genealogy, delving into the past. Who bloody cared where people came from? All that mattered was the present.

That night, when it came time to say goodbye at the lifts, neither of them had been able to. Nothing was said, but Melinda took Eric's hand and led him inside the lift, then led him to her room on the third floor.

He hadn't been able to remember that much about what happened next, but he knew he'd had a bloody good time. A better time than he'd had with Hannah lately, the rolling around on the floor at the farmhouse a distant memory these days.

They said their goodbyes sheepishly the next morning and Eric had returned home to find Hannah waiting. She'd organised for the local authorities to help with her sister, telling her that she was needed back at home. That her husband needed her.

(Jesus, how he needed her *right now*. How he'd give anything to know if this was real or just—)

Though he'd barely been able to look her in the eye when he got back, and he suspected she knew *something* had happened on that trip, he'd fooled himself into thinking it was just a one off. Hannah seemed happy to ignore it, so life went on as usual.

Except it hadn't ended there. Melinda sent the first text a fortnight later, saying that she couldn't stop thinking about him. If Eric was honest, she'd crossed his mind more than once as well.

They hooked up every time he could get away, using the excuse of meeting his agent Ken, or his publisher, or his PR person. Hannah was content enough working on her family trees. It got to a point, though, where Eric was looking at his home life, looking at his secret life with Melinda (oh, some of the things they'd done over those months!), and wanting more than just a few stolen hours here and there. In fact he wanted to swap. Wanted Melinda at home with him so he could have her anytime he wanted – first thing in the morning, in the shower, over the kitchen table if he so desired, smearing pancake syrup all over her.

And for Hannah to be gone.

It wasn't as if they'd ever had kids, was it? Though not for the want of trying in the early days. Maybe that might have changed things – maybe not. Neither of them wanted to be tested in case it was their fault.

Should have been a clean break, in theory. Ah, who was he kidding? After so many years, how could anything like that ever be clean?

Eric resolved to tell her when he got back from one of his 'business' trips, fired up at the prospect of sex with Melinda on tap.

'Look, it's just not working out, Hannah.'

'What are you talking about?' He could see tears welling in her eyes already, the first of many that afternoon. She'd run the gamut of emotions: from misery to anger; from resentment to denial.

'It hasn't been good for a while, surely you've seen that?'

'Please Eric, please don't do this to me.'

('Please, baby, why don't you let me in?')

His turn to look down at the floor. 'I have to, don't you see?'

'Who is she?'

'What do you mean?' Eric replied, looking up again.

'I know you, Eric. You wouldn't throw away what we've got without there being someone else involved.'

'You're crazy.'

(You're going crazy. It *can't* be her.)

Hannah grabbed him by the arms. 'I can still smell her on you!' she'd screamed into his face.

He'd shrugged her off, pushing her back at the same time. 'Hannah…' That's when he'd said it. Those three little words; not the three he'd said to her for the first time the morning after they'd slept together. But just as powerful.

'It's all over.'

But it wasn't, was it? That was just the start.

When he wouldn't speak to her anymore, Hannah packed and left – as far as he knew, going back to stay with her sister. Melinda moved in about a week later.

Next there came the phone calls, pleading at first – 'Why do things have to change? I want to come home!' – and later accusatory. 'I know she's there with you,' Hannah would say bitterly. In the end he began to hang up as soon as he realised it was her.

Then the calls stopped.

A good month went by and he didn't hear anything from his wife, though he was expecting to hear something from a solicitor at some point. Tying up loose ends. (Is that what she'd become: Hannah, a loose end?) Divorce proceedings would be starting soon – yet strangely he wasn't in any rush to initiate them himself. Probably down to the shine wearing off his fling with Melinda. Because that's all it was, that's all it *ever* had been. In the end he understood that, especially when she was going out and spending his money on expensive clothes and jewellery. Eric had made a rod for his own back there, buying her presents in the first place, leading her to think that what was his was hers. While at the same time she was trying to muscle in on those real meetings with his agent, publisher and PR person.

'I can see what you're up to, you know,' he said to her after coming out of one such session.

'I don't know what you mean,' Melinda answered, her sweet face long since replaced with the hard one she wore most of the time around him.

'Come off it. "Oh Ken, don't be silly, you don't have to look at my stories – just because I'm shagging one of your biggest clients".' He fluttered his eyes then, mocking her, and she slapped him.

'Fuck you, Eric.'

Things hadn't gone so well after that. But they'd gone from bad to worse when he got the call. A couple of weeks on his own with no Melinda, flipping through old photo albums (who exactly gave a shit about the past, now, eh?), and he'd started to realise what he'd thrown away. What a bastard he'd truly been to Hannah.

When the phone rang, he snatched it up this time, praying it would be her, praying they could work things out. It hadn't been Hannah, though. It had been *about* her.

'You're listed as her next of kin,' the voice down the line informed him. He dropped the receiver. No, not Hannah. She wouldn't do something like that! Except … except, he'd driven her to it, hadn't he. While he'd been making up his fucking mind and coming out of the other side of this – this what? Midlife crisis? – she'd been going through Hell.

(He often wondered if he was the one who'd died all along, maybe killed *himself* , and this was his punishment in–)

Fast forward several months. Months after identification, months after putting her in the ground. Just when he'd got to the point where he would give anything to see her again.

Then came the first visit. The first of many. In all kinds of weather, out in that flimsy nightgown. Eric recalled the night of the rain; she hadn't moved as the water saturated her, causing the silk to stick to her body, making it see-through, making him hard again.

(And another time, another place, out walking when they were young – not caring about the torrential down-pour because they had each other. 'We've been in this rain, feels like for hours,' she'd said to him. 'So?' he replied, clearing a wet strand of hair out of her eyes.)

Hannah was out there in the rain alone that night, and this time she *had* been there hours. 'Please, Eric. Why do things have to change?'

Because you're dead, Hannah. Things change when you're dead – or at least they're supposed to. You don't just carry on with your lives – ha! – as if nothing's happened. Doesn't work that way.

Night after night, time after time. Yet he told no-one about it. What would he say? 'Hey, Ken, I think my dead wife's coming to see me every night. I think I'm being haunted or maybe I'm just going nuts, y'know?'

'Understandable. Now, when are you going to get that new manuscript to me?'

That wasn't going to happen any time soon. He could hardly focus on existing, let alone working. Now it was Ken's calls he was ignoring, his knocks at the door when the agent came out to visit.

Because there was Hannah, and only Hannah.

Here again, tonight. 'Eric? Eric, *please!* Won't you answer me? Won't you let me in?'

Tonight might be different, he told himself again. *She might not be there when you look, when you flip on the lights. Then that will prove you're okay.*

Dammit! He pulled the curtain back and looked. There was the figure. He didn't need the lights. It was her, same as always.

But something *was* different tonight. Hannah was turning; leaving.

Christ, do something! This is what you wanted – the chance to be with her again. You've hesitated all this time, frightened of what you might find if you just went out there and ... touched her. Remember the feel of her, remember what it was like to hold her?

('Oh God Eric, please!')

To really hold someone you love and care about. You wanted this and now you're about to let it slip through your fingers. If there's a chance, just a chance that she could be real...

Eric ran to the door, undoing the locks and bolts, flinging it wide open. 'Wait! Hannah, please wait!'

The dark figure, in the process of walking away from him forever, paused and turned. He could see the outline of her head. Feel her gazing at him – and though he couldn't see her eyes he knew it was a longing look.

'Baby?' she asked.

'Yes. Sweetheart, is it really you?'

There was a slight tip of the head.

'I didn't dare hope. I thought I was going mad.'

Hannah walked forwards, passing through the floodlight's invisible boundary. He saw her clearly now as they flicked on, more clearly than he ever had before – coming closer and closer as she did so. 'It's me, baby. It's *really* me.'

There were tears welling in Eric's eyes. 'I'm sorry, Hannah. I'm so sorry for what I did, what I said. Sorry I didn't believe. I—'

'Shh. It's okay. Let's go inside and we can talk.'

She'd covered the distance between them quickly, obviously as eager to get to him as he was to reach out and touch her – make sure she was actually there (and God, did she look good in that nightdress, the way it clung to her, just like his shirt had once done ... ignore the cuts on her wrists...) But she was just out of reach near the doorway. Just come a little closer, a little closer.

Now it was Hannah hesitating. *Don't just leave her out there in the cold, she wants to come inside. She's always wanted to come back home.*

Eric pulled back, into the hall, and beckoned for Hannah to follow him. 'Come in,' he told her. 'It's all right.'

Hannah smiled, then crossed another boundary.

She approached him, reaching out her own hands. Letting him touch them. She was real – as solid as anything Eric had ever felt in his life. Hannah took one of his palms and placed it on her breast.

'That's it baby.' She smiled again. 'I know what you want.'

Eric couldn't help grinning. It had been so long since he'd made love to his wife, even before her death, even before the split.

'Yeah, that's right,' said Hannah as he kneaded her. 'Please baby. *Please.*'

'Oh God, Hannah. God, I love you so, so much.'

At that, Hannah tensed up. 'Love?'

'Yes,' said Eric looking into her deep, blue eyes. 'I love you.'

She smiled again, but then the smile grew organically into a laugh. 'You don't know the meaning of the word.'

Eric frowned. Suddenly this whole situation – this whole situation which shouldn't really be happening at all – was turning sour. Had Hannah come back just to tease him, to point out the error of his ways? The 'ghost' of dead wives past? He didn't need *her* to do that! He'd felt bad enough without.

'Fortunately, *I* do. Now,' she told him.

'What—' he began, but she placed a finger to his lips.

'Don't speak, Eric. You've done all I needed you to do. Now it's my turn.' Hannah grabbed him by the arms and swung him around into the wall. It shouldn't have been possible to even lift him, let alone do this, but his wife was incredibly strong suddenly. Stronger than she ever had been in life.

And when she smiled again, he saw her teeth.

'No,' said Eric. It couldn't be possible, he'd seen her corpse. Couldn't be possible that she'd become something he'd written about – albeit only a few shorts, as it didn't do to overuse the classics … unless you had a new twist.

But, as he was about to find out, Hannah was exactly that. 'You didn't think I'd actually topped myself because of you?' She laughed once more, cocking her head right back. Still no bite marks.

Except why did they always have to be at the neck?

'You think while you were having fun with that whore, I wasn't out looking for someone else too? Someone who could stop the pain, someone who could make me feel wanted again?'

There was a shadow at the door, just beyond it in fact. The figure of a large man dressed in black.

'We're going to be together for a long time, he and I. He promised and … I believe him. His family history's fascinating, Eric. Oh, the things we've done together this past year. But I just couldn't stop thinking about you. I knew I had to come back.' She grabbed him by the shirt and shoved him against the wall again – hard. It was now that he saw it – the cuts at the wrists, easily mistaken for razor slashes, but too jagged. Too much like —

Panicking, Eric tried to push his wife back, but he couldn't shift her. 'Please Hannah, please don't do this to me.'

'I have to, don't you see? Please don't struggle, Eric. You'll only make things harder on yourself.'

'No—'

'*Yes* —

('Yes! Please, oh my God… *Yes!*')

'I've waited all this time for you to drop your guard. But I can be oh so patient. Especially now. It was also sort of fun, given your line of work.' She tutted. 'You really should have known better than to let me inside.'

There was another noise from the doorway and Eric saw more figures emerging from behind the broad-shouldered man. Oh, Hannah *had* friends now. So many friends. Crowds didn't bother her in the slightest.

'But now it's time, Eric. Time to tie up loose ends.' Her incisors grew longer than ever, her face altering, contorting, brow furrowing. He had to admit, there was a part of him that had always wondered if stuff like this existed. He'd never wanted to find out this way, though.

('Oh, I'd love a bite, thanks.')

'There's just one last thing I have to say to you,' Hannah managed through her new teeth, pushing against those ruby-red lips. 'And I think you know what it is, don't you?'

In spite of himself Eric nodded.

'It's over,' he whispered eventually.

'It's all over…'

LIFETIME

He couldn't exactly say it felt good to be back, but it felt right.

The town, his old town – his hometown ... once upon a time. Not that he'd been born here, or even grew up here. No, this was the place he'd chosen to make a life for himself. Where he'd *lived* – back when he was young. A lifetime ago now.

Neil sat in the car, not the same one he'd fled in all those years ago – twenty-five years ago to be precise – as that had been stolen, and this was a hirer, but it was an eerily similar make. And here he was again, back where it had all begun ... in more ways than one. He'd already done the tour, because Neil had landed again on these shores a few days ago now, ferry hopping across the channel for the final leg of his journey. As he'd driven down the motorway, one of Brutal's best albums blaring away on the CD player, he'd wondered what he would find when he got here, how it might have changed in the time he'd been away – *stayed* away.

Nothing could have prepared him for quite how bad things had become, though – the shocking state of the economy having done its worst. In fact, it was almost like driving through a ghost town to begin with, hardly anyone on the streets, and those he did spot looked like pale imitations of people – either that or they looked haunted themselves. Storefronts were boarded over or had faded 'going out of business' banners hanging in darkened windows. What few shops remained had to be struggling, Neil reasoned. The library where he'd slaved away for all those years, working his way up to become senior librarian in fact before taking off without even letting them know, had also been shut down. That was hardly a surprise, however, given how many cuts had been made in government funding, and how the 'net had made libraries, vaster than his old one could ever hope to be, available to people at the click of a mouse.

Neil had found himself breaking in for a final look around – especially down at the basement where he used to lock himself away at that special time of the month. He hadn't lingered too long; it was upsetting for him to see the state of the bookcases, the abandoned tomes covered in cobwebs. Forgotten about, unloved, unwanted. Ancient and all alone.

He could relate.

In fact, the town in general seemed to reflect how he felt at the moment. Lost, world-weary and old ... very, very old. It occurred to him that they'd always been connected, that no matter where he'd wandered it had always been calling to him. Nagging at him to return until he could no longer ignore it, until he felt compelled to return regardless of how he'd left things. They'd aged together, it seemed – and in spite of the fact he didn't have as many aches and pains as the average man of seventy (his kind were more resilient than normal humans) he still felt the weight of his years. When he looked in the mirror, it was a white-haired guy with too many lines creasing his face that was staring back at him. But at least he *had* hair, Neil often reminded himself. He'd always have hair – *too much* of it at a certain point in the month, as it happened. And while he no longer had the beer belly he'd developed during his time playing at having a normal existence, his body wasn't in as good a shape as it had been even a decade ago – no matter how many push-ups he attempted in the mornings, no matter how much he jogged or star-jumped.

It was a far cry from the fresh-faced student who'd attended uni here, met his old friends, his pack, here – who'd been just as young, just as naïve. Hadn't worked out just how rotten the world could be yet, how unfair, how unjust. How there were always consequences to your actions – or, as his mate Owen (his *dead* mate Owen) might have said: 'You reap what you sow.'

It took him a while to build himself up to the house, mind: the house he'd lived in for a major part of his life here, after getting married and 'settling down' for a while. After meeting Julie, the catalyst for splitting up his merry little band. The signal for starting to grow up, he'd thought; becoming tamed and boring his friends had probably thought. There was someone else living there when he finally plucked up enough courage to drive by, other cars in the driveway. Which felt weird, as did imagining those other people inside, sitting watching TV in the lounge, making love in the bedroom where —

Neil had shaken his head, tears in his eyes. Wasn't it bad enough that he had nightmares about it, seeing Julie pull her legs up to her chest in bed, hugging her knees the last time… Then lifeless on the floor, neck snapped, yet hearing her voice as he had on the phone, those final words she'd spoken to him:

'Fuck you, Neil!'

She'd just told him she was leaving, and he'd said to her 'Good'. Good, for Christ's sake! But all he'd meant was it would be better for her to be away, out of town and out of danger. Not that he *wanted* her to go. Not after the night they'd just shared, one that topped any of the other night's they'd slept together – even back when they first met. How was he to know that it was already too late, that the maniac who'd targeted Neil and his friends already had Julie in his sights?

Neil had seen the toys then, in the garden. These people had kids – *a* kid at any rate. A kid like the one they'd created, conceived that night; a son whose life had been stolen even before it had really begun. And, worse still, that it was Neil's fault it had happened.

He'd had to drive off then before he lost it completely. Neil wondered if they knew what had happened in that place so long ago? It was doubtful, hardly a selling point – unless you were one of those sickos who got off on murder houses. For a fraction of a second he thought about going back and telling them.

'Don't you understand, my wife and son were murdered here! In this fucking house where you're living your life, completely oblivious and happy!'

It would be unfair to do that to them, but then again that was life, wasn't it? He thought of the consequences thing again and decided against it – wasn't their fault, what had happened there. Why should they have to pay for it? Reap what he and his pals had sown?

'*Fuck you…*'

Julie's words again, drifting through his mind while he was awake now – and Neil certainly had been fucked, hadn't he? They all had. Jack and Adrian even before they'd come back together again, one poisoned the other stabbed. Owen, who'd become a detective since Neil last saw him, and figured out what was happening – that they were being hunted and picked off – had been thrown from the roof of the hospital Ryan had also found himself in after being run over.

Dead. All dead.

And wasn't Neil staying in the very hotel where his last friend, Luke, had met his end? Staged as a suicide, submerged in crimson bath water with a razorblade by the side of him; a *silver* blade, to be precise – had to be. Just as silver was used in all the other killings to some extent, the only way to be sure people like Neil *were* actually dead.

He'd been surprised to find the hotel on Hadley Street was still open for business – though it had been absorbed by a familiar chain and was no longer called The Wanderer's Lodge. Probably not as surprised as the woman at the desk, however, when he'd asked for a room: 'Any room apart from 320.' She'd frowned at him and simply nodded, perhaps assuming he had a thing about those numbers or that he'd had a bad sexual experience in there? He didn't give a shit, he just needed a place to stay and this was the only real option in town... Neil just didn't want to lay his head down in a room where Luke had bought it, even if he wasn't planning on staying for too long.

It had all been a preamble, a prelude to tonight. To this pilgrimage he was undertaking. He'd begun by driving to the park just off Milton Street where he used to meet up with his buddies before a night out when he was in his twenties. Leaving the car by the side of the road, he'd entered the empty park and sat down on a bench by the lake to watch the ducks and geese, to look at the trees – the leaves still green for the moment, though they wouldn't be for long now they were entering the autumn season. It had been quiet, pleasant, and his mind had conjured up more ghosts form the past. Luke leaning over and looking at his reflection in the lake – combing his hair back, making sure those model looks were up to scratch for pulling later on; Jack, fresh from practising with his band – who'd have ever thought they'd make it big? – pushing Luke's shoulder so he overbalanced, but making sure the lad didn't fall in. Ryan and Adrian mucking about, playing 'keepy-uppy' with empty cans of beer they'd drained, and talking about the match... Calling Neil over to join in, which of course he'd been happy to do, while Luke and Jack shared a stubbly cigarette.

Those visions faded soon enough, and before he was ready – but Neil knew it was time to head off anyway, to take in the next leg of the journey. Time for a quick pint at The Oak, which did still have its original name and was still being run by Kev, though he probably should have retired long ago. Once burly, he'd lost weight since last Neil had seen him; looked ill in fact. Neil gave a sniff as the man served him and, yes, detected the unmistakable whiff of cancer. The man only had a year left, tops; shouldn't even be working, let alone on his own – although there weren't more than a couple of people in the whole pub. Nevertheless, he remembered Neil.

'Bitter, right?' Kev had said.

Neil didn't want to correct him, his taste for that particular drink having vanished around the same time he had – replaced by various drinks depending on where he was in the world at the time. But, when in Rome. He'd nodded at the man.

Kev had winked. 'I never forget a customer, *or* what they drink. Been a while, though.'

'It has,' Neil admitted.

'Where've you been hiding, then?'

The landlord's choice of words made Neil flinch, so accurate without him even knowing it. That was exactly what Neil had been doing, hiding away. He'd told himself that he'd fled the area not just because of the devastation he was leaving behind – and the awkward questions that would inevitably follow – but because it was time to get back to the old ways again, to return to the old Neil who'd embraced his baser instincts. Told himself that and lived like it for a long time, until it got boring. Just wasn't the same as when the boys had been with him, plus he couldn't ignore the fact that he *was* getting older by the day. His heart simply wasn't in it any more: the chase. It just wasn't any … fun. Some of that had to do with what had happened because of their antics, most of it was just because he wasn't the same person he had been back then. Events had changed him irrevocably.

Every one of his victims, all the women he'd 'pushed' – necessarily older women now, because his days of hanging around in clubs were long since gone – all the ladies he'd persuaded to come with him, he'd had to force himself to devour. He'd met a lot of them at singles nights, which attracted a certain kind of desperate older person, so in fairness Neil hadn't really needed to nudge them that hard (and he'd seen she-wolves too, doing the same thing with *their* prey at a few of those events – but he'd kept out of their way, because he'd heard that the female could be just as vicious, if not more so, than the males he'd encountered). Many had been willing to go with Neil anyway, thought he seemed like a nice guy. And with each sniff, he'd gained a greater sense of who they were and how they'd ended up alone: divorces; affairs; shyness in their youth. Often he even convinced himself that he'd be doing them a favour by killing them.

But he'd also been cursed with seeing their possible futures, what 'might be' for them. Some had kids, and would have – or already had – grandkids. By ending their lives he was depriving them of time they might be able to spend with their families. One such woman called Silvia, he'd got so far down the line with – had gone back with her to her place – but chickened out at the last minute, partway through the change that came over him. He'd seen a moment in time a few years down the line, where she'd actually have to take over looking after her granddaughter after her son and daughter-in-law died in a plane crash. It would give the woman a new lease of life, give her purpose and make her truly happy. Neil would not only be taking that away from her, he'd be taking away the future of that little girl as well.

He had morphed back, reining in his bloodlust – as hard as that was – and exited to the sound of Silvia's high-pitched screams. It was sloppy behaviour like this that had put the hunters on his tail in the first place. People like those brothers over in the US several years ago – one a little older than the other; he'd barely escaped with his life after they'd come after him and it had taken quite a while to shake them off. Then there was that guy in Holland who claimed he was some kind of descendent of quite a famous Professor – and there was Neil thinking he was just a made up character. But the worst had been that 'league' of hunters which had been tracking him for the last couple of years. Relentless, organised and thorough, once they had his scent it had taken a lot of ducking and diving to evade them; even now he wasn't sure he had.

He couldn't really blame them, he supposed. Neil had been a bit of a menace back there for a while. But he'd also spent a lot of time on the road just helping people as well. Went through a phase of being like the Fugitive or the Incredible Hulk (from the TV series, not the later CG version), or even the Littlest – or maybe that should be the Biggest? – Hobo. The last one was probably most apt, given his unique abilities ... or affliction, whichever way you wanted to look at it. Perhaps thinking he could make up for all the shit he'd done, he'd tried to help people on his way – often attempting to put his particular skills to good use, like when he took out those crooks who were putting pressure on a community with their protection racket. He'd definitely been doing the residents of that town, not to mention the world, a favour when he ripped through them.

Yet there had been times, especially lately, when he'd thought about simply ending it all. Even had the pills laced with silver in his stuff, which he was planning to wash down with a single malt if he got low enough. Neil knew that he would live a lot longer than any human, that his chances of ending up in some kind of home were slim – he wouldn't want to die in somewhere like that anyway. A fucking werewolf in a nursing home? It was like that movie where Elvis was battling a mummy in there or something. Better to go out the way he wanted, *his* choice and his alone. It hadn't come to that yet, but it was around this time he began thinking about returning 'home'. Maybe he was winding down? Maybe he wanted to? Or maybe he was still hiding, as Kev had said – just in plain sight this time, in the last place anyone would think to look for him.

Kev had said something else, but Neil hadn't caught it; he'd been miles away. 'Hmm?'

'I said,' Kev breathed out with a sigh – Neil couldn't tell whether he was pissed off at having to repeat himself or it was his condition – 'you back to see family or something?'

The only family that had lived here were his wife and unborn child, thought Neil. His parents – the ones he'd known about anyway – had passed away a long time ago.

He hadn't even bothered to return to this country when he discovered this, hadn't been particularly close with them. His real parents remained a mystery, even after doing some digging. Neil sometimes wondered if he would have gotten on better with them than he had the man and woman who'd adopted him. Maybe they'd have understood him a little better, especially his wanderlust. It made no difference now, he guessed. Remembering Kev had asked him another question and was still waiting, he shook his head.

'Just passing through, thought I'd drop in and visit.'

Kev nodded, knowing that Neil was lying – he could tell, not only from Kev's expression but from his scent again. The landlord hadn't spent all this time chatting to punters without being able to tell when someone was bullshitting him. So he left it at that, left Neil to find a table and enjoy his bitter in peace. It was obvious this customer wasn't into the conversation, so why bother?

Neil sat down in the same seat he had the night of the reunion, after Owen had brought them all back together – or at least the ones who were still okay – little realising he'd sealed the rest of their fates. Led the killer that was apparently after them right to the others in their old pack. More memory ghosts floated before him now from a Friday night similar to this one, Luke sitting opposite with his drink and Owen striding in, looking every inch the cop he'd become. He'd laid out what was happening, how Jack and Adrian were already dead, that there was someone picking them off. They'd waited for Ryan to arrive, but of course he never had – knocked down by that same killer, left to die in a hospital bed.

He closed his eyes, blinking away the spirits – and finished up his pint quickly.

Neil had other places to pay his 'respects' to.

***

If the town was dead in the daytime, then at night – and especially at the weekend – it truly came alive. If anything, the nightlife here was even better than it had been when Neil was young.

He'd heard the youth of today, in this country, still had plenty of disposable income – where they came by this, he didn't have a clue; grants and benefits probably – and it looked to him like they were intent on spending every last penny of it on a good time. As he nosed his car around the club district he'd known so well long ago, he noticed that, like the hotel he was staying in, the names of these places might have changed – from Harry's, Monty's and The Green Room, to Shapers, All Pink and The Octopus – but what was going on outside, what was spilling out onto the street, was exactly the same … maybe even worse.

At least in his day the girls didn't try and keep up with the boys in the laddish department. Neil saw young women, wearing virtually nothing at all, tumbling out of clubs and crawling around in the gutters. As he passed one, her blue hair being held back out of her face by mates, she was throwing up for England, body jerking with each fresh heave. It wasn't even that late, either. Things hadn't really started to get … interesting until after eleven when he and the guys used to frequent these kinds of places. The sights he was seeing now made him feel just as sick … and *even* older than he had before, if that was possible.

Fed up with all this, he found the side street he was looking for and headed down it. Neil parked the car and walked down the alley. His hands were shaking as he recalled the last time he'd been here, saw the man who'd killed his friends, his wife and son – older than Neil back then, but actually a good ten years younger than he was now. Not a hunter, just a father looking for revenge because *they'd* murdered his fifteen year-old daughter, Tammy, back when they were young. The irony being that was the night Neil had quit to try and make a life for himself with Julie, to settle down.

Cosmic. Fucking. Joke.

He saw the fight now, replayed it in his mind – and projected it in front of him as if he was watching a movie of what had happened over two decades ago. Neil transforming and leaping down, being hit with a silver bolt which he removed (quickly enough it didn't kill him, but not so quickly to prevent his left shoulder aching fiercely now, especially in the damp and the cold, and for the full range of movement in that arm to be impeded when in human form), the chains, tearing into the top of the man's car, then tearing into the man himself... Why hadn't he just done what Neil told him and got out of there?

Because he didn't care if he lived or died, came the answer. Just wanted to avenge his Tammy, maybe even wanted to be with her again? Fathers and their daughters, it was a complicated relationship, but there were few bonds stronger. Neil wondered how strong his bond would have been with his son, had he lived, had this man not taken the child away from him. He'd never know ... just one more regret in a lifetime of them.

The scene segued into the night that had led to all this, the gang stumbling out of a club with Tammy – hair blonde, then strawberry blonde, switching between the young girl's face and Julie's, the main reason Neil didn't want to be involved with this kill. None of them had any idea she was so young, or perhaps his friends just hadn't cared... Their scenting abilities weren't nearly as honed as they would be in their forties, and a fraction of Neil's now that he was seventy. If they had been better then...

It really was true what they said, and a cliché for a reason, but youth *was* actually wasted on the young.

Neil watched, gazing open-mouthed, as the four friends began their attack, unable to do anything to prevent it. Then suddenly it dawned on him. Four ... there were four guys here, and even if you didn't count Neil – as these ghosts were from his point of view – then there would still have been five of them: Adrian, Ryan, Owen, Luke and Jack. And, with that realisation, came a shift in perspective. At first glance, a couple of these boys looked a little like Adrian and Jack – but now he looked more closely, Neil saw that they weren't his late friends at all. And the other two looked nothing at all like either Owen, Luke, Ryan, or indeed himself. For one thing, these boys were a lot younger than he and his friends had been when they'd taken Tammy's life from her. Barely out of university, if they'd even gone there at all – that was another difference in this day and age, fewer kids were going to uni because of the expenses they'd incur. Or simply because they couldn't be bothered.

Neil realised that he was still standing and staring, frozen not in the past but in the present. History was repeating itself right in front of his eyes – he sniffed, getting their scent. Knowing they were near to the change, could no more control this than they could their other skills. The bloodlust coming on them. Above, the brand new full moon shone brightly and illuminated the scene. Even without his sense of smell, Neil could see who was the most important member of this pack. It wasn't Lewis (who worked part-time for the local scrap merchant), the one who had hold of a girl called Alice, not really – even though at first glance it might seem that way, because he was the leader at the moment. It wasn't Pierce, Lewis' 'second-in-command' (who stacked shelves in a supermarket just outside town); wasn't even Rav (living on benefits at the minute, but beavering away on his comic-book art), who should probably have *been* the second because of the way he was holding himself.

It was a lad called Troy. He was the Neil of this pack, he was the glue that held them together, and would wrench them apart if he ever decided to leave it. He was hanging back, hesitating ... and there was something about the way he was looking at Alice, pulling a strange face. He was wearing a blue shirt, jeans hanging down past his waist as the fashion seemed to demand – and his dark hair was gelled so that it looked like a wave on his head ... for now, as it would definitely get messed up when the transformation took hold. Already their eyes were taking on that red and yellow cast, causing Alice – who had probably only come into this back alley with one of the group – to open her mouth and scream. Her cries were immediately absorbed by the thumping techno-beat of the nightclubs behind them.

He should just walk away and leave them to it, leave this girl to her fate... Only when he'd inhaled, Neil had also caught a whiff of her future, of what might have been – what might *yet be* if she ... if Alice survived this. A lifetime of events: studying to be a lawyer; falling in love with several guys – some idiots, one complete bastard, but one kind man who stuck; a wedding; two children, one of each; an old age on her own after her husband died, but with grandchildren to love and care for, just like Silvia. Moreover, Neil also saw the possible outcome of what would happen if they did kill her, a replay of what had happened to him and his friends – not exactly the same, but close enough to send a chill down his spine.

Close enough for him to do something about it this time.

Neil was changing even before he started moving forward, his breathing controlled, feeling every single hair – the change not brought on by excitement or the smell of fear or blood, but sheer will. It was the same will that was masking his scent from them right now, allowing him the element of surprise. All four of the lads were changing (Troy last, he noted) faster then Neil could manage but it was out of their influence; they were simply letting the beast free to do what it wanted. Neil could direct his talents where they were needed, could predict their movements – because he'd made exactly the same ones at their age.

His first task was to get Alice away from Lewis before he had a chance to sink his teeth into her throat, before he could pass her round so they could all take a bite, like she was one of those burgers Adrian had used to flip in the fast food joint. If he was lucky, Neil could do this with minimal injuries to both parties. A slash at the lad's side was enough to spin him around, cause his grip to loosen on Alice. But instead of running, as she should have done, Neil buying her precious moments to get herself out of there, she just continued to scream.

By which time Lewis had turned to swipe at this newcomer, quite obviously after their prey – or so he, wrongly, assumed. Neil dodged his clumsy attack, but where he had strategy and finesse on his side, these kids had speed and strength. They weren't worn out from long years of transformation after transformation.

And there were four of them...

Lewis' second, Pierce, a lighter, orangey fur rippling across his skin, was coming to his leader's aid – as was Rav, though he was sensibly holding back a little. Somewhere in that wolf's mind was probably the thought that if Lewis and

Pierce got trounced he could easily slip into the role of leader himself.

Behind him was Troy, hesitantly bringing up the rear.

Neil bent and rolled Lewis over his back, standing and tossing his opponent into the far wall, growling in satisfaction when he heard the crunch of bone and explosion of air. Pierce's attack was just as furious, but also lacked thought – allowing Neil to sidestep it easily, to follow through with a back-slash which sent him sprawling to the ground. The first setback came when Rav accidentally clawed Neil's shoulder, hitting his weak spot without even knowing it – though he quickly realised when Neil let out a howl of pain.

Alice seemed to be waking up slowly, shaking her head and realising that once the distraction was over and done with she'd be on the menu again, back in the position she'd been before this interloper came along. Neil couldn't really blame her for being in such a daze – apart from the fact that she'd just seen four young guys turn into ferocious animals right in front of her, with another, silver-furred beast wading into the mix. She had to get over the 'push', as ham-fisted as it clearly had been. Good looking as Lewis clearly was, he'd also had help with his conquest, releasing pheromones she couldn't resist, making her susceptible to suggestion. So that when he said to her in the club, 'You fancy coming out back with me?' it had seemed like the best idea in the entire world.

Now it seemed like the absolute worst, and Alice made a break for it.

Rav was coming at Neil harder now, swiping wildly. These four also had the advantage that they weren't pulling their punches, unlike Neil. They intended to maim, hopefully *kill* their opponent. Grunting, Neil grabbed Rav's wrists and head-butted him, sending the younger wolf reeling.

That left Neil facing Troy...

They looked at each other for a moment, trying to weigh one another up – Neil having more success because of his experience. Then Troy snarled, obviously deciding it was attack or *be* attacked. He lurched forward, and Neil shadowed him, like Groucho doing the mirror routine; it seemed to throw the lad completely. But not for long. Thinking on his feet, Troy fell to all fours and then shot upwards, catching Neil under the chin and knocking him backwards. Troy continued up into the air, grabbing a nearby drainpipe and using it to swing round again.

Neil shook his head to clear it, by which time both Pierce and Rav were on their feet – and on Neil. On his back to be precise, claws digging into his sides and – in the case of Rav – his shoulder again. Though it galled him to do so, Neil resorted to trying to shake them off, like a dog coming out of the sea. It worked with Pierce, but Rav held on for grim death – which he seemed determined to cause. Seeing no other way to dislodge him, Neil backed up into the wall at speed, the pain in his shoulder incredible.

Rav struck the brickwork with a thud, and Neil felt the grip on him lessen. Then Rav slid away as Neil took a step or two forwards. He caught Troy looking at him again, but then their attention was drawn to the throng that was gathering at the head of the alley, Alice's screams now attracting a crowd, albeit of drunken revellers.

None of them needed telling: as reckless as the original quartet of werewolves had been, even they didn't want to stick around to perform for an audience. Neil had already ducked back into the shadows, observing as Pierce and Rav helped Lewis up and virtually carried him away. Troy trailed after them, gathering up torn clothes as he did so, looking over his shoulder only once at the scene – at Neil.

Wincing, Neil collected the remnants of his own clothing and receded even further into the shadows, to double back in the direction of his car, skirting the growing number of people who were flocking to a much calmer Alice. A girl who was incapable of explaining exactly had happened to her, and probably never would be able to ... especially as Neil had dosed her with his own pheromones before she escaped, ones designed to fog her memory more effectively than any spiked drink could.

When he reached his vehicle, transforming back into human form, he dug around in the shredded clothing for his keys and gave a silent thanks that they were still there. He unlocked the door, dragged it open, fell inside, breathing hard. It had been a good while since he'd been in a fight that intensive, and certainly not with his own kind. With young pups who had so much energy. It had been impetuous, stupid even, but he'd felt compelled to get involved.

As he slumped back in the seat, Neil was beginning to wish he hadn't.

***

When he woke up the next morning, having entered the hotel late the previous night – he always kept a change of clothes in the car, but had to explain the bruises and bleeding to the receptionist by simply saying 'Rough night' – Neil was still of the same opinion. He should have kept his nose out of their business, let things run their course.

It was the way of the world, wasn't it? You make your mistakes, you have to live with them – he'd done that, others should be allowed the same 'opportunity'. That was just life. But at the same time, wasn't it also normal for the older generation to try and stop the younger one from making those same mistakes, to try and pass on the benefit of their wisdom...

Yeah, right, and what kind of wisdom was it that said I had to get into a scrap with that generation, he said to himself, as he sat up in bed and regretted it immediately. The mornings after a transformation weren't the easiest to recover from at the best of times now, but after what he'd been through the previous evening his whole body felt like one giant toothache. Yes it was true that they recovered faster than normal folk, but it had slowed up in the last couple of decades – hell, in the last forty years... Neil didn't want to think about that. How on earth had he done this day after day in his teens during the cycle? Let alone experienced virtually no after effects the next morning?

He looked at the clock on the bedside table, grateful that he'd had the presence of mind to hang a 'do not disturb' on the door handle outside; he could hear the maids in other rooms, busying themselves with cleaning out baths and changing bedding. Almost half the day had been wiped out already, and he had to force himself upright, each step towards the sink in the small en-suite an effort, the clothes he'd discarded catching in his toes.

Neil turned on the light and shielded his eyes from the glare – the curtains were drawn in the main part of the room. He pulled a face when he saw the reflection, the old man staring back at him looking much older than usual. Then his face creased up even more when he took in the state of his torso, and especially his shoulder. That kid Rav had really done a number on him there, the claw marks having healed over but still angry-looking and – he suspected, because of the damage the silver had already done there – now permanent fixtures on an already-ravaged frame. Ravaged by other scars, the stories of which he had nobody to share with, and ravaged by time.

Experimentally, he raised his arms and almost let out a scream as loud as Alice's from last night – before biting his lip, remembering the maids.

Shouldn't have gotten involved, he reminded himself. But now he was...

Neil hung his head and sighed. Now that he was, he had to see it through to the end.

No matter what that meant.

***

What it meant initially, was tracing one or all of the 'cubs' he'd engaged last night. He had been in no condition to follow them the previous night – probably wasn't now, if the truth be told – but also they'd have been in no mood to listen. All that would have happened was that Neil would eventually have run out of steam and had his arse handed to him.

Maybe, though, in the cold light of day and with no danger of a transformation until it was dark, he might be able to get through to them – explain why what they were doing was so very dangerous. Try to get them to see they were drawing far too much attention to themselves ... (*And who was it who let Alice go, Neil?* he said to himself, *whose fault was it really that the crowd started to gather?*) ... that what they did in the present could have a knock on effect in their futures? Futures they probably couldn't even imagine, and didn't give a shit about. At that age, the next month, or week, was like a lifetime away.

Even so, he had to try. Apart from anything else, Neil felt bad about how they'd left it last night, about the damage he'd done (*they did their fair share of damage as well, don't forget!*). So he decided to start with the one he'd felt the most connection with: Troy.

Hadn't been hard to sniff out his trail, to track him to that estate on the outskirts of town. Neil had driven through the maze of streets, his nose differentiating between the various scents wafting in through the open window. It led him to a set of communal garages, concrete bunkers covered in graffiti, with dented metal fronts. One was open, a car poking out and jacked up at the front – a pair of legs sticking out from underneath.

Neil parked and got out of his own vehicle. The feet, which had been keeping beat to a radio by the side of them, suddenly stopped tapping when Neil closed his door. By the time he was halfway to the car, Troy had slid out from under it and was standing. He sniffed the air himself, but Neil knew he wouldn't get anything from him; wouldn't be able to detect that this was the wolf he'd been tackling the previous evening.

'You lost or somethin'?' asked Troy. It was like looking in a mirror, but a mirror from almost half a century ago. Hair dark instead of grey, face smooth rather than covered in lines, body naturally lean regardless of what he stuffed his face with, Neil was willing to bet. Troy was wearing an old t-shirt and a pair of faded jeans with a hole in the knee, both covered in oil. It was a far cry from the gear he'd been wearing out on the town, but he still managed to make it look like some kind of designer statement.

Neil paused, shook his head. 'No ... but I think you and your mates might be.'

'Me and my...' Troy took a step or two towards Neil. '*You* ... but how come I couldn't —'

'Don't waste your time thinking about it. Just a little magic trick I picked up along the way.' Troy's fists were up, and he was covering the distance between them. 'There's no need for that,' Neil assured him, but the lad wasn't listening. Troy clearly thought he stood more of a chance now that neither of them were changed.

He was wrong.

The same applied today as it had last night. Troy might have youth on his side but Neil saw each swing of his fists coming and was able to step out of the way – much as it pained him to do so. On the third lunge, Neil caught him and spun him around, so that Troy landed on the tarmac. He sat there staring up at Neil, who was trying very hard not to show how much the exchange had hurt him, especially his wounded shoulder.

'I'm not here to fight,' Neil said, attempting to control his breathing. 'I'm here to talk to you.' He walked over and offered him a hand up, but was actually glad when Troy batted this away and got to his own feet.

'You put my mate in the hospital last night, fucker,' spat Troy. 'I had to dump him there.'

'Lewis,' replied Neil; it wasn't a question. Lewis was the only one he'd hurt to such an extent that he might need hospitalisation. The General probably hadn't batted an eye at such injuries; just your average Friday night brawl.

'How the fuck do you know...?' Troy began, before remembering what Neil had said before about his tricks.

'Same way as I know you're Troy, Troy.'

The lad looked at him sideways. 'Just who the fuck are you?'

'Look,' said Neil, ignoring the question. 'I'm sorry about your friend, but I had to step in.'

Troy shook his head. 'What the fuck for? You're ... you *were* like us.'

Neil gave a little laugh. 'I still am,' he said, but realised how lame that sounded. He wasn't like them anymore, not really. But what he'd lost in vitality, he made up for in other ways. Then he realised, that wasn't what Troy meant. Neil wasn't spontaneous any more; he thought about the risks, the consequences.

'Then why ... you didn't want the ... *meat* for yourself? You let her fucking go.'

'Can't you say anything without swearing?' Neil asked.

'Piss off,' came the considered response.

Neil laughed again; well, he *had* asked. 'I let her go because I've been there and done that; I've seen where it leads. I saw where it was going to lead with Alice.'

Troy looked confused again, not able to understand how Neil knew the name of what he'd called the 'meat' (a word he'd seemed quite uncomfortable using). Had he known her? Had that been the reason he was trying to save her? Even if that was the case, it didn't explain how he'd known who *they* were ... unless he'd been following them, snooping around?

'I can teach you it, if you like,' Neil offered. 'It's something you learn with age, but I could teach you.'

'I don't want fucking nuffin' from you!' Troy backed away towards his mounted car and Neil took a step to follow him; they were doing the Groucho thing again apparently.

'Would you just listen for a minute, I'm trying to explain.' And not doing a very good job of it, though in fairness Troy didn't really want to hear it. 'You can only get away with this kind of stuff for so long before it gets noticed.'

'More likely to get noticed when you let the fucking prey escape,' Troy answered.

'Alice,' Neil corrected. 'And don't worry about that, I sorted it. She won't remember a thing.'

'Let me guess, another bullshit trick right? Fuck off!'

Neil carried on regardless, there was a way through to this boy – had to be. 'If you don't believe anything else I'm telling you, believe that there are people out there who like nothing better than to hunt our kind.'

Troy's brow creased. 'Hunters? You're talking about hunters, aren't you? Bloody urban legends,' Troy insisted.

'I've seen them,' Neil countered, his voice hardening. 'I've *fought* them.' He thought he saw something in Troy's eyes then, a flicker of ... what, respect? Envy maybe? *Be careful what you wish for*, thought Neil. 'But that's not all. You make enemies in other ways. People like Alice have families – relations with long memories.'

'So fucking what? Let them come,' snapped Troy. The ignorance of youth speaking. Only somebody who had nothing to lose could say that, but only someone who'd lost it all could say:

'So ... *everything*, son.'

'I'm not your shitting son,' stated Troy.

'No,' said Neil with a catch in his voice. 'My son was killed by someone who wanted that kind of justice, that kind of revenge. Somebody reacting to something I'd done when I was only a bit older than you and hadn't been thinking.'

'Good!' said the boy. Neil reduced distance between them in an instance – and without a thought for how sore he was proceeded to slap Troy across the face.

The lad reeled backwards, not from the force of the blow but purely because it was so unexpected. He reached up and touched his sore cheek. Neil pointed at him with a rigid finger. 'How dare you ... little prick! I *know* you're not my son, and thank Christ for that! I'd be fucking ashamed of you!' There was something about Neil using that word that made Troy flinch even more than the slap had. Neil couldn't help it, he took a sniff – he 'read' Troy without really meaning to.

He saw a kid who'd basically been dragged up, whose real father – who hadn't stuck around past Troy's sixth birthday – had knocked the living shite out of him on a regular basis (the boy curling up into a protective ball), not to mention what he'd done to Troy's mum. He saw a single mother who'd tried to make ends meet by legitimate means to begin with, but had fallen into more unsavoury ways of earning a living and got drunk most nights to try and forget the fact. He saw a succession of 'boyfriends' Troy's mother had welcomed into their home – a council flat on this very estate – many of which were just as bad, if not worse than his own father. He saw bullying at school, Troy being pushed around and spat on because he never really fitted in anywhere ... until he left school early at sixteen to do a course in mechanics at college (a natural, always tinkering with engines) and had met up with the rest of his pack there, bunking off and playing cards. Wasn't long after that he turned for the first time, fed for the first time – his mum's latest waste of space druggie boyfriend who pushed Troy too far after he got high one full moon... Troy's mum had been out of it, but she'd seen the blood the next morning. She hadn't said much about it, hadn't said much at all before she'd overdosed one night when Troy was out. Neil saw him dropping out of college, earning his way by fixing cars on the sly, which was what he was still doing today...

Saw him in some basement somewhere, naked and shackled with silver manacles, two men with baseball caps using torture implements constructed from the same material to make him scream. Just like Alice had screamed.

Hunters. Those same hunters Troy insisted were mythical.

'I... I'm sorry,' said Neil under his breath. He wasn't sure himself whether he was apologising for the slap, or saying how sorry he was about Troy's crappy life. Maybe a little of both.

Troy found his voice from somewhere. 'What the fuck, man! Just what the fuck!' Again, what the fuck was Neil doing there in the first place? What the fuck was the slap all about? What the fuck ... just what the fuck...? Neil was beginning to wonder himself.

'I'm sorry,' was all he could manage again.

'Just get the fuck away from me, man. Get the fuck out of here and leave me and my friends alone.'

Neil opened his mouth to say something, then nodded. But as he was walking away from the scene, he called back over his shoulder. 'Just to let you know, I'll be around tonight in town ... so maybe you and your friends should take a rain check.' He wasn't sure how much of a threat that was, how much of a threat *he* was, but Neil hoped at least it would give Troy something to think about, something to tell his friends about. There really was no point trying to talk to them if he couldn't get through to Troy; they'd be just as stubborn, probably more.

So Neil got back into his car, turned it around.

He watched the boy through his rear view mirror, standing next to the car he'd been fixing. Neil watched Troy, just as Troy was watching Neil drive away. A thought passed through his mind. That they were two opposite ends of the spectrum – young and old. But also opposite ends of the story, the beginning...

And the end.

***

Neil thought about what he'd said, later, when he was driving. 'I'll be around in town tonight.' On the streets, patrolling, like he was Batman or something.

If he was, then surely he'd have a better car than this one. Didn't matter, it was getting the job done, getting him about. He'd been going in circles for a while now with the window open, sifting through the myriad of scents to see if Troy or any of his mates were on the prowl in town tonight. Wasn't easy, it was even busier than Friday night – which was probably only to be expected – but Neil prided himself on such skills.

Eventually, he left the car behind and pounded the pavements, checking the back alleys on foot. He wasn't about to venture into any of the pubs or clubs; if he was too old back in his forties to be seen in them, then he'd definitely draw attention to himself now. 'Hey granddad, move it or lose it!' 'Don't do your hip in on the dance floor!' 'Post office is closed if you're looking to get your pension.'

Though it was tempting to *change* and patrol that way – it would be quicker to get around and his aches and pains had more or less gone by now – he resisted. The moon glared down at him, accusingly. How dare he refuse the gift it was offering? It was safer this way, though: oh, he could control himself when in wolf form most of the time, but there was just too much temptation here for his liking. When he was changed, his bored animal brain might just whisper to him: *Go on, what harm would it do, really? It's not like you haven't done it before.* How ironic would it be for him to be out here trying to prevent that from happening, only to fall off the wagon himself?

Neil saw the pair in the alley, messing about, a particularly amorous couple who'd gone back there for a bit of privacy. He observed them from the shadows, devouring each other in a different way altogether, drunk and excited by the fact they might be caught at any moment. It reminded him of the first few months with Julie, how they'd been together, unable to keep their hands off each other … and that last time, after the reunion, *both* of them like wild animals in bed. He'd never have that again. Before he could help himself, there was a tear rolling down his cheek which he wiped away with the back of his hand.

Teeth gritted, he'd let out a growl then which echoed up the alleyway, causing the couple to stop. They'd looked in his direction, at each other, then started pulling their clothes back on and stumbled off – terrified. That had made him feel a little better, but afterwards he'd felt guilty for acting so childishly.

He'd come across nothing else, however, and called it a night in the wee small hours of the morning, heading back to his hotel room to crash for a couple of hours' sleep. Neil was happy that his words seemed to have sunk in with Troy – or at the very least that none of the young pups wanted to encounter him again.

A couple of hours turned into several, and once again he was glad he'd left the 'do not disturb' sign on his door handle. Blinking wearily, Neil saw that it was after midday. He lay back on the pillow, groaning. Then he reached for the remote control and switched on the TV, searching through the channels for something that wasn't country-related or religious (it *was* Sunday). He settled for the local news, which he watched for a few moments before deciding it was too depressing and muted it, wandering off into the bathroom to pee. He was just about to begin when he saw the reflection in the mirror – not his own, but familiar all the same. On the TV. A young girl he'd seen the night before last.

'Alice?' said Neil under his breath. He rushed back into the main room and snatched up the remote, quickly pressing the mute button again and catching the end of the report.

'...missing now since yesterday. Alarms were raised when she failed to show up at her parents' home for an anniversary dinner. Once again, if anyone has any information about the disappearance of missing Alice Timberland then could you please ring...'

The newsreader continued on, but Neil wasn't really listening. He was thinking about Alice, about how it couldn't really be a coincidence that she'd vanished. In his experience there weren't such things as coincidences like this. Neil was thinking that one of the young wolves had done this, maybe because they were frightened of her saying something about Friday night – or simply because they were too proud to let the 'meat' escape.

He ground his teeth together, even gave a little snarl.

It was time to have another word with Troy, probably with the rest of them as well. Before tonight, preferably.

Before the third and final night of the full moon.

***

Troy wasn't at the garage today, but Neil had very little trouble tracking him down from there.

He found him on a nearby stretch of scrubland, watching a makeshift football match. Troy, this time wearing trackies, was standing with a bunch of people on the sidelines – with them, but quite obviously not *with* them. They were following the passage of the ball from one end of the field to the other, where the player with it would try and kick the thing through a goal made from jumpers. The more things change, the more they stay the same, Neil thought – recalling matches just like this when he was growing up;

kids making their own entertainment.

It had been an age since he'd seen football live, and before he realised Neil soon found himself watching the game too, getting caught up in it, trying to figure out who was playing against whom – it was harder than it looked when they didn't have differently coloured shirts on, plus allegiances appeared to keep changing all the time. Troy seemed to be able to decipher it all, though, and gave a cheer when the goal was finally scored. It was only now, when he turned, that he spotted Neil.

He thought for a moment Troy was going to bolt, make a run for it just as Alice had finally done when she'd been freed. In the end he remained where he was, perhaps reasoning that it would draw too much attention to himself. Maybe the people here would think the cops were after him, and word would spread. How many folk would then bring their cars to him for fixing? Neil was glad he didn't run, as he wasn't sure he'd be able to keep up with him – keep him in sight – let alone catch him.

Once he was certain Troy wasn't going anywhere, Neil approached and inserted himself into the crowd. 'What the fuck do *you* want?' Troy whispered; in fact he was barely speaking, but he knew Neil would be able to hear.

'A word,' Neil whispered back through gritted teeth.

'Got nothin' to say to you.'

Neil produced something from behind his back, then turned and slapped it into Troy's chest. It was a local paper he'd picked up from the hotel foyer, folded at the moment. Puzzled, Troy opened it up, looking left and right to see if anyone had noticed. Neil couldn't work out whether it was the act itself the lad was worried about, or the fact he might be seen holding a newspaper. The paper was already on the page Neil had been reading, and that was the first thing

Troy saw after he'd unfolded it.

'The fucking meat,' Troy mouthed when he spotted the photo accompanying the piece on page four.

'Call her by her name, Troy. She's not meat, she's not prey.' At that moment the football was kicked over in their direction. Neil stopped it by trapping it under his foot, then – without even looking – he kicked it back into the middle of the players who shouted their thanks. He continued: 'I saw the way you were looking at her on Friday night, you know that yourself.' Or at the very least Troy was on his way to figuring it out. 'Call her by her name.'

'Alice,' said Troy, a bit too loudly.

'So, still got nothing to say to me?' Neil took him by the arm, but Troy wrenched it away. Then he looked at Neil and nodded, began to walk away from the match with his escort close beside him.

Once they were far enough away from the match to talk, Troy spun around and repeated, 'It wasn't me … it wasn't fucking me,' over and over, like some kind of disciple of Shaggy's.

'I believe you,' said Neil. 'I'd know if you were lying anyway.'

'When you left yesterday I got in touch with Rav and Pierce, told them what you'd said, told them you were a fucking headcase. They agreed it was better to lay low at the moment, at least this month.'

'That's what they *told* you,' said Neil. 'But obviously one of them had other ideas. Did you tell them I fixed it, that she wasn't going to tell anyone?'

Troy nodded.

'And they believed you? I'm not even sure you believed me.'

'Man, it wasn't fucking them either. I was Pixchatting

them last night, they were both at home.'

'What the hell's Pixchatting?' asked Neil.

Troy got out his phone, a smartphone, the kind Neil hated; what did he need one for, anyway? He had nobody he needed or wanted to keep in touch with. And somehow, while his back was turned, mobiles had transformed into things that connected you to social media sites or had facile games on them that turned the users into zombies. Troy showed him the Pixchat app which, as far as Neil could see, involved taking pictures of yourself or the things around you and adding lines of dialogue to them in an effort to have some kind of inane conversation (in this instance a lot of derogatory remarks about Neil). Didn't anyone simply talk on the phone anymore?

Nevertheless, Neil could see the timestamps next to Pierce and Rav's faces; could see that the 'chat' went on periodically most of the night; could see the background of their houses, the pictures of their TVs, walls and whatever that marked them as being at home, just as Troy had testified.

'See?'

Neil shook his head. He didn't trust this modern technology, and still didn't believe in coincidences. 'Get your friends together, I want to meet with you all.'

Now it was Troy's turn to shake his head. 'They won't fucking go for it, man!'

Neil grabbed his arm again, this time harder than before – but when he saw the fear in the boy's eyes, saw the memories reflected there of his father, he let go again. 'This is serious, Troy. It's a big deal for a place like this. The police are looking into it already.'

Troy held up a hand. 'All right, all right … *where* do you want to meet them, then?'

'Where all this began,' Neil said without missing a beat. 'And where it's going to finish.'

***

The alleyway looked very different in daylight.

Neil and Troy waited there in silence for a while, his friends late for the meet, but then the quiet grew uncomfortable.

'I'm not the enemy, you know,' Neil ventured, leaning back against the wall – looking across the way at Troy sitting on a fire escape, his legs dangling down.

'Could've fooled me,' the youth said. 'Must've been someone else who got stuck into us on Friday, then?'

Neil hung his head. 'I've explained about that. I had to do it. I could see where it was heading.'

'Yeah, you fucking said.'

'It's only because I've gone through all this that —'

'But that was you. Newsflash: *I'm* not you. My friends aren't fucking *you*.'

'No, that's true … but, believe it or not, there are definite similarities to me and my old mates.'

'Did they have an old fogy on *their* backs complaining about what they were doing?'

Neil shook his head. 'But I wish someone *had* spoken to us back then … because my friends might still be alive now if somebody had done what I'm doing.'

'Right, and of course you'd have listened,' said Troy sarcastically. 'But hey, why don't you just travel back in time and fix it all, I mean you can do everything fucking else. Magic, like you said.'

Neil sighed. 'Trust me, if I could, I would.'

'All that Jedi shit, all that knowing everything and seeing into the future. Fucking give me a break.'

'I'm *trying* to give you a break, Troy.' The lad muttered

something, but he didn't ask what it was. Just the same old crap. 'Look, I get it – I understand what you've been through, and why you're so defensive but –'

Troy scowled. 'You don't know shit about me.'

'I do actually,' Neil said, with a certainty in his voice. 'You said it yourself, the Jedi shit.'

The lad shook his head. 'You don't … don't know shit,' he repeated, but there was less conviction this time. A silence settled between them which, surprisingly, Troy broke. 'Was that true, what you said to me yesterday?'

'Was what true?' asked Neil.

'What you said about … about your son, about the hunters?'

Neil gave a single nod. 'It was the road you were going down as well. I saw it. And Alice was the key. *Was* being the operative word.'

'I told you man, it –'

'Wasn't you, I know.'

'And it wasn't Pierce or Rav.'

Neil folded his arms. 'I'd like to hear that from their lips. No offence.'

Troy shrugged.

'So maybe you should just come out and we can get this over and done with,' Neil said with a smirk.

'How the fuck…' came a voice from some distance away. Rav, hiding round the side of the building, revealed himself, dragging Pierce with him. Now, in the light, Neil got a better look at them both. Rav's dark skin, his stance like some kind of ancient Prince. Pierce's washed-out look, the ginger hair topping it off. They ventured down the alley, but kept a reasonable distance between themselves and Neil.

'Look, he's just an old man,' Rav pointed out.

'An old man who was beating the crap out of you the other night,' Neil replied.

'How about we try that again right now, then?' Rav was sneering.

'Ready when you are,' Neil answered him. It was the bluster and bravado of youth versus the confidence of age. He'd learned a long time ago that even if you weren't particularly confident, if you appeared it then that was half the battle – especially in a pissing contest.

'Guys ... it's okay, he just wants to talk,' Troy assured them. 'It's about the girl from the other night, Alice.'

'Our meal,' Pierce corrected, running a tongue over his lips. He pointed at the older man: 'The one you made us miss out on.'

'Maybe. Maybe not,' Neil said. 'She's missing, and it's been noticed.'

'What's that got to do with us?' asked Rav, touching his chest.

'I think one of you followed her, went to finish the job.' Neil stated.

Rav and Pierce exchanged looks, then said almost as one: 'Wasn't us.'

Neil sniffed the air. Even if he didn't trust the photos on Troy's phone, he did trust his own senses: they were telling the truth. So where did that leave them?

'What a second,' said Rav. 'Has anyone heard from Lewis?'

All three of them shook their heads. 'Not since the hospital,' Troy admitted. 'I just assumed he was still there.'

'You don't think...' Pierce was looking to Troy for answers. Suddenly it had become their conversation, these three friends.

'Naw ... he was pretty fucking out of it when I left him,'

Troy told them, looking over at Neil. The transformation back to human wouldn't have helped with the injuries, that's for sure. They were in a more vulnerable state then.

'But we do heal faster than other people,' Neil reminded him, trying to convince himself. It wasn't inconceivable that Lewis had gone in search of that which had been denied him. After all, he'd put in the groundwork. And then, when he was stronger, maybe he'd come after Neil. But wouldn't he have included the rest of his pack in his plan? Wasn't there safety in numbers?

Still…

Rav had his phone out, was tapping away on the screen. 'Just texted him.'

Neil sighed. 'Can't you just ring him up?'

They looked at him blankly. 'We could send him a FaceSpace message,' Pierce suggested. It would appear that unless they happened to be in the vicinity, this generation would much prefer 'speaking' via words on a screen. But it struck Neil that as connected as they were, these people really couldn't be further apart; they hadn't even bothered to find out how Lewis was since he'd been dumped at the hospital. And *Neil* couldn't be further apart from them.

He went over to Troy and demanded the boy hand over his phone so he could call Lewis. 'No fucking way, man!' They were also apparently the most precious things these youngsters possessed. Neil turned and strode over to Rav instead, snatching the phone out of his hand.

'*Hey!*' he shouted, reaching for it back.

'Leave him, he won't be able to fucking work it out anyway,' said Pierce. 'Look at him.'

As much as he hated to admit it, Neil was struggling with the workings of the thing in his hand. The last time he'd used a mobile, they'd actually had buttons on the front, numbers you simply pressed to dial. He heard sniggering coming from the trio, and threw the phone back at Rav – who fumbled but caught it. 'Shithead!'

'*Ring him!*' Neil barked. 'Get him here!'

Rav glared at him, but eventually did as he was told, looking down at the screen and tapping things into it, doing what Neil had been unable to: finding Lewis' number and dialling.

He was in the process of bringing up the phone to his ear when Rav suddenly paused, shuddered, then let it go – let it clatter to the floor. That made no sense, not when he'd been so angry about Neil's mistreatment of the thing. Then the boy staggered forward a couple of steps, looking down at his chest where a bloom of red had appeared. He touched it, bringing his fingers up to a confused face, before his eyes rolled into his head and he collapsed face-first onto the ground.

'Shit!' said Neil, then to Pierce: 'Take cover!' The ginger kid was still trying to work out what had happened to his mate, but Neil already knew. '*Get down!*' Pierce just stood there, like Alice had done when they were attacking her; it was only when another bullet pinged off the floor behind him that he started to get his arse in gear, to shift sideways.

Neil was sniffing the air, but getting nothing. He wasn't the only one who could mask his scent apparently. A spark hit the alley wall not far from his head and he lunged across, towards Troy and the fire escape.

'W-what's happening?' he asked.

'You know those hunters that don't exist,' shouted Neil. 'Well, they're here.'

Troy's face was white as Neil joined him on the platform. 'No … it can't—'

Neil took his face in his hands. 'Listen to me, I need you

to focus – they've come for us in the day because they think it's safe. Because they think we can't change.'

Troy was simply staring at him.

'But we can! You just need to concentrate. It's not dark yet, but we're still in the cycle. The moon's up there, you just have to connect with—' A bullet pinged off the fire escape; they were shooting from a rooftop somewhere. Neil squinted, his eyesight not perfect but good enough to trace the trajectory of the projectile. He let out a growl, then breathed in, closed his eyes. Maybe if Troy saw it for himself, he'd believe… Another little trick Neil had picked up over the years, though more a realisation, really.

Neil reached out and began to feel it, the power of the sphere up there – the pumping of the blood in his veins, hairs just waiting to push up through his skin. He knew his eyes were changing because of Troy's reaction, a mixture of surprise and awe. Now, when he looked down at himself, Neil saw that change – shirt and trousers being replaced by fur, muscles bulging as he readied himself.

Then he was away, up the fire escape, dodging another bullet that ricocheted off the struts. He was angry and it fuelled his actions, helping him to claw his way to the top of the building and bound onto it. Neil spotted the sniper almost immediately, one rooftop away – but he could cover that distance easily enough. The man had his long hair tied back in a pony-tail, out of his eyes – one of which was pressed against a scope on top of his rifle. There was a long extension on the end of this, a silencer so that they'd have no warning at all. Still there was no scent to him, as close as Neil was – some kind of spray perhaps?

Now the man saw him, rose from his position and swung the rifle in Neil's direction as the wolf leapt across the gap. Neil angled himself sideways, so that the silent bullet – obviously silver – whipped past. The man was swearing in a language Neil didn't recognise, cursing and firing another shot that missed its mark. He dropped the larger weapon in favour of a handgun he drew out of the back of his dark jeans. Holding it straight, he let off a succession of shots that were also dulled by a silencer. Neil dodged left and right, before finally crouching then springing forward to ravage the guy. He ripped into him, biting and clawing, tearing into him before lifting him off the roof and tossing him down into the alley itself.

The blood told him all he needed to know about these people, even before he saw the van pull up at the head of the passageway. The league... Neil let out a howl of despair. Down in the alley, more armed men were pouring out of the vehicle, some wearing caps; one pulled a gun on Pierce and shot him in the head, in the eye to be precise; blood and brains exploded out of the back of his skull. Trained and professional, these men were also cowards – expecting to face their quarry in a weakened state.

And then there was Troy, who hadn't really moved from his position on the fire escape. He had his eyes closed, body curled up into a ball – terrified, paralysed with fear. Neil had no choice: he had to get down there as quickly as possible.

He ran to the edge of the rooftop and jumped.

Neil felt the rush of wind as he speeded up, plummeting into the alley. His aim was as good as the shooter he'd just taken out, landing on one of the men, pushing his shoulders down into his body with a crunch, but then hitting the ground awkwardly – feeling the vibrations up his legs, the bones not taking the impact well.

Now he was surrounded. One move and he'd be riddled with silver bullets.

'Alive!' came a voice – sounded American. 'Take this one alive!'

Neil paused, breathing in and out. No sudden moves. So this was how it was going to end, captured and taken to some dungeon somewhere – or maybe even sold on to some covert government agency so they could experiment on him? After so many close calls, Neil guessed he couldn't argue with that and it was probably no more than he deserved.

Then it happened. Something was moving quickly, circling the men and slashing at their hamstrings with razor -sharp claws. The first couple dropped, letting off shots into the air as they fell. Neil seized his chance and clawed at the closest man, raking up and slicing the rifle he was holding in half, then continuing on into his chin so that the claws exited at his cheeks.

More cries in foreign languages – one Polish maybe? – as the men started to panic. Neil bit the throat out of another, as a couple more dropped to their knees – crippled by the blur that was still racing round them. He caught a glimpse of it between the figures; Troy, half-transformed, as much of a change he could muster in the daylight, but still deadly. He looked more like those old-fashioned film versions of wolfmen than a giant full-blown wolf – he still had his trackies on – but in time he'd master the process, Neil felt sure.

Between them they were taking down the shocked hunters, who'd been expecting to simply pick off these creatures in their human forms. One pulled out a silver knife and slashed at Neil, maybe hoping that close quarter combat would be better, but Neil just dodged it and wrenched off his arm.

Then Neil saw something flying through the air, heading

towards them – something small and black, tossed from the van. Some kind of grenade, it would land closer to Troy than Neil … but the youth hadn't seen it.

Without even thinking, Neil dove in Troy's direction, shoving him out of the way as the black object landed and exploded. It wasn't like any kind of explosion Neil had seen before, though; there wasn't much of a flash or bang – instead the air just sparkled. And then it hit him, going in through his lungs, being absorbed through his pores.

Silver. Not a shrapnel bomb, no – this was worse than that. Particles of silver that were burning him up from the inside out. Neil let out a howl of actual pain now, his turn to curl up on the floor, coughing and spluttering.

Troy was on his knees, starting to work out what had happened. He made to move over, but Neil waved him back. The older wolf grunted, attempting to stand. They'd felled the men in the alley, but there was one still left who'd thrown the grenade. Who was emerging from the front of the van, dragging someone with him and holding a pistol to her temple.

Neil recognised the hostage immediately. It was the missing girl, Alice. She'd been beaten, had one black eye and a split lip, and she was crying.

'Yeah, you know who this is, dontchya?' said the broad-chested man, his bald head covered in sweat. He was addressing Neil, but cast a glance over at Troy as well. 'I can see that you do, monster! Saw the way you were protecting her the other night. What is she to you, some kinda relation?'

Neil just growled. She wasn't anything more to him than another ghost, a reminder of a girl he should have saved when he was younger. He'd got it all so wrong, though. The young pups weren't the ones who would bring the hunters here, he'd already done that himself – they'd trailed him from abroad. And it hadn't been Lewis who'd gone after Alice, it had been them. In fact, Lewis was probably dead, just like Pierce and Rav, and then he and Troy probably soon. The league was nothing if not thorough. Neil had made it easy for them, gathered those left in one place to make their task simple.

The hunter dragged Alice forward, then removed the gun from her temple, aiming instead at Troy. 'You, I don't give a shit about. Just another dead growler, though I've never seen any who could shift in the day before. But you...' He kicked Neil in the side. 'You're gonna come quietly with me, aintchya?'

But Neil had one last trick up his sleeve, something they could all do but he'd refined. He didn't even have to growl. His own form of 'texting'.

When I say now, Troy – take him out... Troy's brow furrowed, trying to work out how Neil was talking to him. But then, he'd seen – he'd *done* – stranger things that day.

Now!

Neil bit into the hunter's calf, causing him to cry out loud. His aim shifted, allowing Troy to leap straight at him. The young lycanthrope careered into the guy, and he let go of Alice – who tottered sideways like a crab, out of the way. Neil watched as Troy relieved the hunter of his firearm, then slammed him up against the side of the van.

The man gave a defiant laugh. 'Might not be today, but one day you're gonna to get yours, freak!'

You reap what you sow, thought Neil.

Then the hunter spat in Troy's face and, seconds later, he had no mouth to spit with. Troy had opened his jaw wide, locking on to his enemy's face as if Hannibal Lecter himself had given him lessons.

When he was done, he turned. Alice had backed up into a corner of the alley, was sitting and shaking, still crying her eyes out. Neil was struggling to get up, struggling to get a breath.

Troy walked over to him, stood over him.

And then he offered him his paw.

***

The hunters hadn't been the only thing Neil had been wrong about.

It hadn't ended in that alleyway, not really. While Troy had cleaned up as best he could, eating his fill and gathering together all the weaponry that was left behind, he'd left Neil and Alice alone in the van so the old wolf could do his thing, or try to, at any rate. Neil was pretty spent, each time he took a breath it hurt him, but he managed to wipe the images of the wolves from her mind again ... then paused, adding something else.

They'd dropped her off a little way from the alley, putting in an anonymous call to the police using one of the mobiles, before breaking them all – even Troy's. By now they'd both changed back, and it had become clear than Neil badly needed medical attention. Not only had the silver ruined his lungs, his legs were pretty screwed from that jump. Troy left him wrapped in a blanket at the hospital gates, where he knew the man would be found, and drove off in the van – without even so much as a goodbye.

Neil only remembered bits and pieces; he'd been pretty out of it at the time.

The people in casualty did their best, stabilised Neil enough for him to be transferred to an elderly day-care facility where they could devote more time to looking after him ... supposedly.

That's where Troy had found him again a week or so later, after blagging his way inside by saying he was a volunteer visitor, something they always welcomed. Neil had been propped up in bed, staring out of the window. When he'd turned to look, he'd wheezed, 'You lost or something?'

Troy had smiled at that. 'No, but I thought you were, back there... Sorry I had to bail, man, but I had to get rid of all that stuff, the van. The ... well, the rest of it.'

Neil had nodded, he understood. The important thing was, Troy had returned, had actually gone out of his way to track Neil down. Just like Alice had apparently tracked Troy down.

'Found me at my garage,' he said. 'Your doing, I suppose?'

'Well, she is a pretty girl,' Neil said, then began coughing – hard. So hard, Troy asked him if he needed a nurse. Neil shook his head, and took a drag on the oxygen from the cylinder they'd left beside him. 'You ... you could do a lot worse.'

'She wanted to thank me, but didn't know what for.' He laughed. 'The police think she was taken by some kind of trafficking ring, you know. That she got away ... she remembers men, being manhandled.'

Neil nodded. 'All I could manage at short notice.'

'So...' said Troy, taking a seat.

'So...' managed Neil.

'So how're you doing for a start?'

'To put ... to put it in language you ... might understand: I'm fucking fucked. My legs are fucked and my lungs...'

Troy nodded, looked down. 'I'm sorry.'

'No need. I made a choice,' breathed out Neil. 'But for

once I don't regret it.'

'And what happens now?' Troy had asked.

'What … what happens is we talk. Y'know, the old fashioned way.'

So they did, they'd talked that day and for many more to come; sometimes out loud, sometimes not. Neil had told him his stories, tried to warn him about the pitfalls – things he should look out for as a member of this unique clan. He'd also offered him some options: to live as he had been doing, or to simply *live*. To see where things might go with Alice, if he wanted. To stay or to leave

They'd played cards – it wasn't Elvis and the Mummy, but it was nice. And Neil had shown Troy how to do a few more of those magic tricks of his, things it had taken a lifetime to learn, or at the very least set him on the path to learning. Some of it really did only come with time, with age. 'You just have to keep practising,' Neil had told him.

He'd done all this, not because he felt guilty, but because he wanted something in return. Troy had already hidden Neil's hire car away, and when they were coming to the end of their visits, he asked a favour of him. Asked him to bring something from the glove compartment, smuggle the items in.

Looking over his shoulder, Troy had passed him the pills and the flask. Neil opened it up and sniffed. 'Ah, that's the good stuff.'

'And … and you're sure this is what you want?' asked Troy. Neil wasn't certain, but he thought he saw tears in the lad's eyes.

'Yeah, I'm sure. I don't want this to drag on. I'd rather go out on my terms. One last choice.'

Troy said nothing, but Neil could see that he understood.

'You know, I once said I was glad you're not my son, but

the truth is … I always sort of felt like you were. I know that's pretty odd, but—'

The boy got up and made to leave. Was a couple of steps towards the door before he stopped, turned, and went back to hug Neil. Just wrapped his arms around him. Neil hugged him back. 'You … you take care of yourself, son. Okay?'

He felt the boy nodding into his shoulder.

Then he was gone. Neil wiped the tears from his cheeks, before taking out the pills, popping one into his mouth and swallowing with a swig of whiskey.

It was time, he thought.

Finally, it was time.

***

Troy was wiping away the tears as well, as he stepped out of the day-care centre for the last time. As he made his way towards his car.

It was almost a month to the day since the old man had come into his life, since he'd exploded into it as devastatingly as the grenade that had done all the damage during their last fight. He'd sat and listened to Neil, come to think of him like a father – as bizarre as that sounded. But, like a father, he wasn't sure whether to take the man's advice or not. Whether to just go his own way, be his own man. There was no way he would make the same mess of things anyway.

Yeah, he had some decisions to make, definitely. But they were his choices and his alone.

Troy slid behind the wheel, looked up at the darkening sky. It was Friday night, a full moon. He knew Alice would be waiting for him to call her, but truth be told he was thinking about a night out. Was starting to become bored, was missing the thrum of the clubs and pubs. He was only young, when all was said and done.

And there really was nothing like a good night out, thought Troy.

Nothing like it in the world.

AFTERWORD: STORY NOTES

'The Ugly': This poem was done as part of a bunch, at the request of editor Peggy J. Shumate for a book called *Cemetery Poets: Grave Offerings* back in 2003. The idea of this little monster, quite a pitiful thing really, came to me pretty much fully-formed and the ending was inspired by my love of all things freakish and carnival-like, as evidenced by the book I co-edited with my better half Marie for PS Publishing, *A Carnivàle of Horror*.

'Nightlife': By the late '90s I'd already tackled those other fundamental horror staples, zombies and vampires, so I figured it was high time I turned my attention to werewolves. Upon approaching this one, I was very conscious of the fact that the subject had been done to death in films and fiction, and I knew that probably even my idea would be similar to something else from the past. One of the ways I got around this was by withholding the fact that it's a werewolf tale until the climax, and this means that when you go back and read it again a lot of the lines have very different meanings.

'The Disease': Here we have one of my favourite all-time stories. I first had the idea to do this one in 1996/7, when I was taking a course in fiction writing. Don't ask me where the initial notion came from because I can't remember, but the first draft of it was called 'Drawing Board' (I know –

gives the game away, doesn't it?) and the protagonist was originally a cartoonist. That first draft also had stuff in it about secret government conspiracies to cover up the disease and men in black suits carrying guns. My tutor – thank goodness – told me to get rid of all the unnecessary stuff and pare it down into a lean, mean, fighting machine of a story, concentrating on the victim's plight and his relationship with his girlfriend. I've had quite a lot of experience with hospitals myself, due to sick relatives, so I felt fairly confident about the medical bits, and somewhere along the line it just seemed to take on a life of its own; the way decent stories do. Altogether, I'm still pretty pleased with the finished result, and have had some really positive feedback about it – the story is even being turned into a comic by Hellbound Comics. I was going to send this to the Waterstones' magazine *Alien Landings*, but didn't want to overwhelm them with material as I'd sent them a few stories at the time. Luckily, there was a new science fiction horror publication out back then called *Sci-Fright*. The editor Sian Ross, who has since married – sorry Sian I don't know your new surname! – was very complimentary and she used it in her millennium special.

'Sabbat': Turning now to another interest of mine, witchcraft. I wanted here to combine some of the aspects of my academic life with my fiction (I actually studied Art, Design and Film, but the trappings of university life remain the same). I hadn't been out of uni all that long when I wrote this one, and it was all based on genuine stuff I researched. I tell you, all us horror writers and fans would have been burnt at the stake in those days! Because it's got a certain antiquarian style to it, the wonderfully-named Michael Pendragon took this one for his magazine *Penny*

Dreadful and I think it worked pretty well in there.

'Dig (This)': This one was sort of inspired by hanging out with my friends as a teenager, in a rural community with very little to do – although we never spent any time in the graveyard, I should point out. We did get into other sorts of mischief, as bored kids do, so I just took this to its extreme: the Devil makes work for idle hands, or at least someone does in this story. It was published in the Australian magazine *Dark Animus* in 2007 and I'm delighted that I managed to creep out Nick (who very kindly did the introduction to *Monsters*) with this one, as he told me in a test for his 'Chattering' show back in December, just after reading it.

'A Chaos Demon Is for Life': This story holds quite a special place for me, as it's the only one I've ever won an award for so far (The 'Dead of Night' Editor's Choice Award for best story, 2008). I've come close, with multiple British Fantasy Award nominations and so on, but this one finally bagged the prize. It came about when Steve Upham at Screaming Dreams (publishers of my supernatural serial killer novel, *The Gemini Factor*) was looking for stories for a Christmas edition of his *Estronomicon* magazine. There were adverts on the TV around this time warning people not to buy dogs and cats as presents, so I just thought: what if you were a kid and your parents were into the occult? What if they decided that a demon might make a better present, or pet, so they summoned one? Obviously, you and I know that's a spectacularly bad idea, but it makes for a great premise – and some pretty black humour too. For the ending I was trying to tug at the heartstrings – this is still the boy's pet, after all – whilst at the same time presenting a homage to movies like *Godzilla* and *Cloverfield*, which I absolutely adore.

'St August's Flame': There are countless legends and stories about candles helping people to see visions or focus on the past, so I thought it might be different if there was a flame that allowed you to see into the future. Just imagine the lengths someone might go to in order to find it – you only have to look at how many people read their horoscopes every day. This tale is definitely Barkeresque, and I make no apologies about that. What can I say? I love Clive's work (as books like *Hellbound Hearts* should tell you). The protagonist could just as easily have been searching for the *Hellraiser* puzzle box as the Flame of St August, though obviously for different reasons. There are even demon-worshipping monks, as well as monstrous fire creatures that come up through the ground. This was accepted by the first magazine I sent it to, the much missed *Strix* edited by Anna Franklin and Sue Phillips – who are extremely talented authors in their own rights – and I felt very honoured to feature in issue 14 in early 1999. Anna even used it again when she set up the *Strix* website two years later because she thought it 'deserved another airing'. My thanks again, ladies.

'Keeper of the Light': When Maria Grazia told me she was putting together a second anthology after *Return of the Raven* (which featured my story 'Masques' a sequel to Poe's 'The Masque of the Red Death'), and that the theme was fear of the dark, I was all ears. I've never liked the dark, and this is something that's cropped up again and again in my writing ('Shadow Writer', 'Blackout', *Of Darkness and Light*…). This time I came at it from a different angle, with quite a bit of misdirection. I firmly believe that darkness will engulf the world at some point – hopefully when I'm long gone – and this might just be the result. You won't have to worry about the dark then, more the things that *make up* the dark. Maria also kindly asked if I would pen the foreword to the anthology, which I was delighted to do. It was the first intro to an anthology I've ever done; I've only written them for people's collections before. So my thanks to both her and the team at *Horror Bound*, who have been great supporters of my work.

'Dracula in Love': People who read my fiction across the board will be familiar with my more comic stories, such as the Dalton Quayle adventures – which I do as a bit of light relief after writing about death and destruction all the time. This was one of a clutch of stories that sold to one of the only magazines I've ever come across which published humorous horror fiction, or as one of my ex-writing students once termed it 'Horredy'. The mag was called *Dead Things* and 'Dracula…' appeared in its fifth issue in 2000, reprinted in my 2005 collection *FunnyBones* – this is the first time it's been seen since then. I thoroughly enjoyed writing it, and found that it also plays well when read out to an audience, especially if I do my Bela Lugosi impression!

'Half-Life': When I was looking for new material to write to go along with my novellas 'Pain Cages' and 'Signs of Life' for Books of the Dead in 2011, I started thinking about 'Nightlife' – about maybe dropping in and seeing how Neil was doing these days. More and more as my career goes on, I find myself revisiting stories and doing sequels, most recently working on the sequel to *RED* for SST publications, which – along with *The Curse of the Wolf* from Hersham

Horror – also ties in to Neil's life. And, as I was approaching middle age myself, I thought it might be a good time to comment on that, on lost youth and how the mistakes of the past can sometimes come back and – quite literally in this case – bite you. I had such a good time with this tale, writing about what Stephen Volk (who was introducing *Pain Cages*) called 'Chav Werewolves', that I started to think about Neil a little later on in his life and maybe tying up the whole thing in a trilogy … but more on that later.

'Guilty Pleasures': My love of demon stories is pretty well established, but when I was asked to contribute to an anthology called *Demonology* back in 2004 I wanted to do something a bit different with the sub-genre. I started to think about why sometimes we get this irrational guilt when we're thinking about things, often way beyond what the actual 'crime' might be, and wondered if there might be a devil, if not on your shoulder, then maybe behind you whispering into your ear. And I began to wonder if that Guilt Demon ever felt guilty about any of the things that *it* did. The result was a story I'm still very proud of to this day.

'Speaking in Tongues': This was a fun little short which was, again, greatly influenced by Clive Barker's work – specifically a story from his *Books of Blood* called 'The Body Politic'. In Clive's tale, one man's hands revolt against him, to the point where they murder his wife and one cuts the other off to set it free. Tongues don't actually feature in Clive's story that I can recall, and the body parts in question aren't alien in origin (to my knowledge) so I thought it would make a nice homage to have those wriggling things inside our mouths be just that: symbiotic creatures that latched on to us, let us use them until the time was right to detach themselves once more. Again, this was accepted by the first place I sent it, *Necrotic Tissue* magazine (though it's more like an anthology). Never look up pictures of their covers without typing in the actual word 'magazine'. Big mistake!

'Star-Pool': This is another very early 1998 tale and it's heavily influenced by Lovecraft, a writer whose work I read voraciously as a teenager, plus the *Terror Tales* publications I was reading at the time. It was the editor of those, John B Ford, who suggested I try Dave Price over at *Tales of the Grotesque and Arabesque* with this one, and am I glad I did. He absolutely loved it and raved about how good it was at every writers' gathering afterwards, which did my reputation no harm. It was also beautifully illustrated by an artist called Wendy Down, who sent me a signed colour print of the picture; this is still hanging on my wall in the office. Strangely enough I got the idea for 'Star-Pool' on the way back from the local post office one day. I'm not suggesting that I live in some kind of jungle populated by alien creatures with thousands of eyes and tentacles. Although, come to think of it... No, it just popped into my head as I was walking up the steps to my house, the way some ideas do. No explanation, no warning, just a complete story from start to finish. I jotted it all down and then wrote the piece over the next couple of days, when my schedule would allow. Simple as that, really.

'Rag and Bone': A story that was written for a specific anthology which never came out – this time for Steve Upham's *Dead Ends* – but ended up being an original contribution to my PS Publications' collection *The Butterfly Man*. It was kind of the end of a cycle of stories for me, before I started writing new ones. I've always been interested in where words and phrases come from, and as we used to have a Rag and Bone Man in our neighbourhood – right up until a few years ago – I thought this subject was ripe for exploring. It was interesting finding out quite where the name came from, which you'll have read in the story itself, and even the words themselves 'Rag' and 'Bone' cry out horror, don't they? Anyway, this is the story that they suggested to me – with apologies to *Steptoe and Son* – and I was delighted when it was subsequently reprinted in Stephen Jones' *The Mammoth Book of Best New Horror* the year after.

'The Weeping Woman': I have a real soft spot for this one, mainly because I like short, sharp horrors with a twist. A lot of people have mentioned the fact that the narration is from the point of view of someone who dies (I've done this a few times, but did it much more when I was first starting out). How can he be telling the tale if he's dead by the end of it? I've never really been able to come up with a satisfactory answer, maybe it's a ghost talking? The real answer, of course, is that I just like the device. Perhaps it's the fact it lulls you into a false sense of security, thinking he might actually make it out alive – keeps you guessing. I've always been a fan of creepy children in horror, from Damian in The Omen to Samara in The Ring. These mutant kids are my take on that, but in a much more hands-on way. I might come back to this one day, create a mythology around them – because I find what I haven't said here much more interesting. How did they come to be born that way, what's the mother doing out in the middle of nowhere? It was published first as part of the *Terror Tales* e-mail magazine, and subsequently filmed by award-winning director Mark Steensland (something you'll see for yourself if you bought the limited hardback of this collection, as the DVD comes free with it).

'Pay the Piper': Zombies are one of my favourite things in the world! I love all kinds: the fast and slow moving sort, the brain-eaters and more discerning diners. It was a dream come true when my own zombie story 'Dead Time' was turned into an episode of the NBC/Lionsgate TV series *Fear Itself* (and I have Masters of Horror creator Mick Garris to thank for that, so thanks again Mick). Here is one of my early attempts to do something new with it all, and these zombies are more Hammer's *Plague of the Zombies* than anything else. I wanted to do a sort of zombie fairy tale, so I started to imagine what would happen if the Pied Piper could control dead people rather than rats. Next came his background, and from there came the kind of person he was – or had become. This one had a life – if you'll excuse the expression – after appearing on the *House of Pain* site: in an Australian anthology years later called, simply, *Zombies*.

'It's All Over...': A tale I wrote originally for Mark Deniz at Morrigan – for an anthology based on one of his favourite albums of all time, The God Machine's *Scenes from the Second Storey*. Mark sent me the lyrics and from that I came up with this vampire story, drawing heavily on my background as a writer and attendee of literary conventions. I've even run a few in my time. You might also spot the reference to one of my other stories 'Suicide Room' (which you'll find most recently in GHOSTS published by Spectral Press), not to mention my favourite horror film of all time, *Hellraiser*. And there's also a nod to *I Am Legend* thrown in for good measure. I really like character building, as you've probably guessed, and it was interesting to see where the couple's relationship went in this one.

'Lifetime': We finish with an ending, but also a beginning. I'd always wanted to tie up Neil's story, the 'Life Cycle' trilogy as I've named it, in a book of monsters – so thanks again to Peter and Jan at Alchemy Press for allowing me to do that. I think it fits perfectly in amongst the other tales here. This novelette allowed me to imagine what Neil might be like as an old man (I'm not there yet, before you say anything) but also comment on the generation gap as I see it and have experienced it. They say 'youth is wasted on the young', and nowhere is that more apparent than when Neil is attempting to pass the wisdom of his years on to Troy. It's an ending because of how we leave Neil, but it's also the beginning of Troy's story – which brings things round full circle, I think, especially with the final line. They also say, 'the more things change the more they stay the same', and that's a pretty good note on which to finish this Afterword. Thanks for reading the stories in this book and I hope you've enjoyed them half as much as I enjoyed writing them.

Paul Kane
Derbyshire, February 2015

ABOUT THE AUTHOR

Paul Kane is an award-winning writer and editor based in Derbyshire, UK. His short story collections include *Alone (In the Dark)*, *Touching the Flame*, *FunnyBones*, *Peripheral Visions*, *Shadow Writer*, *The Adventures of Dalton Quayle*, *The Butterfly Man and Other Stories*, *The Spaces Between* and *GHOSTS*. His novellas include *Signs of Life*, *The Lazarus Condition*, *RED* and *Pain Cages*. He is the author of such novels as *Of Darkness and Light*, *The Gemini Factor* and the bestselling *Arrowhead* trilogy (*Arrowhead*, *Broken Arrow* and *Arrowland*, gathered together in the sell-out omnibus edition *Hooded Man*), a post-apocalyptic reworking of the Robin Hood mythology. His latest novels are *Lunar* (which is set to be turned into a feature film), *Sleeper(s)* (a modern, horror version of *Sleeping Beauty*) and the short YA novel *The Rainbow Man* (as P B Kane).

He has also written for comics, most notably for the *Dead Roots* zombie anthology alongside writers such as James Moran (*Torchwood*, *Cockneys vs. Zombies*) and Jason Arnopp (*Dr Who*, *Friday The 13ᵗʰ*) and as part of the team turning *Clive Barker's Books of Blood* into motion comics for Seraphim/MadeFire. Paul is co-editor of the anthologies: *Hellbound Hearts* (Simon & Schuster), with stories based around the mythology that spawned *Hellraiser*; *The Mammoth Book of Body Horror* (Constable & Robinson/ Running Press), featuring the likes of Stephen King and James Herbert; *A Carnivàle of Horror* (PS Publishing) featuring Ray Bradbury and Joe Hill; and *Beyond Rue Morgue* (Titan), stories based around Poe's detective, Dupin.

His non-fiction books are: *The Hellraiser Films and Their Legacy; Voices in the Dark;* and *Shadow Writer – The Non-Fiction. Vol. 1: Reviews* and *Vol. 2: Articles and Essays.* His genre journalism has appeared in the likes of *SFX, Fangoria, Dreamwatch, Gorezone, Rue Morgue* and *DeathRay.* He has been a guest at many conventions, including: Alt. Fiction five times; the first SFX Weekender; Thought Bubble in 2011; Derbyshire Literary Festival and Off the Shelf in 2012; Monster Mash and Event Horizon in 2013; Edge-Lit in 2014; and Horrorcon in 2015. In addition he has been a panellist at FantasyCon and the World Fantasy Convention.

His work has been optioned for film and television, and his zombie story 'Dead Time' was turned into an episode of the Lionsgate/NBC TV series *Fear Itself,* adapted by Steve Niles (*30 Days of Night*) and directed by Darren Lynn Bousman (*SAW II-IV*). He also scripted: *The Opportunity,* which premiered at the Cannes Film Festival; *Wind Chimes* (directed by Brad Watson [*7th Dimension*] which sold to TV); plus *The Weeping Woman,* filmed by award-winning director Mark Steensland and starring Tony-nominated actor Stephen Geoffreys (*Fright Night*). You can find out more at his website www.shadow-writer.co.uk, which has featured guest writers such as Dean Koontz, Robert Kirkman, Charlaine Harris and Guillermo del Toro.

PUBLISHED BY THE ALCHEMY PRESS

Astrologica: Stories of the Zodiac
Beneath the Ground
Dead Water and Other Weird Tales
Doors to Elsewhere
Evocations
Give Me These Moments Back
In the Broken Birdcage of Kathleen Fair
Invent-10n
Kneeling in the Silver Light
Leinster Gardens and Other Subtleties
Merry-Go-Round and Other Words
Monsters
Nick Nightmare Investigates
Rumours of the Marvellous
Sailor of the Skies
Shadows of Light and Dark
Swords against the Millennium
Tell No Lies
The Alchemy Press Book of Ancient Wonders
The Alchemy Press Book of Pulp Heroes
The Alchemy Press Book of Pulp Heroes 2
The Alchemy Press Book of Pulp Heroes 3
The Alchemy Press Book of Urban Mythic
The Alchemy Press Book of Urban Mythic 2
The Komarovs
The Paladin Mandates
Touchstones: Essays on the Fantastic
Where the Bodies are Buried

www.alchemypress.co.uk

Dead Water & Other Weird Tales

By David A Sutton

From weirdness on the Welsh coast...

Whatever it was, the object was too large for a bird, too slim for a boat, too streamlined for flotsam... She pressed her face closer to the glass, fascinated and terrified at the same time. In the net ... bilious white, flesh that might have been partly consumed by some predator. ("The Fisherman")

A visit to Lovecraft's Innsmouth...

My eyes could not block out the sight of the shapes, flopping, wading, barking as they inexorably massed in my direction... the texture of their skins bore the suggestion of the final stages of gangrenous flesh. ("Innsmouth Gold")

In the depths of winter in Arthurian times...

The sound of battle clamoured through my brain. The field of Arderydd, soaked in blood; Liddel Water running with blood; Gwenddolau's fortress hard by ... splattered with blood... Perhaps it was not Myrddin's great age that sapped him of his powers. Perhaps it was the Romans and their priests... The new faith has made us all weak. ("Midwinter")

On board Venturer, about to land on Mars...

The texture of Mars, the texture of its red facade, the sub-liminal texture of its history and mythology and the baggage of the many fictions. Mars was larger than itself... The three of them had sat in the rec. area and watched as Earth's dark soul was lit up again. ("Landfall on Elysium Planitia")

And more ... eighteen stories of horror, fantasy and science fiction from award-winning editor and writer David A. Sutton

NEW FROM THE ALCHEMY PRESS

Leinster Gardens and Other Subtleties

The ghost stories of Jan Edwards.

Fourteen short stories from Jan Edwards, including the BFS award short-listed 'Otterburn', plus a previously unpublished tale.

Concerning Events at Leinster Gardens: *He handed the maid his hat and replaced it with a coronet of silk holly leaves and tinsel. She gave him only the smallest raise of an eyebrow. 'Ghost of Christmas Present,' he said...*

The Waiting: *She picked up the hem of her night-dress and ran the length of the gallery. She wanted to race them to the door, to greet her father. Why, then, did a tiny part of her hesitate? Why should she be afraid? From the landing she heard the doors of the great hall being flung open...*

The Ballad of Lucy Lightfoot: *This had been in the planning for a very long time, for centuries – to the where and the when that the Wite had sent her. Across an entire continent to the edges of the Ottoman lands, to a place and time long before the Lightfoot name had ever begun. Her children, and her children's children, for more generations than she could count, were dust. Only she remained.*

From the introduction: ...Ghost stories. Adeptly told, often with a sense of locale and time neatly placed within the narratives. Her family history informs and inspires some of her stories. Folklore figures as a focus in more than one story, whether urban myth or historical lore. But ghostly they are and deceptively disturbing.

Lightning Source UK Ltd.
Milton Keynes UK
UKOW02f1034080615

253077UK00001B/94/P